B·A·C·K

COUNTRY

B·A·C·K
COUNTRY
Two Tales by Joe Back

Johnson Books: Boulder

ISBN 1-55566-019-3
LCCCN 87-82331

Cover design by Molly Davis

Printed in the United States of America by
Johnson Publishing Company
1880 South 57th Court
Boulder, Colorado 80302

Contents

MOOCHING MOOSE AND MUMBLING MEN

THE SUCKER'S TEETH

MOOCHING MOOSE AND MUMBLING MEN

Preface

In offering this book to the public I'll admit I've stuck my neck out; and while it's some shorter than that on Nosy the moose, it's a gambler's neck.

Much of this story is based on actual happenings, encounters, and life with the moose family. A few squirts of mustard and a dash or two of applesauce have been added to enliven the proceedings. Although the names of the human characters are wholly fictitious and some of the incidents more than border on the imaginary, many of them have happened to me, to my friends, and to other inhabitants of the moose country.

As most of us are more familiar with the human than with the deer family, it may be of interest to some to take a peek behind the moosehide curtain.

It seems to me that the moose has had more insulting slurs cast in his direction than any other member of his family. Beauty is only skin deep, some say, and, brother, this critter has a thick one.

If the human, needing swamp salad, would dive down in a deep and muddy pond or slough and grope around to snap his snout about a lily root to have a little chew, when he came up he'd be a little snooty, too. The moose is one of the original skin divers, with a hair shirt on, of course. His built in air supply, nose valves, and knowhow was developed long before his two-legged critic ever thought of it. Maybe they stole his patent. Some moose have been clocked to stay under for a minute and close to two.

You should see him or maybe her rare up on a tangled willow clump to flop that rubber kisser around a thumb-thick willow. To strip the leaves and twigs off, a beaver can't beat this slicker. He leaves the trunk to maybe grow more next year. And watch him stand in snow hip deep to a tall Indian, reach up and shred the bark off trunks of live green quaking aspen, cottonwoods, and sometimes fir. All this with no upper teeth in front. Now he can't brag about this too loud. The other deer are fixed the same way for upper front teeth; except that elk and sometimes caribou do have two canines up above; but they're too far back to do much good.

Some folks say the moose *don't eat grass*. Now some folks don't stray too far from town, and when they do, they don't stay long. Mr. and Mrs. Big Nose don't eat *much* but they do eat *some*. I've watched them do it and so have many others.

And we'd get bored with the grub that nature built his insides to handle. Like us, the moose has bilious tantrums. He'll stand close up to haystacks that tease his smell and taste buds to bore large holes chest high and shoulder deep. He's after cured willow leaves, seedy twigs, timothy and wild grass heads and blossoms. The gut he's got can't stand a bender like this long, though. The bellyache he gets from this kind of digestive hangover drives him to a quick willow diet for cure; or he finally flops to become a feast for the coyotes and a dainty for the birds.

While he's taking the willow cure, let's consider some of his other peculiarities. You would think he likes music, because he wears a bell; but it never rings. His tail is too short to shoo the flies; it's just for balance. He uses bog holes and makes a wallow to knock the bugs off. His ears are long and floppy, but most times he can hear good. The moose is morose because he's near-sighted and can't wear glasses. What he lacks in humor is more than made up in temper. His legs are long and his neck is short. You've maybe seen him stand spraddle-legged, giraffe style, to try to reach the ground. In winter, tired of eating snow and scared of trappy, open, icy water holes, he'll stand on lake or river ice, to spraddle out and flop his long tongue in and out and back and forth to lick up moisture for a paunch full of soured old willow twigs. He can't help it, if his neck is nearly a half shorter than that long head he's so proud of.

He may not be nearly as articulate as his noisy cousins, the elk and the deer, but his own kind understand him. Personally, I think the moose is jealous of the elk. The elk is the most intelligent of the deer family, and the moose is afraid of him and with reason. But somebody has to be boss and it's a lot of trouble anyhow. Besides, everybody can't be foreman.

The moose, I believe, is the most primitive of the deer family, as a thinker, anyhow. That's what makes him a character. He seems to be proud of the fact that he don't know what he's going to do next and you don't either. Somebody's got to be erratic or they'll quit using the word. When he gets mad, he stands there staring straight at you, just like a mad bill collector. He'll run his tongue in and out in time with those dangerous long legs and feet stamping up and down. Just like you and me as kids. But watch *this* kid. He's about to make up his mind, if any, and you're in front.

His fastest gait is a trot. You should see him travel through deep mucky swamps, and up steep mountain sides chock full of down timber and soggy snow. When he's scared, he don't like to let on. This moose has pride. Lots of times he'll casually walk into the timber until he thinks he's out of sight, then his imagination hits him. He'll bust up through the jungle like a locoed locomotive. He probably forgot to trot, and tried to gallop or run, got his pistons all mixed up with his connecting rods, and fell down. He flusters to his feet, then he'll trot away from there.

The tracks he leaves on dry ground are sometimes hard to tell from elk tracks. Moose tracks are usually larger, longer, and pointed more than elk. But follow walking tracks for twenty yards— usually dim prints of dew-claws can finally be found. Usually means moose.

When in deep snow or mud, you're sure of moose tracks if the animal *doesn't* drag his toes much. To see this willow chomper travel in deep snow is to watch an efficient machine built for the work. He lifts his legs up, front and back, nearly vertically each step, then plunges them down rapier style for forward movement. Not much drag. He may not be compact, and he's lost his fins, but boy, the moose is a graceful machine on the job.

There have been many instances of moose pets. Some moose have been broken to harness and driven. A man sixty miles from here brought up a cow moose from a calf and used her as a trick animal on exhibition in several of the large cities. Her end was tragic, as with lots of other pets. Some brave jackass hunter shot her for a trophy close to her home shed in a settled district.

Here's a lot to the moose and a little to the men. When next you see a moose I hope you'll remember little Nosy. And I also hope you like this book.

> So long,
> Joe Back
> Dubois, Wyoming.

The Bird Watchers

It was fall, and many birds were flocking together to make plans and dates for migration to warmer climes. A bird watchers group from the Nature Club was having a picture contest and bird list race. George Takum and his hefty mate, off on a lone trip, were way ahead in the contest.

Nosy had taken a much needed dietary vacation from his lunches on handouts and sometimes filched provisions. He'd had a change of food in the past week of roaming the timbered expanses above Bill Thompson's ranch. Now on his way home, his stomach adjusted for a new campaign, he had spotted the big car on the hill road, and was modestly hid in the nearby willows shyly surveying these interesting humans just getting out of their car.

George Takum was the junior member of the Casem, Loanum, and Takum Investment Company, and was on his way up. Having finally acquired title to several ranches in an oh, so sorry, way, Takum felt that any wild game around was his for the taking—especially because he had seen members of the deer family grazing in the meadows of his several ranches at odd times. The pious-looking loan shark felt that fair exchange was no robbery. Of course, one had to discreetly observe the proprieties. The Game Department men had to do their jobs, of course, to keep down the hungry appetites of the nearby ne'er-do-well ranchers and the local riffraff natives. Although Jayne genteely frowned on these wicked little habits of her Gawge, she had to admit privately that she got a distinctly peculiar thrill whenever her clever provider brought home some illicit bacon—especially when she met the game warden or his wife on the streets of Roaring River.

"Ouh, Gawge, my deah," her Grim Mahwr accent had commando undertones, but hearing no "Yayus, Jayne, muh love," didn't bother this militant stage managuh of the Little Theatuh. She couldn't take her bulging eyes away from her Bird Watchuh Specials for fear of losing sight of the rare bird. The lady firmly held the binoculars in a be-ringed grip. George had stopped to tighten up a loose lace on his boots on the steep hillside just below the car. He thought he'd seen a moose calf down in the swamp below the road. His big calibre,

13

"The Go Git 'Em Special" he called it, was in the back seat of the station wagon within easy reach.

After calling several times to her husband to hurry up and identify the bird she'd spotted, the angry stage manager lowered her glasses and turned around. There was the investment counselor kneeling down in the tall yellow grass, his ought-six rifle aimed down the hill. She turned her powerful glasses on just what tidbit Old Thrifty had located now. Bill Thompson's little brown milk cow had gotten out of the pasture. The grazing Jersey never will find out that she owed her bovine life to the main member of the Little Theater Group. Jayne caught the sound of Annie's bell, and from her different point of vantage, saw that Takum's avarice had gone just a little too far. When her shrill yell of warning reached the slightly deaf loan man, he had taken up the slack on old Go-Git-Em's trigger. But he took his itchy finger away in irritation at the yowling of the bird watcher. A fat moose calf was just what the doctor ordered, and so Gawge was peeved.

Popeyed, George stood staring down the hillside at the Jersey cow now moving into the open, her clanging bell audible now even to the chagrined hunter.

"If you'll put that nasty old gun back into the cah, I'll try to locate that bird again," Jayne fumed at Old Dead-Eye. "I'll declah, trying to kill a poor little old Jersey cow."

"I'll swear, Jayne, that was the first time I've ever seen a fat moose calf turn into a milk cow." Takum looked back down the hillside as he put his disappointed rifle in the big station wagon. The line of willows bordering the swiftly falling creek looked innocent enough, as the little brown Jersey grazed out of sight behind a stand of timber.

"You should know there's no moose within miles of heah at this time of yeah." The irate bird watcher walked over towards her original stand and was again trying to spot the strange bird. Watching the antics of this couple, the hidden bog trotter had decided that they weren't worth his while, when the wind shifted. The smell of Big Money nauseated the calf, but the scent Mrs. Money Bags used was intensely interesting. So Nosy trotted out of the willows straight for Mrs. Takum, who was snooping through her B.W. Specials in the other direction. Gawge T. was disgustedly walking over to his beckoning mate when he heard the grunting mutters of the long-nosed customer on his way over to the new perfume counter.

The single-minded calf, seeing Takum's hurried and speechless

14

ascent of a nearby pine out of the corner of an eye, was now up close to the interesting lady in the well-filled pants.

Jayne Takum mistook the pleased whines behind her for her helpmate's usual smothered comments. Keeping her eyes grimly fixed on the pretty birdie, impatiently she held the leather loop high in one hand, and the field glasses ready for her tall husband's confirmation in the other.

Takum himself had by now got his wind back. Seeing the potbellied pet about to look through those expensive binoculars, he couldn't take it. He howled a frenzied warning at the waiting bird woman. When the investment counselor's wife whipped her head around, to meet the softly affectionate gaze of the short-tailed party of the third part, she gave a theatrical screech and dived into the nearest haven of safety, the huge shell of an ancient fire-killed tree lying close by.

Old Lady Badger had found what she considered the ideal nursing home. The hollow-end log was long dead, but the still thick shell extended inward four or five feet until the interior ended in a blank wall. She lay on her back at joyful ease, while her three fat babies lunched at their leisure. When Mrs. Takum went calling, she usually was more polite and rang the bell, but this time was a little different. Mrs. Badger got kind of ringy, to say the least, at Jayne's unceremonious entrance. She bared her teeth and hissed that no painted up hussy can come into my home and show me how to raise my kids.

Nosy, in his short life, had been handed a lot of odd things, mostly edible. This gift that dangled under his chin was kind of bothersome, but the moose was polite and didn't ask the reason why. When he tried to follow his new-found friend into her hollow tree for better acquaintance, his formal education started with his lady friend kicking him on the snoot on her way out.

When Jayne Takum came galloping backward out of Snuffy Badger's unfriendly apartment, the calf moose sensed an unwelcome attitude in the gathering. He whirled around and trotted off into the heavy timber. He didn't even notice that the descending junior member of Casem, Loanum, and Takem was again on his way up.

Tony Belknap had spent a few hours visiting with Velma and Bill Thompson, and was now untying his saddle horse from the backyard fence. His two friends were saying their so longs, when Nosy walked out from around the corner of the corral. As Bill and his wife stood staring at the calf, Tony hurriedly stepped on his

15

He howled a frenzied warning.

horse and started to ride off. They could hear the startled cowboy mumble, "By gravy, Ol' Bill's shore slipped his pack. Furnishin' that damn near-sighted pest with a pair uh glasses! Wait till *this* gits around. *By hell,* I've seen *everything* now!"

Hay Stealer

Whoa, now, I'm getting a little ahead of the story about that little moose. Maybe it would be better to start at the beginning of what happened, that early winter at the head of Roaring River. The hunting camp and gear were all packed into the ranch. Most of the pack and saddle horses had been driven below town on winter pasture. The two men put in a wood camp a few miles above the ranch to get out logs and firewood till deep snow stopped their operations. Up to now, things had been going pretty good. Snow was getting deeper up high in the mountains, and more moose were showing up.

This one stamped her feet in a sort of crazy dance and kept time with her tongue running in and out of her mouth. The coarse mane rising upon her short neck and the "I'll gitcha" look rolling in her near-sighted eyes completed the picture for Tony Belknap. He gave a scrambling hop off the sled-load of logs and plowed through the deep snow for the nearest stand of spruce.

Bill Thompson calmly see-sawed the leather lines on his team of roans who were trying to jacknife the front bob in the deeply rutted snow. He wrapped the lines around the chain boomer handle, reached into the canvas nose-bag he kept tied to the binding chain, and came out with a slingshot and a rock. Ignoring the stomping of the cow moose ahead, he let fly at a clump of willows in back of her. There was a surprised squeal from a big calf, hit dead center. The ungainly mamma whirled around with a grunt and plunged off, with her gangling offspring trailing along in her wake.

Tony plowed sheepishly back to the bobsled. Bill bit off a fresh chew and said, "OK, sissy, git on 'n' we'll go t' camp. Ain't yuh never seen a locoed cow moose before? Yu' only been around 'em for sixty years!"

"Yuh dumb wrinkled-up ol' fool," barked Tony as he bowlegged up behind Bill, "them Mizzouri tricks'll git you killed yet. You an' that crazy bean-shooter!"

"Aw, hell," says Bill, and pops the team on the rumps with a loud yell, "why don't you get modern? These rock-throwers is plenty handy t'have around, don't hurt a thing."

18

They saw one more moose as they stopped the team on the brink of a steep hill just above camp. While they put the roughlock chains on the back runners, Tony kept a wary eye on the bull as he crunched the crowns off small green spruce and lodgepole trees. When they clambered back up on the load of dry logs and started the team down the drop-off, the screeching of chain-bound steel on snow and rocks made the big moose take off, trotting smoothly in the direction of Bill's camp on Mosquito Creek.

"Damn him," says Bill. "Didja see that hay stickin' up there, tangled in his mane?"

"A sign he's one o' yer nosy friends, I reckon," says Tony. "You sure take up with some onery lookin' characters."

"Well, by hell, if you went 'n' left those poles down when you hitched up t' the sled this mornin', some o' that forty-dollar hay'll be comin' outa yer wages, my big-hatted friend." Bill slapped angrily with the lines to hurry up the horses.

Down in the next park they took off the roughlock chains and drew up in front of the rickety buzz saw and truck engine Bill swore by and at. The small cook shack looked intact. The corral looked okay at first glance, but as they started to unhook the team, a roaring grunt warned them. Bill held on to the plunging team as a huge moose dashed past them, with a mass of baling wire tangled up in his horns and around a bunged-up front leg. When Tony came out from behind a standing tree, he says, "If this ain't a hay-wire outfit, I'll put in with yuh!"

While Tony led the horses over to the creek for a drink, Bill hurried over to the hay corral—four trees he'd nailed poles to. The gate poles were up, all right, and the baling wire loops that held them were intact. But a couple other poles were knocked down, lying on the snow covered ground, the big spikes still in the ends. The moose, pushing hard to grab at the precious bales of tasty native hay, had finally made the grade. Bill always hung the wire from the bales on a tree limb for emergency repairs, thus unconsciously setting a trap for four-legged thieves. But the trap was sprung after the bait was eaten.

Whenever he got enough ahead, Thompson would haul logs to his ranch and firewood to town twenty miles below the wood camp. Every time he hauled wood to his customers, he would haul grub and hay back up. The hay had a lot of cured willow leaves and stems and other native seeds and grass mixed up in it.

The moose population, weary of the early heavy snows and bored by their natural diet of willows, bark, and other forest tidbits, had taken to raiding Bill's hard-won horse feed. They wasted more than they ate while searching for what they could digest. Their natural erratic behavior was making the two loggers uneasy.

"They kinda resent us birds invadin' their private domain," Bill remarked to Tony. "Y're dead right, partner," Tony had just about his fill of moose. "Them dang critters also don't know whut they're goin' t' do next and we don't either."

He unharnessed and fed the horses while Bill nailed the poles back up to the trees, and reenforced the spikes by twisting wire around trees and poles.

"Winter's sure early," Tony grunted as he hung his hat over his coat on the inside of the cookshack door, and pulled off his head the wool sock that protected his ears. "Huh," Bill was loading the stove with kindling and striking a match, "Yuh wouldn't feel th' cold if y'd wear a Scotch cap 'n' quit tryin' ta be a cowboy fashion plate." He bent down to the wood box, rammed the door with his head, and knocked it open. Out into the dark rolled Tony's precious headgear, and out leaped Tony to its rescue. Bill shook his head and stoked up the stove.

After supper Bill rolled the logs off the bobsled onto the skids by his saw rig. He hobbled the horses, put a bell on old Dick, and turned them loose for the night. He knew they'd be right there at the hay corral for breakfast next morning. He re-piled the bales of hay in the center of the little corral, and raked up the scattered leavings of a broken bale with a pitchfork. He leaned the pitchfork against a tree trunk, and crunched over to his truck for a few blocks of sawed wood to split for the breakfast fire. As he stacked it handy by the shack, Tony, who'd washed the supper dishes, unhooked the door and threw the dishwater out on the trod-down snow just outside. Bill looked up and said, " 'Ja bring yer skates, Tony?" No answer. Tony was too busy wrangling the dishpan, catching his hat in the air, and getting it back on the nail, all at the same time.

In the dim light of frosty morning, Bill woke to hear the horse bell's loud clanging. He prodded Tony back to cold reality from his dream of a big ranch and many cows. After he got dressed, he opened the door and stepped out—to put one shoe-pack square in Tony's big hat, the other on the frozen dishwater. At his loud skiddy fall, the horses and Tony all showed up, to see him brushing snow and profane anger all over the cowhand's messed-up hat and the echoing timbered landscape. Tony was grieving loudly as he started the breakfast fire, while the bruised logger haltered the two horses and tied them up to the corral poles.

He hung the hobbles on a tree limb, and was just reaching up to unbuckle the bell strap from Dick's frosty neck, when he heard a musty belch. He looked over the poles directly into the unbeautiful face of a willow-cruncher with a half flake of cured willow leaves and native hay crosswise in his mouth. All of a sudden Bill lost his philosophy of "share-the-wealth". He grabbed the pitchfork by the handle, aimed its sharp business end at the boarder, and gave a forty-dollar lunge at the moose's flopping smeller. In just about a tenth of a second, a mess of tangled-up broken poles, hungry horses, scared logger, and murderous moose were headed hell-bent in the same busy direction. Hare-lipped now and dripping blood, the hay-stealer cut Bill out from the small and frantic horse herd with a deadly precision that amazed cowboy Tony, watching the show from the open shack door. Big hat tipped on one side of his head, he stepped closer to see the sights better. The moose had Bill all lined up and was closing in to make the deal final.

There was no affection in the moose's passionate breath on his neck. Bill didn't stop to check with his compass but speeded up in a desperate scrawly rush for the shack and solid shelter. Seeing the parade approach, Tony turned too fast, slipped, and fell ka-phump on the frozen dishwater and lost his big hat in the snow banked up nearby. He just made the door in time and yanked it shut in a hurry. Bill, at a high lope, howled, "Open th' door, yuh damn' sap, this moose ain't a-foolin!"

The fat was in the fire—Tony had backed up too far while holding the door shut. When he felt the fiery sizzling on his rump from the booming cook stove, he thought the moose must have come in through the back window. So he kicked the door open, and made a running jump to, he hoped, safety. He and Bill collided, and Tony fell underneath. Bill's eyes were blinded by the spurting snowy rush of Tony's exit. He thought he was on top of the cantankerous moose, and grabbed for his mane, but all he got was a mane holt on Tony's shaggy black hair. The moose had missed his aim at poor wind-broken old Bill. He stepped right into the cowboy's waiting hat and poured on speed straight up the logging road. Distant moggy coughs told of his fears of the Stetson trap now flopping just below a hock.

The two worn-out loggers sorted out who was who, and at last were painfully gulping hot coffee in the shack. Tony was sadly

A mess of tangled-up poles, hungry horses, scared logger, and murderous moose.

figuring how many cords of sawed wood it took to buy a new hat. Bill gave old Bowlegs a long, hard look, and says, "Why in hell didja shut that door?" Tony felt of the burned place under his singed wool pants, and yelped, "Why, yuh danged ol' coot, there wa'n't room fer three of us in here!"

The Water Bucket

The deep snows came early. They kept piling up so bad that Bill and Tony had to pull up stakes and call it quits. With truck and bobsled they got the whole outfit hauled down to the ranch. Tony got a job shoveling hay for a cow outfit. Bill planned to put in the rest of the winter building a log barn on his own place.

Moose showed up early in the bottoms along Roaring River, glad for the shelter and food in the miles of willow jungle. You could see them every mile or two—groups of four or five cows and calves, sometimes solitary old bulls or grumpy cows enjoying their own company. You could see those snouty swamp-lovers, in groups or singly, breath steaming, standing up and reaching high, to snap their pendulous upper lips around the succulent stems of the head-high ropy growths. The deep snow served as beds and generous water supply.

With a huge thumbnail Bill scraped some of the frost away from a window and peered out over the willow flats below the hill. No moose in sight. The leaden sky was just beginning to lighten up Bull Ridge, the timber covered hill crowding the far side of Roaring River.

Bill's wife, Velma, was bustling around the humming kitchen range, getting set for breakfast. She was full of pep and impatient with Ol' Bill. He was taking turns looking out the scratched streaks of window and staring glumly at the two new galvanized pails he'd brought back from town, ten snow-coverd miles away.

"Well, if you want any breakfast *this* morning, you'd better get a hump on, and go fetch a couple buckets of water. I'm tired of melting snow," Velma said, putting a fresh stick of wood in the stove.

Bill quit scraping peep holes in the frosty glass and warmed his cold thumb by adjusting his new store teeth. He reached up for his ragged wool coat on a nail behind the door, mumbling, "OK, but you'd better keep the dumb dog in here. I've got sore bumps all over me from yesterday." The beautiful white collie, safe behind the wood box, sniffed in the direction of the frozen slab of elk meat Velma was sawing at. His long patrician nose wrinkled with disdain at Bill's voice.

"If you'd be a little considerate of Moocher," Velma pointed

24

Bill's hunting knife in his direction, "he'd be more considerate of you. Besides, he's only a pup. He's just growing up. That's what his papers said. About his age."

"Yeah, and what a pup! That fancy-pants brother of yours told me the strawberry roan he traded me for that load of logs is young, too. I looked in his mouth—he's been four years old for ten years anyhow."

Bill limped over to the table, grabbed the new pails, and started for the door, favoring his sore leg. The spring water supply had failed—the water froze up in the shallow pipe system before Bill got it shut off. The spring creek flowing from the timbered mountain up behind the cabins would freeze and thaw and terrace up in frozen knobs and boils. The day before Moocher had brushed Bill off an icy plank at the spring, chasing a snowshoe rabbit who played daily games with the useless warrior.

Mittens and Scotch cap in place, old Bill warily opened the door. Just before he got it jerked shut behind him, Moocher flashed past him and out. Bill was thrown into the cross chains of a log sled just outside the door. The heavy snow muffled his curses and the sounds of flying pails, but cushioned his fall. Moocher was chasing a weasel. Its black tail tip flipped in derision as it disappeared under the log storehouse.

Bill got up, wordless now in the gathering light. He gave an angry glance back at the cabin, but its closed door was no help. He found the pails and started plowing through the fresh snow, past the gloomy deserted summer cabins. As his feet felt for the snow-filled trail, his eyes automatically looked for stray moose in the willows on each side of his path. Near the river he looked up the trail to the cowshed and corral, thinking he ought to have given the little Jersey more hay last night.

Moose tracks were everywhere, criss-crossed through the deep snow from one dense willow clump to the next. Hummocks and dead willow roots made it rough country for walking, down here where the river's roar sounded from the water hole, where the frosty mist smoked up from the dark rushing water. Trotting warily along, Bill wished he'd worn his sheepskin coat. His loose teeth chattered in time with his shivering limbs. The intense cold was eating its way in under the ragged henskin jacket. Bad footing here; glassy from spilled water. No animals in sight among the willows of the jungly cafeteria; but some melted beds showed where they'd been.

Bill set his pails down to get a good look around before filling them.

These willows had seen foot-races before, Bill so far staying the winner. Now he wished he'd slung his trusty '06 on his back. Just as he started to kneel down on the ragged edge of the chopped-out water hole, he tottered on the slick ice and nearly fell in—Moocher had arrived in a snowy rush, just brushing the hillbilly's pants as he passed. Scared and enraged, the water packer stood and wildly informed the snowy landscape of his very low opinion of the collie and his alleged pedigree. Moocher, meanwhile, white tail proudly high, was gaily disappearing down the river on a moose trail.

Bill hurriedly knelt down again. As the rushing water filled his pail, he jerked it up and set it brimming on a flat place on the slippery trail. The bail of the bucket stood upright, frozen into place. Another shivering look around, and old Bill grabbed the other pail and quickly bent down.

Just as the furious water yanked at it, he heard a ki-yi-yi-ing of desperate come-help-me anguish. He looked up to see Velma's registered pride and joy flying to him for protection, with a big bull moose close behind. The pail made a choked clatter as the river grabbed it, and Bill took off, waiting for no formal introduction. Believing in straight lines, he pounded his packs toward the closer cow's corral and safer quarters. A cold hollowness inside him promoted record time. The mighty Moocher left a trail of woeful wails up the longer trail toward the cabins.

The moose quickly transferred his hostile intentions and now wanted to get acquainted with the water packer. But as he swerved to his new course he saw the bucket and plowed to a stop, his big toes and dewclaws raising a cloud of snow. He snorted and blew through his bulbous smeller at the thing in his way. Nothing moved. He pawed, then hooked at the bucket. As he brought up his antlers, the long brow tine on one side hooked into the waiting bail. Bill's reprieve was over; the jar broke the surface ice on the filled pail; it cracked like a gun. Old Snooty took off in a hurry after the mountain man. Poor Ol' Bill heard the whanging and banging of metal and horn, but about that time he didn't feel curious. Just short of the corral, he skidded to a hard fall. The cow trail dipped down and over the deep ruts of Bill's sled road to timber. There Bill sprawled in a frantic wrestle with frosty gravity.

Up came the moose, full speed ahead, muttering querulous grunts at the tinny rattling. One eye was hidden by icicles and hoarfrost, the other rolled in a vicious calculation. But he was off a little on windage and elevation, for he missed the scrambling man by a yard.

He was off a little on windage and elevation.

Bill got up and galloped up to and over the corral in one frantic surge of speed. He'd had a cold canine start, but his arrival was a race-horse finish. He sounded like a wind-broken Caruso.

His pet, the little milk cow, was bedded down in the open-faced shed, chewing her cud in sleepy comfort, when she was thus rudely interrupted. Her rest had been disturbed by nightly observations by curious moose peepers, and now, by alfalfa, here they were again, and in the daytime!

She got up in a furious Jersey tantrum, sharp curved horns down. With an unladylike bellow, her bell clanging, she charged out of the flimsy shed at the first thing she saw, poor old sweating and heaving Bill. This was Bill's second race. He scrambled for the highest corral pole. It wasn't high enough, and the moose belched willowy blasts into his face. So Thompson raced around inside, pursued by the bellowing Jersey, while the moose raced outside. He got the pail dislodged and stomped it into a tinny mess. His squealing roars kept encouraging the Jersey.

Bill finally made a damn-near-too-late Orville Wright to the top of the shed. In the race, he'd lost his Scotch cap and a mitten. As he jumped, he hoped that the slight loss of weight would be enough to keep him from going through the flimsy roof.

He tried to sweet-talk the Jersey into remembering him. The moose stopped to listen. Through with her moose-mare, the cow finally calmed down and let Bill get off the roof.

He was getting chillier and chillier, chattering and shaking with cold. When he pulled the jacket up to warm his cold head, his back was exposed. He tried to put both hands into one mitten, with no luck. The bull moose just stayed there, re-stomping the battered bucket, making muttering squeals at the corral. Bill shouted and hollered for Velma, with no luck so far. The cabin was west of the corrals, and the wind was wrong. A heavy stand of timber muffled the sounds of his hoarse calls for help.

Yelping up the cabin trail, Moocher was stopped by the closed door. Sure that Bill was in a tantrum at some prank of her pet, Velma let him in. She gave him some milk, and went on mixing up flapjacks for the three of them. By now she began to get worried about Bill. She put on her heavy coat and her overshoes and went out into the bitter Wyoming weather, with Moocher along for protection.

First she went to the brink of the hill to look toward the waterhole. She yelled and yelled and peered through frost-rimmed eyelids down at the clusters of willows. No sign of Bill, but her screaming intrigued the remaining lodge brothers of Ol' Bill's big bull moose. Seeing those dark big ears coming into sight, Velma remembered how Bill, a member of the Elks, said the B.P.O.E. had the Moose skinned all to thunder. She became alarmed, thinking Bill was mebbe being initiated into an order he detested. Moocher barked to the universe. The west wind carried the barks and yells down to the corral.

Velma remembered the corral. She retraced her steps to the cabin, then went eastward on the bobsled tracks till she could see out of the timber to the corral and shed below. At first, in the numbing cold, she could see nothing but a moose moving slowly round the outside of the snowy corral, and the Jersey inside. She was just about to turn back when the wind died down, and Bill managed to turn loose one last loud yowl for help. The Jersey, startled, shook her head, and her bell set up a hollow bonging. Moocher dodged Velma's fingers and dashed down the hill, looking for an exhilarating cow chase.

Velma trotted bravely down the frozen ruts, her fear of moose overcome by her love of the dog. The moose looked up when he heard her shrill calls, and saw the small red-coated figure and the spurting gusts of Moocher-driven snow. He gave a weird rolling snort and took off at a swinging trot for the heavy timber, his long hairy bell dangling sidewise in the wind.

Bill had only a hoarse greeting of "That blamed dog." Velma gasped angrily, "Why, you old stoop, he saved your life, and you still run him down!"

Crouched by the roaring fire in the stove, Bill gradually thawed out. Velma poured coffee and set out breakfast. Now in a more genial frame of mind, Bill even gave the collie a furtive grin. But when he started to eat the tender and fragrant elk steaks, he let out a howl of frustration. "What in the world is biting you now?" asked Velma, surprised and angry.

Bill choked out, "It's me, biting this elk meat! Now it ain't only that confounded collie and no water pails, but where in hell are my new store teeth?"

Innocent Hell-Raiser

Bill pulled up the team, with only another hundred yards to go. "Danged if the chain didn't slip off again. Better not take a chance. These horses are still spooky from them moose last winter." He kept a tight hold on the lines, and walked over to tie on to a standing tree beside the rocky skid trail. The load was a light one—some poles for the buck fence he was building—but he'd been hauling plenty of them this spring. The tired rancher mused, "If I don't see another blamed bog-trotter in a hundred years, that'd be too soon."

Ol' Bill took the chain off the doubletrees and wrapped a couple hitches around the pile of long poles. He got the slide hook adjusted. He was about to hook into the clevis on the doubletrees when the team of roans lunged ahead, snorting their fright at something coming out of the willows along the creek below the skid trail. Bill saw that the tied lines stopped the jittery horses, and looked around. There was a long-legged moose calf staggering up out of the rocky creek. His reddish coat was splotched with mud, and the eyes in his homely big head were half shut. A long gash on one of his knobby hind legs was sticky with half-dried blood.

The logger put his big hands over his eyes and moaned, "Oh, not again, oh, no! All winter long, and here's one o' th' dang babies come to gimme hell." As he stared at the short-backed, long-legged infant of the swampy jungles, the ugly little fellow gave a weak whine and fell down, right at Bill's unwilling feet. Now, you couldn't fool ol' Bill, not with this kind of "Come on, sucker" play. He knew that maw was handy, and when a mama moose mislays her baby there's hell to pay. Bill didn't feel like paying any bills, not then, and not to any damn moose. He knew that moosenapping is a dang sight more dangerous than kidnapping. He was about to leave those poles and take him and the horses to a safer place as of now. "Damn the snooty things, anyhow." Then Bill furiously untied the lines and drove the anxious horses at a trot further up into heavier timber. He looked back down at the dense growth of willows. There was no movement except the moose calf trying weakly to regain his feet. Bill took down the halter ropes and tied the snuffy team to a big tree. He decided he had to see what the mystery was.

"I ain't too old t' climb a tree," he mumbled to himself, "but mebbe I won't have ta." He looked cautiously in all directions as he walked down through the trees. He made a sneaky circle through the jungle of willows, crossed the roaring creek on a handy log, and was about to head back toward the moose calf, when he saw a couple of ravens fly up out of a clump of small spruce just below him. He went to look and came on the dead body of a huge cow moose. Her hind leg was trapped in a snaky loop of a tree root. The broken leg, the torn up earth and rocks, the peeled bark on the spruce told the story of a futile battle. Now it looked like her forlorn heir still had hopes there must be friends somewhere in these hills.

Bill paused just to look at the starved swamp baby. But when the ugly calf swayed suddenly to his feet and grabbed Bill's fingers to start sucking, the hillbilly knew he was lost.

"I don't give a hoot what Velma says," Bill tells the wall-eyed little starveling, "a feller can't let ambition like this go to waste." With a bunch of green branches tied on to the poles with one halter rope, and the struggling orphan tied to this bed with another, Bill skidded the whole wooden ambulance right down in front of the cabin.

Velma was making butter in her new churn, but when she heard the snorting horses and dragging poles she came out on the back porch. There followed exclamations, valiant struggles by the moose, explanations, and then a bottle of milk. During its administration, Velma delivered her ultimatum on the whole moosey deal. "Now, Bill, as soon as this poor little rascal is able t' fend for himself, you'll have to run him off. From what I've seen of all your pets so far, if you don't, he'll try t' run us off before he's done. You've had 'em in your hair all winter, and now you bring one right inta the house. Looks like you don't feel natural 'thout a moose bein' close around."

In a week or so, it looked like Nosy would make it. Velma and Bill figured out some kind of a milk formula that seemed to agree with him. "Maybe it's un-Christian, but I'm afraid he's going t' live," Velma said to Bill one day, when Moocher the collie got kicked in the ribs for taking a jealous nip at the calf. "He's gotta defend himself, ain't he? If Moocher bit you on the rump, what would you do?" asked Bill, rubbing Nosy's big head.

The bull calf and Moocher made up. They would romp around like a couple of kids. But Nosy hated the cat and would vainly try to stomp on Tabby with his sharp toes. He didn't like strangers. Any who came visiting caused him to hide behind Velma or Bill, mane hair straight up, and even the hairy fringe on his sharp little rump standing

31

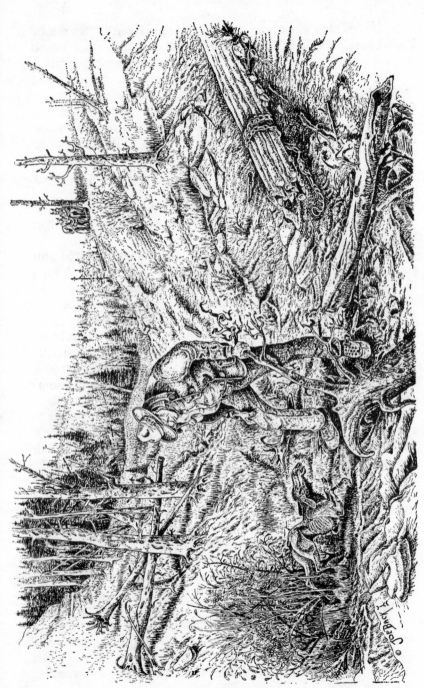

Bill paused just to look at the starved swamp baby.

Velma and Bill figured out a milk formula.

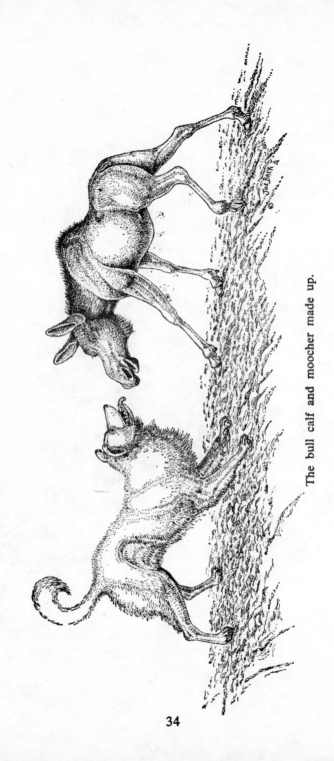

The bull calf and moocher made up.

34

Velma was showered with flapjacks.

35

erect. He began to figure he was the most important one in the family. He would come like a dog when he was called. He learned to pry his way into the kitchen and would sprawl on Velma's linoleum looking for handouts of celery leaves or other vegetable tidbits. She drove him out so many times he finally quit trying that. He grew fast. By the end of July he began to change color. His reddish brown started to become a grayish black on the body, and his legs up to the knees and hocks turned grayish white. He got into so many jackpots and caused so much trouble that both Bill and Velma began to wish they'd never seen him. "Adolescent moose get teen-aged a swamp sight quicker'n kids do," said Velma one day. Bill, who had suffered that time, said, "You mean a damn sight."

One morning Velma put some sourdough pancakes out for Moocher. The moose calf happened by, chased the dog off, and gobbled the cakes down. The busy housewife in the kitchen thought she heard a far-off train whistle and ran out the door to see how civilization could have got there that fast. There stood the ungainly swamp angel with his first case of hiccups. His short body was bunched together on those extra long legs, and his round belly was going like a blacksmith's bellows. He had his ears back, and his bell-shaped snoot high in the air, snuffling like a wind-broken horse. Ol' Bill was starting to saddle a horse in front of the barn when he heard Velma yelling. That was when Bill really got in the doghouse, for he came running up to the long-snouted calliope and brought down a heavy saddle blanket ka-whompie on the heaving calf's back. That stopped the hiccups in a hurry. But poor Velma, standing unstrategically in front of the bull calf, was showered with her own damp flapjacks.

Moocher came out from under the safe porch in a yelping hurry to bite the belcher on the hind leg. Nosy's kick missed the collie, but Bill got it on his belt buckle. As the moose was growing fast, being fed on things people say moose don't eat, that was a hefty punch. When Mr. Thompson got his wind back, *he* had the hiccups, but that didn't keep him from whacking the disillusioned bull calf clear across the creek. The coughing man realized this was a huskier baby than he'd thought. His belly hurt.

No Butter on Sunday

"The minister and his new city wife are coming up for dinner, Bill." Velma was pulling fresh loaves from the hot oven. "Now, this is Sunday, and I don't want them to think we are heathens even if we are hillbillies. So if you can, just for once, keep that so-called pet of yours out of the way, maybe we can have a peaceful day." She had just got a new hairdo yesterday and felt as chipper as she looked.

Bill said he'd put the calf moose in the new horse corral just back on the barn. So he got some watercress from the fenced-in spring and tolled his bulb-nosed pet down to the corral. Next chore was the Jersey. She'd somehow got out of the cow corral last night, gathered up her calf, newly broken to drink, and hadn't shown up to be milked. As Bill saddled up a horse to ride the big meadow in search of her, he saw the moose calf still peacefully chewing watercress in the horse corral, and Velma was in sight, bustling around, sweeping the back porch. The horse snapped into a fast trot when Bill popped him with the reins. As he rode off, the thought occurred to him, "Mebbe that dang moose *is* gettin' t' be kind of a halfway pest at that. The blame thing *is* kind of rambunctious." Now, some pets are gentle and all lovey-dovey; Bill Thompson thought his moose was, but then he was bunkhouse raised, you might say. As a guide, packer, and mountain rancher, his ideas were a little basic and down-to-earth. Ol' Bill believed that Nature was gentle, if you understood just what was natural with some of Nature's children.

Everything was percolating just right, Velma thought, as she watched through a window in her trim kitchen. She could see part of the road down past the lodgepole pines and expected the minister and his wife to show up on it. "Better get fresh eggs for the cake icing," she thought, and left the kitchen and walked down the path to the log barn. She found six or eight in the manger. On her way back she went to check the long-legged menace in the horse corral. She opened the gate and saw Nosy asleep in the shadow cast by the barn. She had trouble with the pole slide lock on the gate but thought it was OK. Then she started round the barn for the house.

A new red jeep was just chugging up the road. So Velma hurried up, went in the kitchen to put the eggs away, looked in the mirror on

37

the wall to put any stray locks in place. Then she dashed to the front door, just in time to welcome the tall and smiling minister and his very dainty and feminine little wife. Velma noticed the new jeep roll forward slightly, then stop, a front wheel against a large pebble. After she'd made her visitors comfortable in the living room, Velma excused herself to put dinner on the table, saying Bill would show up soon. "Our Jersey strayed off and Bill's gone to find her. He should be here now."

As she went to the springhouse she saw Bill unsaddle his horse at the barn. The cow and her calf were in the corral gently nosing each other.

The ambitious calf moose must have pushed open the corral gate right after Velma thought she'd fastened it. In the course of his survey of what's new he saw the jeep. He had a violent dislike of any stranger or strange thing, so he smelled this suspicious object, gave a few angry squeals, backed off, and then rammed the machine into movement. As the jeep started slowly ahead, he figured that's that, the durned thing's leaving. So he trotted around the cabin just in time to see Velma leaning in the door of the springhouse. Velma had reached past some crocks of cream half immersed in the cold water to get a jar of butter, when Nosy, playfully asking for attention, gave her a very firm affectionate nudge with his big head.

Bill had decided to milk the Jersey out before he went to the house, so there he sat, with his head in her brown flank, milking away at a great rate. The peace of the Sabbath and of Bill's mind were soon shattered by the most hideous sounds ever heard on this mountain ranch. Suddenly, with deadly precision, the gentle little Jersey kicked old Bill in his unsuspecting and empty belly with one set of hooves, then rammed another set, jack-hammer style, in the nearly full pail of rich milk. The poor wrinkled-up old milkmaid sat down hard and lay back on his elbows, slathered from stem to stern, while the cow ran bellering over to the calf bawling through the corral bars. And here came his moose pet desperately whining for help. He was in a fast trot, with Velma beating on his numbed differential with a ripped-off 2x4 studded with rusty nails. The air vibrated with hideous imprecations. Bill Thompson was startled by the sudden knowledge that women can swear without cussing.

Velma's Sunday dress was all streaked and blobbed with rich Jersey cream, and her hairdo was buttered up, Mongolian style. The mountain stillness of the sunny Sabbath was punctuated with, "Either that horrible bat-brained moose has gotta go or I do, *and* it's not go-

The Jersey kicked Ol' Bill.

Gently nosing his milky overalls.

ing to be *me,* I can tell you *that!* Mr. 'Oh! he's just an innocent animal!' *Blah!* So *there!"*

A tinny crash of metal and tinkling glass in front of the cabin brought the moose- and cow-smeared pardners up there in a stumbling run, just as the tall minister and his new bride came out of the front door at an undignified trot. There was the new jeep in the rocks of the tumbling stream, with its proud red front in a pile of snaggy driftwood. As the four people gazed down together, Bill felt the huge nose of his innocent pet gently nosing his milky overalls.

Salad Days

Things weren't always at a crisis. Nosy, the pest, would disappear for a week or so at a time on business of his own. Velma was relieved, but Bill, though he wouldn't admit it, sort of missed the trouble-maker. One day he was down the road putting new poles in a section of buck fence where a falling tree had wrecked it. Some cattle passed him. When the cowboy driving them saw Bill, he got off his horse and came over to visit. It was Tony Belknap. No sooner had they howdyed and started passing news of the mountains when out of the timber came Bill's bog trotter. He walked up behind his friend, rubbed up against him, and stood glaring and snuffling at the startled cowhand.

Tony, taking no chances, hopped on his snorting pony and backed him away. "Well, I'll be damned. After all the hell them things gave yuh, yuh had ta take one in ta raise. Man, are you bushed!" Tony grunted, staring at the raised mane and laid-back ears. As he reined his horse around to leave, he sent a parting shot, "Tell Velma t' quit feedin' yuh willows!" Bill grinned and threw an arm over Nosy's withers.

The moose had disappeared another time, when Bill stopped his old pickup in the yard. Velma came out of the house and picked up the box of groceries Bill had brought from town, while he headed for the woodpile. She carefully set the grub down on the porch chair and started to open the kitchen door. She heard a crispy crunch behind her and turned to see the long stem end of her precious celery just going down Nosy's big maw. That was too much for Velma. She galloped off the porch and grabbed the nearest weapon handy, a garden rake. The young bull with the longest nose on Roaring River dodged, but not fast enough. Velma was raking his gray rump with every step. If you don't think ranch women can run and holler at the same time, you should have seen this race. Moocher, tagging along behind, enjoyed it, but Nosy didn't. In the short time it took the speeding moose to get to the woodpile, the ferocious housewife had a crossword puzzle pattern engraved in red furrows on the robber's back. Velma's fellow members of the church guild would have been

Velma was raking his gray rump.

43

dismayed to hear the descriptive comments that came down with every vicious stroke of their chairman's weapon.

Bill Thompson, the alleged head of the house, had ten good toes, but nearly lost half of them when his falling axe missed the block of wood. The squealing calf had run right into Bill's long legs, looking desperately for protection.

"If you don't run this hateful big-nosed pest off the place, Bill, I will." Poor Velma was heaving and the rake was waving. "He's going to eat us all out of house and home." The four-legged menace hid squarely behind the tall woodchopper, rolling his little eyes and squirming his aching back up against his protector.

"Well, now, I reckon that's my fault. I was goin' t' put th' fence up around th' cabin, but I ain't got enough poles out yet. I'll start in tomorrow." Bill sat down on a block of wood. His prized pet gave him an affectionate nudge, and Bill narrowly missed slicing his hand on the double-bitted axe.

Velma, tired out and still exasperated, glared at the moose. "Well, I just hope the game warden catches up with you. Keeping that thing around here is against the law." She waved her rake. The calf ducked his head and pushed closer to Bill. "Now, *look,* this little devil can leave *anytime*. What th' law says is, no game animal can be kept in captivity." Bill waved his hands at the timbered mountain back of the log buildings. "He's free as the air."

"Well, they'll have to change the laws, then, or I will," said Velma, starting back to the house to get dinner. "That ornery little bog trotter has got *us* in captivity, and *I,* for one, am getting awfully blamed tired of it."

"Only time he ever *was* in captivity was the day the minister came," Bill called after her, "an' you're th' one let him out that time!"

That was a sore point with Velma. She slammed the door.

The Suitor

A few weeks after this, Velma's prim old maid sister came up for a visit. She was a retired county school superintendent and an active despot in her church. Minnie had an ill-disguised disapproval of Bill's way of life, so her visits were painful for him. This time Bill had a good excuse to get away for awhile. He had to drive the old pickup into town to get plumbing fixtures, as the indoor facilities had gone out of kilter.

The old gal used the very latest perfume, a heady mixture that attracted nobody but the pet moose, and he had a pungent odor all his own. This militant old sister detested the bog trotter, but Nosy was the only suitor she had ever had in a long life of pedagogical frustration. She rarely came to the ranch, mostly because of him and his delighted attentions. For this Bill was privately grateful. When she did show up, the moose was Johnny on the spot, if the wind was right. Her violent reactions didn't bother this gangly-legged suitor; on her visits he'd try to push open doors and bust windows. On one historic occasion he tried to cram into her car with her.

Ol' Minnie had just gone out to the Chic Sales when the assistant county assessor drove up to the house. He was a deacon in Minnie's church, and they had small charity for each other. His job took him over a lot of the county, and he had developed a newsy neighborliness. This habit made him welcome at lonely ranches and helped to soften the blow of more taxes. Velma and the assessor were in the kitchen talking over county happenings, when weird screams and delighted squeals brought them on the run to the back porch. The old school mom stood in the door of the rickety Chic Sales throwing heavy mail-order catalogs at her detested sloppy-nosed admirer. Her lurid invective was highly interesting, but her aim was poor. Evidently the affectionate willow-cruncher thought his beloved was only playing a game, for he was up close, snorting his happy approval. Poor Minnie was out of vocabulary and ammunition when her giggling sister and the interested assessor rescued her. Velma ran the young moose off with her broom, and the scoop-heavy deacon soon left on more official business.

The dictator of many a schoolroom, long skinny arms akimbo,

stood on the back porch staring in rage at the fast disappearing car. As the lodgepole pines hid the joyous reporter's bouncing vehicle, she whirled on her sister. Velma retreated into the kitchen and stood at the table rolling out pie dough. She expected Bill home for dinner, and this was a bang-up meal she was fixing up in honor of Minnie's visit.

The irate old maid stood glowering at her sister. Velma was choking down mirth as she lined her pie tins with dough. "Never in my born days has anything so embarrassed me, or have I been subjected to such insulting indignities." Minnie's bejewelled horn-rimmed glasses trembled on her long intellectual nose. "Between that misbegotten, moth-eaten, malicious moose pet of that mule-headed husband of yours, and that hypocritical, tongue-wagging church mouse of a cheap politician," she paused for a righteous breath, "I'll be the laughing stock of the whole stupid county!" Her long pendant earrings jangled in tune with her vibrating jaws, as Velma shoved the pies in the oven, and put more wood in the shining stove.

Nosy in the meantime took his disappointed majesty back around the barn. He spied his arch-enemy, the tiger-striped tabby cat, stalking a mouse. The frustrated yearling sensed honor regained and took after Tabby. The cat whipped around the log barn, hell for breakfast, with the humpy calf in close pursuit. After losing the chase to the hay shed, Nosy was shoving his long snoot up against a bale of hay, wondering where in Hades she'd got to. He found out in a hurry, for the cat's kittens were in a warm pocket under that bale. She had no catalogs to throw, but she thought maybe moose eat kittens. So she came out of her chute with a snarling yowl, lit on Nosy's high withers, sank her sets of sharp spurs in his humpy shoulders, and went to scratching, Cheyenne style, rowdy dow.

This moose didn't buck but he sure did bawl. And then he suddenly decided misery loves company. The tigerish contestant was making a buzz-saw ride on the lonesome calf, but left her mount and jumped up on the porch roof when the frantic pet burst up against the screen door to the kitchen.

Bill was just coming in the front door of the cabin with his arms full of store plunder when he was knocked down and run over by his terrified, high-heeled sister-in-law. He got up in a bruised hurry when he heard the screaming hullaballoo at the back door. Running around the cabin, Bill was just in time to get a second and third dose of moositis, for he was knocked down and run over by the fleeing calf

The contestant was making a buzz-saw ride.

He was knocked down and run over by the calf and Velma in turn.

and Velma in turn. She had her broom working, and her flow of language showed that education ran in her family.

Breathless, his wife helped poor down-trodden Bill to his unsteady feet. He could hardly stand. The tough old hillbilly had moose and woman tracks all over his aching carcass. Velma suddenly thought of Minnie when she heard a muffled screech. A heavy door slammed, and down the road went her sister's new car. Right behind it, his long nose high in the air, was the calf moose. He was in an ungainly trot, but making good time.

After he had heard the story of Nosy's last exploits, Bill agreed that the youngster would have to find a new home. "When he shows up again, I'll run him off." Bill privately hoped, though, if Nosey did show up it would be when Minnie paid them another visit. That would help some.

Nosy and the Pin-Ups

Ol' Bill started to swear when the worn pipe wrench slipped again, then he remembered the company Velma was entertaining in the front room. He could hear the voice of Hector McBain, a deacon in Velma's church.

"Ol' Fact 'n' Figgers tryin' t'sell Vel some more insurance," Bill blew on his skinned-up knuckles. He just got a fresh holt with the wrench when he heard hoarse whispering back of him.

"Say, Bill, I know your facilities are not in order now." Old McBain was leaning over the bowlegged plumber and looking furtively over his shoulder towards the teacups rattling in the next room. "But I need to go, and do you have a place?"

Thompson wearily got up from the jumble of pipe fittings on the floor and pointed out the window. "See that building right next ta the bunkhouse? That's what we're usin' till I git this layout goin' again."

The portly man pursed his lips, then started out the back door at a half trot. Thompson saw McBain go in the Chic Sales, and then he sat down on the floor again to tinker with the assortment of pipe fittings.

The hornets figured that their nest was anchored plenty strong under the eaves above the door of the shaky building. They got kind of waspy when their home was half shook loose as the deacon slammed the door. When those angry bugs in the yellow jackets started to swarm through the many cracks in the building, the distracted insurance man was stung to violent action. He kicked a couple of shaky boards loose in the back of the trembling edifice, squeezed through, and galloped off in the direction of his car, parked in front of Thompson's cabin. Moocher, from under the back porch, saw the frantic man in a high lope, slapping at his head with one hand and holding his britches with the other. He helped speed the frustrated deacon on his way.

Life seemed sort of uncertain lately for the moose. He sensed an unfriendly atmosphere around the ranch. He had sneaked out of the timber and was now chewing his cud behind the barn. When he heard Moocher's enthusiastic barking over by the bunkhouse, Nosy heaved

The peppery and astonished face of Mrs. Hector McBain.

up on his hind legs to investigate the proceedings.

The moose calf happened to see the loose boards lying on the ground behind the sittin' and thinkin' establishment, so he walked up to see about the new opening in the back of the building. The hornets by this time had given up and buzzed away elsewhere to discuss a new location for their headquarters. Having become quite a student of human nature, the nosy calf stuck his long head and short neck through the deacon's door. He got to studying the pin-up pictures that Tony Belknap had nailed to the inside of the old door last fall.

Lulu McBain got uneasy over the long absence of her crusty old husband. Finding where he'd gone, she called several times. Old Heck didn't answer, so Lulu got alarmed, ran up to the small and silent building, and jerked the door open.

The moose hadn't yet come to any nearsighted conclusions on the lithographed dreams of Tony the cowboy. He was now patiently chewing his cud, still staring at the pictures. His attention was rudely diverted from a pretty pin-up to the peppery and astonished face of Mrs. Hector McBain.

Belknap was having his jug ears lifted in Harry Clipper's barber shop when he heard the story. "Yuh don't believe it, huh? Why, you birds don't know the half of it. You'd be surprised at whut ol' Bill teaches that dang moose. Sure he uses th' Chic Sales. Why, that nutty packer regards th' blasted thing as a member o' the family. Wouldn't supprise me none if they feed 'im at th' table next!"

Just Married

"My gosh, Jeannie, we forgot to bring a lantern." Colvin Larsen put another small branch on the campfire. "I just looked through all our things, and no candles or flashlights, either." Jeannie, the young bride of a few hours, sat on a log close by her young husband. "M-m-m, Colvin, I like it dark."

Nosy, on his way home from visiting some upland swamps, was coming down a trail when he smelled the smoke. Over in a small timber-surrounded park he saw the dim shape of a car lit up by flickering firelight. The sounds and smells coming from the two vague shapes sitting close together on a log aroused Nosy's sense of conquest. Maybe this *was* a closed corporation, but the dark night and his ever-present appetite decided the moose to look over the prospectus. The honeymooners were reaching into a well-filled basket and feeding each other tidbits. The dying embers of the small fire didn't give much light, but the two young lovers, engrossed in their new status, didn't need any.

About the time Jeannie reached into the basket for another cookie, the infernal triangle thrust its long nose in between the happy affairs of the newlyweds. As the happy bride handed a nice mayonnaise concoction up to Colvin, Nosy daintily took the offering and started chewing it with gusto.

Jeannie said, "Oh, Colvin, dear, isn't this a dream, just like we planned!" Nosy, busy chewing a pickle, gave a little simpering whine. Colvin, not to be outdone by Jeannie's generosity, answered, "Here's a real nice olive and lettuce deal, honey." As the bog trotter very delicately received the choice tidbit, Colvin didn't want to look. He thought, "Jeannie sure does make a lot of noise eating." His beloved, reaching down for another morsel, was really put out. "My, Colvin is sure a sloppy eater. Funny I never noticed it before." Oddly enough, both the newlyweds were feeding themselves, too, besides supposedly feeding each other. With the new development, the erstwhile happy couple couldn't bear to look at one another.

It occurred to them both that "this must have been a strenuous day, the way we're disposing of this food." As they blindly handed up food to the new member of the troupe, the moocher, not wanting to

Nosy, busy chewing a pickle gave a little simpering whine.

show favorites with such generous new-found friends, rested his chin alternately on each shoulder, and entered into the slowed-down conversation with gulpy gargles. As the chompy smacking continued, both Colvin and his wife were privately thinking of all they'd heard and read of what it takes to make a solid, long-lasting marriage. "Smackey smack. Chompety chomp." "This fifty-fifty business of give and take." This business of such gusty and vociferous appreciation of food would be hard to take for a lifetime. "Oh, my," she thought. "This is terrible," he shuddered. As they fed themselves, and, unknowing, their guest, the disillusioned couple kept their gaze averted. The three-way disposal of food continued.

The distracted young lovers suddenly became aware of a new crisis. The wind rose slightly, just as Nosy nestled closer, in breathless ecstacy, to these fine providers. They wondered simultaneously how in the world so delicate a subject as halitosis should come to their minds. As this fresh danger to a continued happy marriage showed up, the random thoughts became intense. "It's a touchy situation" . . . "What friends could I ask to approach the subject?" . . . . . "These short engagements, hmmm" . . . . . "Never woulda' thought it could be *so terribly awful!*"

The unhappy couple, busy worrying about this noisy and smelly flaw in their early wedded bliss, let the campfire die down. Their attention wasn't on food. In the dark their selection became hit and miss. Jeannie handed up a pickled pepper, which found its spicy way into the bogtrotter's busy jaws. The resulting wheezy expectoration suddenly blew up the coals and put a different light on the situation.

At the first strangling wheeze, thinking to put their arms around each other in alarmed protection, the pair found themselves hugging the hairy moose. The sadly reproachful stare of Nosy's little pig eyes didn't soften the screamy yells as the honeymooners climbed two separate and surprised trees.

During the flurry of his sudden abandonment, Nosy found that he had stepped on a hot coal and now had a burned place on the underside of a front toe. Seeking solace and help from his friends in the upper brackets, he wore a path between the trees. His mournful come-help-me squealed whines made the separated lovebugs sure a bear had joined the joyful procession, and the darkness helped the illusion. The anxious queries of the divorced providers were rudely interrupted by the floppy-nosed member of the triangle. He would limp back and forth from tree to tree, and at every desperate attempt at communication would belch his whiny complaints.

The bridal suite had branched out into two barky roosts through no previous plans of the besieged couple. "If this is togetherness," the pet mused bitterly in his boggy mind, "I'll put in with yuh. Home was never like this." Jeannie and Colvin entertained similar thoughts. For them it was lucky the night was warm, as their clothes weren't the class for that type of high living. Being young, they didn't suffer much. This bridal couple was different from the general run. It wasn't darkness they craved, it was light, that would identify the unknown menace at the foot of their trees.

It seemed like eternity to the people up above. But it was only a couple of hours before one of the coals from the scattered campfire decided to help them out. A slight breeze whipped the coal into igniting some vagrant and very dry branches under their perches. When the blaze flared up, the cold couple saw a small moose rise up from their wedding gift blankets behind the log. Colvin recognized Nosy from a former visit to Bill's ranch. He scrambled down out of his tree with a relieved yell. He got hold of a dead limb and whacked the moose across the nose a few times. Nosy took off in a scared hurry and disappeared into the heavy timber.

The two new Larsens soon had a big fire going. By the time they had their tent pitched they were able to laugh at the only moose shivaree they'd ever heard of.

The rest of the night was very peaceful.

The next morning after a late breakfast they decided to move camp to a small lake just off the forest road. They'd packed everything into the car before Colvin discovered the ignition key had been left on.

"Well, darn it, Jeannie, looks like I'll have to go down to Thompson's ranch." Colvin kicked at a tire. "Maybe I can get Ol' Bill to come up in his pickup and give us a pull. There's enough juice for ignition if we can just start her." The bride sat on a log and stared at her husband, then she started to giggle. Colvin got mad for the first time in his young married life. When she kept on laughing, he started to splutter. Then the thought struck him that she had been too long up in the air, and might be just a trifle touched.

"Oh, honey, with all those cuts and scratches you got going up the tree last night, you wouldn't dare." The bridegroom had his jaw dropped down on his brisket now as he looked his new wife over. She had a cut over one pretty eyebrow and some scratches across her throat and chin. Otherwise she looked the loveliest bride he ever saw. Larsen looked at the old model car, then back at Jeannie. "Are you *sure* you feel all right, Sweetie-pie? Why shouldn't I dare?"

56

Jeannie giggled when she pointed to all the soapwritings their friends had plastered on the car. "That's why, you big ninny."

Colvin had a small garage in town. Lots of people thought he was the best mechanic in Roaring River. Some said he had only wheels in his head. But when he saw "Just Married" printed on the back window a great light dawned. He had to sit down beside Jeannie and laugh, too.

Finally he jacked the hind wheels up in the air and cranked his engine by turning a wheel in gear. The motor caught. Soon they were chugging up the road. As they passed an opening in the timber they could look down on Bill Thompson's ranch cabins in the valley. Just below the corrals they caught a glimpse of Nosy, on the edge of a willow bog. He was looking at their moving car with a moldy stare. The couple waved at the moose and drove laughing up the road.

Picnic

A row of shiny cars was lined up over in the shade of pines on the far side of a big park. Not far off, a laughing crowd of brightly dressed people were clustered around some fishermen, who were showing off their fine catches of trout. A few children were trying to climb trees, playing tag, and skylarking around in the tall yellow grass.

The meeting of the Federation of Fair Play to Nature was a great success. Some of the big city members were there, and the Grand High Potentate of all the national clubs had given a speech. The picnic following it was to be held in Moose Park—"Oh, sure, a lot of us have fished up there." The Boy Scout leader knew the country. He said, "Well, it's a big meadow surrounded by timber. Creek runs through the edge of it. We'll have a good time. Safe for the kids." A member of the local ski club said, "We go up to the Pass to ski, go right by the park. Never saw a moose there. Not many left. Named Moose Park by early settlers. What moose there's left are probably higher in the mountains this time of year. Only takes a couple hours to drive. Good road."

Maybe clothes don't make the moose, but Nosy didn't know the difference. He'd had a bath, in his private wallow a couple miles above Ol' Bill's ranch. After he'd scrambled out of his cozy mud hole, he gulped a few snorts of the delicious brown liquid that floated on the surface of the pool nearby—this thick liquor of spring water and years of rotted willow leaves, swamp grass, and deceased frogs makes moose act the way they do. So the young bull, strutting out of his spruce shaded bar, felt like he was able to face the world again. As the swamp angel walked over to the edge of the mountain park, he heard sounds over by the creek. Surveying the scene from behind a tree, he saw some women spreading blankets and white cloths on the ground, and scurrying back and forth from automobiles on the far side of the grassy park.

Those jolts of willow liquor from his private stock were just getting hold of Bill's pet. He flapped his big ears and rolled his eyes to get control of himself. The moose felt that the brave deserve the fair, and the small breeze told him that there might be a fairly edible meal for a young moose bound to get ahead. So he backed up into the heavy timber to take a sashay around for a more strategic assault. Things had started to look up on Roaring River. The closer he got to the line of cars, the surer his sensitive snoot was that prosperity was just around the bend. But his dreams of sudden subsidy were shattered by the kid up a tree.

A small girl standing on the ground was applauding the brave efforts of an older boy. He was perched eight feet or so up a tree, poking a stick at a chattering pine squirrel in the top. The girl caught a glimpse of Nosy moving close by, suddenly screamed, "Bear! Bear!" and took off at a yelping run for her mother over by the parked cars. The bog trotter's plan for collecting tribute for the invasion of his mountains was deferred for awhile. Irritated by all the yelpy screams, he was forced to make a wider detour.

The big game hunter was so startled by the scream, "Bear!" and by the noisy desertion of his ally, that he lost all holts and busted down through the branches to the ground. He lit on his eight-year-old rump, breaking the jar with his brace of quick draw six-shooters; and he had twice the lung power of any four little girls.

Galloping across the meadow, yelling, "Timmee, oh Timmee," came a big lady in pink shorts. She was waving a pan in one hand and a big long-handled spoon in the other. Several of the crowd running behind her skidded in the trail of purple pudding, but soon most of the local chapter were grouped around Timmy and his breathless Mommy. She had her arms clamped around him, and was yelling, "Get a doctor, oh, get a doctor, why doncha, somebody!"

When the small actor on the ground saw all the attention his audience was giving him, he squirmed out of his mother's arms and wailed, "I run 'em off, they was after Suzie." He pointed with his one good six-shooter, "They went that-a-way. Three big bears." While the women were collecting the kids, the men were ka-whacking tree trunks with dead limbs, throwing rocks, and shouting into the dark timber, careful not to go farther into the mysterious jungle.

In the meantime, on the far side of the grassy park, the young moose, closing in on the line of deserted cars, found several with open doors. Before the women got back to the autos to start assembling food for the hungry gang, the long-nosed investigator was suddenly given more time to evaluate the hidden assets. Their fears subsiding, the chattering women were coming back to the base of supplies, casually followed by the men, when they were electrified by some new screams down by the creek. "Wah, wa-a-a-, ouee!" A strong snag had a fat boy firmly by a hip pocket. "Oh, Dadee, help me-e-!" He was kicking and flailing his arms. One chubby hand bristled with quills. "Oh, Dad-dee, the cactus kitty hit me with his tail!"

Three or four men ran to stand underneath the tree. "Hold on, sonny, hold on." — "Hope that pocket holds." — "Man, look at that paw." The pine needles and twigs showered down into their eyes.

While the experts on the ground shouted advice, the plump youngster, full of tears and quills, was lowered to his hysterical mother. . . . "Hey, there's Johnnie Brown up there." All the eyes had been on the porcupine, and now they saw the lad higher up. He was staring down at the quill pig just below him. Frozen with terror, he was draped around the rough bark, and couldn't make a sound. The defendant in the case wasn't lifting a quill. He was out on a limb and knew it. "That murderous porcupine" was soon dislodged and now lay null and void on the ground.

The high-climbing explorer in the treetop had an athletic father who was also the executioner. He couldn't sweet-talk his boy down out of the tree, so he was soon in a bear-hugging climb up the rough ladder. The long-nosed collector of internal revenue was lucky. All the rushing back and forth of his clients had given him time to sample some of the best products of several chain stores. He found an especially appetizing bowl of salad on the back seat of a new station wagon. Both doors were conveniently left open. As he braced his long hind legs on the ground, he was comfortably resting his folded front legs on the luxurious carpet of the car floor. While daintily discarding unwanted portions over the seat, he could watch the actions of his patrons through the hospitably open door on the opposite side. He was having a snuffling good time when he heard some shouts of laughter mixed with muffled ungenteel curses.

What intrigued the young moose and delighted the sympathetic crowd gathered around, was what happened when the exasperated father deposited his son on the ground. His new high-heeled boots slipped on the slick pine needles, and he slid down the grassy slope right on top of the recently deceased. When he was helped up, he knew that there was some sticky fine print in poor Porky's last will and testament. The angry man had gathered more souvenirs with his aching differential. When the climber had started up the tree he was hungry, but now he was the only one in the bunch whose mind wasn't on food.

When the mayor's wife wasn't playing bridge, she was organizing new plays, with the lead somehow or other usually falling to her own modest self. This time she had missed a lot of dramatic potentials, for she had lost or misplaced her hearing aid. While the tree climbing rescue expedition had taken place, she was gathering spruce and pine cones for bridge favors. When she had an armful she went back to her station wagon. Just as the near-sighted lady came around a small green tree close to her car, her glasses lost their grip on her patrician nose, and fell dangling at the end of the golden chain attached to her ample bosom.

Nosy was still in the same position. He was comfortable, and the sights and cuisine suited him. But when the plump lady came up behind him things happened fast. Mistaking Nosy's jaunty gray-clad rear quarters for her husband stooping over to get cigars out of the glove compartment, the lady playfully cried, "Boo!" and dropped her load of pine cones close to his hind feet.

Thinking that Velma Thompson was on the job, the young boarder dived out the open door in a conscience stricken hurry. When his front feet hit the ground, his hind feet struck the big brass salad bowl. That leverage helped the fleeing moose escape, but the heavy bowl was shot backwards onto Mrs. Jones's twenty dollar permanent. While she lay screaming on her back, clawing ten thousand islands of dressing out of her just built silvery locks, Nosy was trotting right through the tempting feast spread around on the grassy meadow. The shrieking and screaming of the arrangement committee, as they crawled and fell away from the flap-eared pet's frontal retreat, reminded Nosy of sounds he had grown used to from more youthful days, only louder.

The mountain meadow calmed down now. The people gathered round, ready to partake of most of the delayed picnic. Everybody quieted down, waiting for the blessing. One member looked around: "Say, folks, our Grand High Potentate is missing. The last I seen of him, he was fishing, just down the creek. We'd better look him up. He's to ask the blessing. Let's just hold up a minute. I'll go get him."

The highest officer of the federation had been asked to visit this local chapter and attend their annual picnic. He was a philanthropist and very conservative. Besides being highly respected, he was an avid fisherman. While several men went down to the creek bordering the park to locate the missing man, the disgruntled calf moose was back in his private bar. After a few quaffs of the Fountain of Moose, his swampy confidence was restored. He was soon headed back toward the picnic.

The searchers didn't have far to go. Moose Park wasn't misnamed; it was in the middle of the local concentration of the long-nosed animals. But no such thought entered the head of the Potentate as he stooped to go through the heavy growth of willows below the big pool. He'd caught some nice brook trout and thought he'd make a last try before he went back to the gathering. His fishing hat, full of hand-tied flies and spare hooks, fell down over his sweaty forehead, as he lowered his rod tip to squirm through the ropy growths. The natural doorway he crawled through turned out to be the hind legs of a huge bull moose and cut short his ambition for one last brookie.

This bull was sampling some of the delicious tips of the luxuriant willow growths and was at peace with the world. When his tender belly was suddenly pricked by a hand-honed Royal Coachman, he felt that his privacy was invaded, so he left the dining room in high-geared dudgeon. The noise the moose made couldn't hold a candle to the one the Potentate made. He was a solid business man and was used to being on top, even if he was a small sort of Napoleon. One of the members later named this particular spot the Exodus Pool; that is, after they extracted the disarranged fisherman from the water he was drowning in.

The kids had waited long enough, so to restrain them, their mammas had sneaked stray bits of sandwiches and had done a little undercover nibbling themselves. Even the disgruntled heir of Porky's last quill and testament had regained some of his hunger. A dentist member of the group, with emergency instruments and snickering helpers, had relieved the beneficiary of most of the fine print from his anatomy.

Now everything was under control, and everybody was waiting. The Federation President was about to come out of his car, where he had gone for surface repairs and to change clothes. The high mogul was in the midst of hurriedly completing the overhaul, when he thought of something to give him more profound inspiration. He just ducked his head behind the back seat when his secret ritual was rudely interrupted. Nosy, casing the various rubber-tired joints, had come across the fanciest yet. And a window was open.

Just as the hammer-headed epicurean stuck his snout into the window, he stepped on the wreckage of an English-built fly rod lying on the ground. An expensive bamboo sliver gleefully inserted itself between two of the grafter's toes and jabbed with devilish abandon. Young Nosy gave an ouchy squeal right in the worshipping man's face, then wheeled around to disappear into the safer timber.

The hungrily waiting members of the Federation were astounded to see their barefooted Grand Potentate burst from his station wagon and run toward them. His shirt tail flapped against his colorful shorts, and he had a deathlike grip on a flat bottle halfway out of a fancy leather

Nosy gave an ouchy squeal.

case. The sounds he made indicated to the appreciative picnickers that here was no blessing; but that this Napoleon did have mule-driving ancestors.

The Bell

The only church the cowboy had ever attended was the Big One where he had spent his life. Now the canyon walls below Cathedral Cliffs re-echoed the sweet tones before the rider on the roan horse believed his ears.

"I'd know th' sound o' that bell anywhere. It's got a high ringin' sound like th' ol' mission bell down in town. Them chimes has gotta be on that Spook horse. Jest gotta be." Tony ran his big horse into the dark jungle of deadfalls, trying to make a circle above the musical sounds in the timber higher up. "Every time I hear his bell and take to him, he heads for the tall timber, an' I ain't seen him yet." Belknap had been hunting the bunch-quitter off and on for a week, and now figured he had the spooky pony dead to rights. The horse had strayed away from the cow-camp cavvy, and Tony needed him. Holding cattle on the mountain was rough work. His other ponies were overworked and this lone feeder had hid out from the job.

Ducking low limbs and jumping down timber, the horse hunters were making good time. From the sound of the noisy horse bell, Tony figured they were about to close in and nab the shirking renegade. The strawberry roan had the same ambition, but his smeller told him that *this* bell wasn't on any relative he'd ever claim. The cowboy spurred his horse over a huge deadfall. Roany hadn't heard about fools and angels, but he knew which was on his back when he high-centered on a snaggy tree trunk.

"By gorry, I've hunted Ol' Spook fer a week an' I'll be dad-burned if he's goin' ta git away this time!" The cowhand jabbed his hooks into the struggling horse. Tony's weight and his own 1000 pounds didn't tickle the roan's suffering briskit, so at the next jab the outraged horse whipped his head around and grabbed a mouthful of Tony's gittin'-on leg, just above his boot top. With an anguished howl, the horse-hunter fell out of his saddle and lit in a bramble of tree limbs.

The next morning Belknap was barely able to hobble out of the cow camp cabin. He'd spent half the night soaking his chewed-up leg in salt water. "I sure made uh poor trade," Tony mumbled. "Uh horse bite fer uh horse bell ain't what I had in mind."

The crippled-up cowboy had piled up limbs and green branches on both sides of Roany's teeter-totter until the horse had enough footing to scramble off the dead tree. "Ol' Roany didn't need no lawyer, I'll say that fer him. It was a clear case o' self defense. But why'n hell did he hafta wear out th' cinch on that tree he was perched on?" Tony felt of the bruised rump on his off side. When the cowboy had mounted Roany for the painful ride back to cow camp, the horse walked a few steps and the saddle fell off; the old cinch had parted. The horse hunter had a crippled left leg and a sore right hip to sort of make a balanced ride. "By gorry, it ain't ridin' that makes a hand bowlegged, it's th' things that happen when ye're jest a-trying to."

Tony thought awhile and groaned to himself, "I think I'll quit this here cow-punchin' before my carcass gits bent up too late ta weld. Mebbe I kin git me a job washin' dishes, my arms're long enough so's I won't drownd."

A few days hard riding kept Tony's mind off his sore leg. It was healing and showing no sign of infection. He found a bunch of his cows and calves down on the wrong side of the divide and threw them back on their own range. Things looked pretty good now, outside of the strayed horse he hadn't caught up with.

One warm sunny morning Tony decided to clean up the cabin and wash all his clothes and blankets. He had a couple of five-gallon tins of water heating on the cabin stove and was washing out the last of the job back of the cabin. The old tub and the piece of corrugated roofing tin nailed on a board did the job good enough for Tony. The store-bought scrubbing board had come up missing last hunting season, so Tony had a new machine. The clothesline, from a tree down by the creek up to a cabin end log, was hung full of blankets and most of Tony's forty years gatherings. The cowboy was feeling pretty good to have this job about over. He had on an old ragged hat, his oldest undershirt, and a wornout pair of Levis on his skinny carcass. He was playing a tune on the tin roofing with his best shirt and was soap-suds from his wet boots clear up to his knobby elbows.

He was wringing out his polka dot prize when he heard, "Sure is a good washday, Tony." Startled, he bumped the old washtub off the stump, slipped on the fallen soap, and sat down on the wet ground. A wrangler friend of his and a row of laughing dudes sat their horses just beyond the cabin.

Tony'd eaten his dinner and was down to the corral saddling up a horse when he heard some of the dudes talking to their guide as they were fitting their fly rods together, down on the creek.

He sat down on the wet ground.

"Who, him? Why, that'll all he's ever done," Elmer the wrangler had a deep voice. "Punched cows mostly and worked for hunting camps. Born down below Roaring River. Doubt if ol' Tony's ever been outa th' state."

"Are you *sure* he's the real thing, Elmer? On television, and even down in town, they're always well dressed and polite. When I smiled at him and said, 'Howdy, partner,' he just grunted past his whiskers and waved a bar of soap. Are you sure he's not just the flunkey for the *real* cowboy?"

Tony gritted his teeth at that one. He was viciously jerking the cinch tighter when he heard a young voice pipe up. "Elmer, when you brought me up yesterday to meet a *real* cowboy and he wasn't home, I peeked in his cabin to see how this one lived. He must be taking a correspondence course. There's whole stacks of Wild West magazines piled close to his bunk. Maybe someday he'll graduate."

The day had started out fine for Tony. He felt lucky, he'd got the washing all done, and he was determined to run down that lost Spook horse if it was the last thing he ever did. He was now in a foul mood. "Damn dudes, they're dumb, damn 'em." He rode down to the fenced horse pasture to catch a fresh mount, when he found out who the dumb one was. A couple of the dude fishermen were tinkering with their fishing rods behind a clump of spruce close to the gate. When he got off his horse to open it, he heard, "I wonder if these mountain cowboys ride moose." They didn't see the cowboy or his ferocious mug, so the voice went on talking. "I was riding along this morning at the end of the bunch when I noticed those saddle horses grazing back of the fence. Two of them had bells tied around their necks. Sure make a loud noise. Then when I dropped my pipe I got off my horse to pick it up. As I was about to step back up on him, I happened to look past a long neck of trees. There, feeding in a small lily pond, was a young moose. He had *two* bells, one was natural and the other was strapped around his neck. Sure make a loud noise."

No grizzly could have equalled the sounds the enraged cowboy made when he nearly wrecked the old gate open. When Tony came out of the pasture on a high lope, his fresh mount was already in a sweat. The two scared fishermen perched high in the same snaggy spruce heard "the crazy cowboy" yowling to himself, "Damn that moose-lovin' Thompson, damn him anyhow. I'll fix that long-nose-moose lover, damn Ol' Bill anyhow!" Tony didn't even stop to shut the sagging gate. The big cloud of dust down the trail was settling before the uneasy fishermen climbed down to look for their thrown away fly rods.

By the time Tony had ridden the steep six miles down the mountain trail to "Moose-lovin' Thompson's" ranch, his leg was giving him what for, and his mind was set on "turnin' ol' Bill every way but loose," if he could catch that ol' pet-makin' Bill where he could get at him.

As he rode down off Bull Ridge he got a good glimpse of Bill's place. There was Velma working in her backyard among her delphiniums. Tony caught sight of Bill peeling some poles down by the barn corrals, so he rode around out of sight of the cabin, figuring on having it out with Ol' Bill without any rolling pin interference.

Just as he rode up to the corral, all hot and bothered, Bill looked up. "Well, by hell, Tony Belknap, jest in time for coffee. Yuh look like yuh need it. Down in the mouth and all lathered up." Tony got stiffly off his horse. He was about to tell Bill off when Nosy the pet moose came around the barn. He took one look at Tony and his mane came up. He started to stomp his front feet as he came toward the astonished man. He had only one bell and it was his own hair-covered one. While the crestfallen warrior watched, Ol' Bill picked up a stick and run Nosy off.

As the hostile moose disappeared around the barn, Tony sat down on a pile of corral poles and wearily pulled out his tobacco sack to roll a smoke. The cowboy felt that he was a fool twisted by knaves to make a trap for moose, but he didn't dare admit it.

"By hell, Bill, them danged Bar Zee dudes's got the cow camp surrounded. I thought I'd come down t'associate with humans while them dern city slickers fish th' creek out. Besides, I aimed t'go t'the ranch ta tell the boss I'm outa salt fer th' cows."

While Bill and Tony walked up to the house for coffee, Ol' Bill noticed the limp Tony couldn't control. "Jest hit a low limb while I was ridin' through some timber, tryin' t'bend back some cows," was the quickest lie Tony could think of. He was sure that if he let the true story out, he'd be christened "The Hungry Horse Kid" from then on.

By evening the disillusioned cowboy was down at the home ranch. The boss said he'd pack some stock salt up to the cow camp in a day or two. After supper and a good sleep in the bunkhouse the cowboy felt better. He ate breakfast, and felt strong enough for the ride back to the cow camp.

"By hell, Tony, you shoulda been here a week or so ago." The boss was laughing at the joke he'd played. "Bill Thompson's pet moose showed up here, and he got t' jumpin' over inta a new stack yard full of hay, 'n' foolin' around th' barn. I thought I'd play a good one on Ol' Bill, he's so proud o' th' dang thing. I roped th' dang grafter, tied 'im down, an' strapped a bell around his neck. You'da laughed yer head off when I turned 'im loose. He took off in a clangin' hurry, stampeded th' milk cows when he piled over th' new buck fence we built this spring. Th' last I seen 'im, he was jangle-bongin' through th' heavy timber, straight up Bull Ridge. You cud hear 'im a long time."

Tony stared at the boss. "Say, now, when we hazed th' cows up th' mountain this spring, I took *all* the bells off'n the ranch fer my horse string. Where didja git hold of th' bell?"

"By hell, Tony, I fergot t'tell yuh." The boss grinned. "That horse Spook showed up here about ten days ago. That's his bell I put on Bill's moose."

The cowboy thought of Nosy staying home and minding his own business, so he didn't tell the boss he'd wasted a bell on a wild moose. Tony rode off up the trail mumbling to himself, "Mebbe I'd better wait before I git me a job a-washin' dishes. By gorry, I kin still hear good, even if I ain't yet graduated."

Travois

While she was sorting out her freshly washed clothes, Velma happened to look out a kitchen window and saw Bill crawl out from under his decrepit old pickup. When he sat down on the running board of the "Old Maid," as they called the eccentric truck, Velma went out to hear the verdict. Bill sat with his head in his hands. "I guess I'll hafta give up, Velma. We c'n git ta town with th' old girl, but I'm afraid she's on 'er last legs." Bill stopped talking to rub the butting head of Nosy, who had come up to get in on the deal. "Near's I c'n figger she's got th' gallopin' consumption. Her rings has outwore her engagement. The Old Maid's gotta go. We'll hafta deal for a better one."

Moocher, behind Velma, growled at Nosy.

Remembering other deals, and how trusting and gullible Bill was, Vel started off with, "We've got to watch our step, Bill. Some car dealers are like some lawyers seem to be." Bill reached into a pocket for his mouth harp, to tantalize Nosy with. He played a high-pitched whiny tune. He and Velma both laughed to watch the moose calf in a stiff-legged trot, squealing and bunting at the pickup's crumpled fenders. Old Moocher, the dog, sat off to one side howling and yelping at the sky.

"What's lawyers got t'do with car dealers anyhow?" Bill, out of wind, got tired of watching Nosy's and Moocher's gyrations, and was hammering out the harp's moisture on his knee. He just grunted when Velma replied, "Lots of car dealers are like lots of lawyers, they're masters of subterfuge and evasion."

"Look, Vel, you're thinkin' o'Nosy. He *likes* my music. He just *pretends* he don't."

Velma stared at Bill and Nosy in exasperation. "I give up. Well, I've got to iron a dress and get ready. It'll take me about an hour. Then we can go to town to see about another pickup."

Bill got up off the running board and started towards his shop. "I'll git some tools and stuff. I might as well fix that corner of roofing on the back porch while you're a-gittin' ready."

Her irons were hot—been heating up all morning on the wood stove. Having tested one with a wet finger, Velma was busy ironing a towngoing dress in time with her record player. Out a window she saw Nosy scratching his rump on a fender of the forlorn pickup. Remembering the show he'd put on for Bill's mouth harp, Vel stopped ironing for a minute to put "The Irish Washerwoman" on the record player. She opened up a window, turned the volume up high, and giggled at the antics of the long-legged bog-trotter. He was trotting around the pickup, squealing and grunting in frustration. Every once in a while he'd stop and bunt at the truck. Finally he went out of sight at a fast, humpy trot.

Velma had the volume turned up so high she didn't hear the yelling hullabaloo around the corner of the back porch. She resumed ironing, and was dreamily listening to one of her hifalutin (Bill called it) college records, when she heard hoarse mumbling as somebody fumbled at the screen door on the back porch.

When Velma saw the black and bloody streaked figure in tattered clothes stagger toward her, she instantly thought of the morning's radio report of a crazy man on the loose. She grabbed up Bill's big game rifle off his gun rack, hurriedly threw a live shell into the chamber, and was aiming wildly at the dripping apparition in the doorway when she realized it was her Bill, in a crude and painful disguise.

Vel doctored up Bill's cuts and scratches. He insisted she use his special sulpha-bear's-grease salve on his skinned-up face and knees. She didn't know whether to laugh or cry at the moose-maimed old hillbilly. So she did both.

"I was standing halfway up on that ladder," Bill muttered through his puffy lips. "I had just tacked down that last piece of roofin' and was pourin' tar when it happened." Bill, leaning over, had his head over a washtub. Velma was gingerly picking roofing tacks out of his sticky toupee.

Just a week ago Ol' Bill had undergone one of the town barber's grizzly bear crew cuts, for which he was now grateful. His smiling housewife was using turpentine to get the tar out of his hair, and Bill just knew the hair would come out. "Gittin' thin up there, anyhow," he muttered to himself. When he had to stand up suddenly to straighten out the kink in his neck, some of the turpentine dripped down his back a little too far. Bill dern lear lost his temper when Vel fell over into a chair in a giggling fit as Ol' Bill danced around howling and holding his backsides, his tattered and water-soaked overalls and shirt fluttering in his war dance.

Finally the dilapidated guide was some calmer. He was peacefully drinking coffee and eating some of his wife's delicious pie.

72

Nosy's pretty good with a travois.

"When you started playin' that record and I heard Moocher barkin' and th' calf a-squallin', I figgered somethin' was goin' on. I *knew* there was when th' top of th' ladder left th' roof edge in a hell of a hurry. All th' time Nosy is squallin' 'n' Moocher is bawlin', but I was kinda busy. There I was a-ridin' th' ladder down. Th' can o' tacks 'n' th' bucket o' tar musta been travelin' neck 'n' neck, but I lost th' race. What brought me to, was ol' Moocher lickin' my face. I was still a-layin' on what was left o' th' ladder. That there Nosy's pretty good with a travois. He crossed th' deepest part o' th' crick before he lost me in th' bog. Musta been travelin' right smart. Course Moocher probly was helpin' out the percession.

"Velma, when you was mixin' up them lawyers an' car dealers, you musta got them words twisted." Ol' Bill had spent last winter's evenings studying a dictionary a dude hunter had given him. "When you played that there 'Irish Washerwoman' on your juke box it musta acted like a *vermifuge* on Nosy. An' your last word shoulda been *invasion,* cause that little devil hit the ladder dead center."

"Well, I never," Velma exploded, "I'll bet the politicians love you. You vote a straight ticket every time. Nosy nearly kills you and you still stand up for him."

The Poacher

Al Payton, the forest ranger, happened by and was visiting Velma and Bill. As he sat on the edge of the back porch, he kept an eye on the calf moose over on the edge of the timber close to the road. His hot-blooded saddle horse, tied to a tree, had just clipped the sniffing Nosy with a quick hoof. The baffled moose backed up into the shadows of a big spruce. His spindly mane was standing erect, and he was stamping with his front feet.

As Velma came out of the kitchen to refill the coffee cups, a new car drove up and stopped with an important flourish. A flashy dressed man stepped out, leaving the car door open. When the three friends saw who it was, they sort of stiffened up, but put on their best grins when the man dressed up in the cowboy uniform walked over and shook hands all around and pulled cards out of his pocket. About then, the ranger saw the calf moose leave the unfriendly horse and walk over to the shining car.

Duke Johnson had spent many hours practicing his acts before a big private mirror at home. Now he picked out the one that fitted this kind of local yokels. No use to waste the best acts in his political poke on country people.

"Of course, you good people know I'm running for State Senator." He tilted his big William J. Bryan hat back on his noble forehead and poked a fat cigar in his mouth. "Now, I know you folks are *for* me, but I just dropped by to remind you it's getting toward voting time." Velma's ear drums thrummed as she went back into the house for another coffee cup. The town sharpie talked on and on about the great platform he'd erected. "I want to congratulate you forest ranger fellers on the fine job you're doing, Al." A pudgy finger snapped a blob of cigar ashes off his bay window. It lit in Bill's eye, but Patrick Henry didn't notice. He had his bulging peepers up on the high peaks of achievement. "But some other things in these parts I'm going to change. I know that the more important guides and out-fitters, and like Ol' Bill here, are with me, and the people are standing squarely behind me, when I re-organize that coffee-coolin' game department."

As the hot-shot garage owner adjusted his string tie, he didn't notice the sly grins exchanged by his restless audience. His ardor didn't arouse any enthusiasm in anybody except Al Payton. When the sharp-eyed ranger saw the calf moose hop in the open door of the car and disappear, he gave Duke Johnson a big handshake and said, "We're for you, Duke, give the big game poachers the works."

Nosy, busy chawing away on the head of lettuce, thought that this rubber-tired chuck wagon looked interesting. He hadn't yet had time to investigate the rest of the groceries on the back seat beside him.

Duke Johnson figured he had the upper end of Roaring River Valley all sewed up. So he shook hands again, and was soon headed, hell for leather, down the country. The politician, deep in his hazy cloud of heaven for all hands, hadn't noticed the long-nosed grafter in the back seat of his glory wagon. The hell-fired takeoff threw Nosy on the floor and the whanging bumps of the rocky road kept him from getting up. The calf was soon lying flat, and he was a very car-sick moose. The ranger knew he was the only one in the crowd to see the long-nosed boarder get on the gravy train, so just after Duke's car disappeared down the road, Payton stood up and said, "Bill, I see you got your telephone put in. Do you mind if I use it for a minute or two?"

"Help yourself, Al. Call up the State House and tell 'em we done elected the new senator."

Soon Velma and Bill could hear the ranger talking to somebody, and there seemed to be a lot of laughing on the country line. Al stayed awhile longer, then he stepped on his horse and rode off. Nobody missed the moose. He was in Velma's doghouse again. He'd chewed up a lot of the iris plants flourishing by the house, so Velma had put the run on him with a strong club. Bill and his wife figured Nosy's latest lumps had driven him down to the swamp behind the springhouse for his own private meditations.

When the two-legged grafter jerked the car to a stop, the four-legged one next to the back seat was deluged with the rest of the groceries. But the angry driver didn't hear the noise. He viciously jerked his big hat down and opened the door.

Just in front of him was a game warden's pickup parked squarely across the road that led to the ranger station and the town just below. One game warden sat on the running board reading a paper. His pardner got out of the cab and came over to grin at the angry politician. "Duke, old boy, sorry to git in your way, but we're lookin' for poachers."

"Look here, smart guy, you go polish up your badge with some

Gave a lusty squeal.

other cute jokes. I'm in a hurry and got no time for foolin'." Duke Johnson had caught too many fish several years ago. He still smarted from the small fine he'd got, after being caught by this particular warden.

"OK, OK, now keep your britches on, Duke." The other game warden was now leaning against the car fender. "We know that you're running for senator, and *if* you git in you'll make a good one, and mebbe some good laws. But we can stop any suspected poacher with the ones we got now."

Johnson burned a deep purple and started to splutter about damned smart alecks holding up decent citizens. "When I get in office, I'll put a stop to you badge-happy birds. You can't pull any funny stuff with me." The long-nosed grafter in the back seat had now got his sea legs, so he scrambled up, shoved his messy smeller under the back of Duke's big hat, and gave a lusty squeal. The cigar stub Duke swallowed before he jumped out of his car didn't make him half as seasick as the roaring laughter of the two game wardens.

The bog trotter scrambled out of the same door he'd went in, and was off at a grumpy trot up the timber fringed road towards Bill's ranch. The maybe senator crawled out from under the game department pickup, where he'd dived when the calf moose had told him off. Popeyed, the politician stood staring up the road as his short-tailed prisoner made his escape. Duke's new hat lay crumpled on the ground and the fancy cowboy uniform was smeared with dusty grease. Johnson had never heard of Bill and Velma's pet moose, and the whooping game wardens didn't tell him.

Slim Atkins rubbed his badge and told his pardner, "My gosh, there goes our evidence, and we caught old Duke red-handed, too." They got into their pickup and got out of the way. As Duke drove his car past them, he heard Slim, "I don't believe he'll cut the mustard. It takes a real poacher to make a good Senator." The flustered driver rammed his car down the rocky road, smarting at that last jibe. But what really boiled his radiator was that he couldn't put his finger on the frame.

Jam Session

It was later in the fall when the calf moose showed up again. Velma and Bill thought that the swamp angel had finally gone back to his own kind. They were much relieved at his absence, and so was the white collie. It was peaceful again.

In October, Velma and some other ranch wives had been down to the lower country, gathering buffalo berries. Now she had pots and pans filled with sugar, pulp, and berries, in the process of making jam for the coming winter. The hot stove was booming a tune with the sizzling juice and bubbling nectar. The tables and chairs were all occupied with glass jars and other containers, some full of this rich jam and some waiting. Bill was taking a rare nap on the old couch in the living room. He took time out, once in a while, to sniff the delicious odors from the busy kitchen. Velma was humming a tune in time with the bubbling jam, and had the jelly job about half done.

She heard some desperate whines, and in through the open kitchen door trotted Bill's shovel-nosed pet, his smeller decorated with a halo of porcupine quills. The moose calf skidded on the slick floor, Velma's hard-earned pride, and slid slam crash into the jam factory, head over tincup.

Electrified by the screams and squeals and crashing bangs, Ol' Bill bounced up and lit in the steamy kitchen to see a sight that durned near made him resolve to swear off making pets of the universe. His beloved wife and the glary-eyed moose calf were all sprawled out together in a conglomerate mixture of broken glass, mushy berries, and wine red jam spattering the kitchen landscape. The bog trotter's squealing mixed with Velma's screamed imprecations were more vociferous than articulate. When the bewildered hillbilly pulled his purple wife out from under the wreckage, the jam saturated moose blundered his needled nose out the door, leaving a trail of broken glass and crumpled aluminum kettles in his wake. His tracks dripped wine red clear up to the safer timbered hillside.

Just as Bill set the mumbling woman on her feet, the sourdough jar, teetering on the shelf above the stove, saw its chance and fell on poor Ol' Bill's gray head. Stunned, he sat himself down on a glassy space on the floor. He began wiping the yeasty sourdough out of his eyes, but he came out of his trance in a hurry when he heard two quick shots in the doorway. There stood his red-dappled

Levering another shell into his old rifle.

wife levering another shell into his old rifle, and taking a shaking aim out towards the peaceful mountain side.

Velma, stern-faced, lay at her silent ease on the old sofa in the living room. She had a copy of "Will Power and Its Influence on the Universe," and was all dressed up in her best clothes. The sound of scrubbing and polishing came from a disillusioned bowlegged man on his weary hands and knees. The kitchen was beginning to have a lived-in look, but a purple tinge still pervaded the edges of this food dispensary. Every time Velma heard the faintly mumbled comments from the kitchen, she had a little smirk all her own, remembering an old proverb, "Spare the rod and spoil the child."

Bill, now and then, would get up and go outdoors to shake the cramps out of his legs. Once he looked over and saw his pet in a willow bog below the corral. He had his schnozzle thrust into the black mud, and was very quiet. The skinny mountain man reflected that maybe he *should* teach Velma to shoot accurate, just maybe. She sure must have been excited, anyhow!

Ol' Bill went back into the kitchen and started scrubbing again.

The Clipper

The wind blowing past his sweaty head went on down the mountain carrying the message of U2, the best hair-growing oil in the world. Harry Clipper didn't know who would be interested up in this neck of the woods, or care. But his druggist friend down in Roaring River had assured Harry that the formula, concocted especially for the clipper, would even grow hair on Old Baldy, the highest peak on Roaring River.

The tired barber finally heaved himself off the log and started pussyfooting warily up the steep trail, careful to avoid breaking branches and rolling rocks. He kept traveling into the wind coming faintly out of the dark green jungle. Several times he swung around, his heavy rifle at the ready, but he couldn't see a thing. Maybe those muffled footfalls and low whines were his imagination working overtime.

Most everybody in the mountain town of Roaring River loved the barber. He had the only shop in town. This loquacious gent claimed to be not only the best tonsorial mechanic in the whole region but also one of the best hunters. Harry was an enthusiastic joiner of just about everything. He was a sucker for every hard luck ne'er-do-well in the country and was always broke. But that didn't hurt his ever present good nature.

Most of his customers enjoyed the tales of his hunting prowess. You could always spot the ones who had undergone his most vivid bear hunting adventures. No matter what their tonsorial preferences had been, they always sported crew cuts.

The trimmer was also an ardent member of the town's little theater group. His sonorous voice and theatrical gestures usually frightened new customers. Harry hadn't yet stabbed anyone, although some hardy souls admitted to some close shaves.

Of late he hadn't been chosen for any of the more juicy parts in the plays the L.T.G. had put on. The disappointed Thespian had put this down to his rapidly thinning locks, but by no means to any lack of histrionic ability. His generous use of the pungent hair remedy had shown, he thought, some remarkable progress on his re-seeding program. Also, the banker's wife, who was the main

82

director of the dramatic society and the Little Theater Group, had been less distant of late.

The clipper was sure he was staging a comeback. Besides, if he could manage to bag a big bull elk or some other large game, Clipper was sure that the entertainment department of his fleecing emporium would be well supplied for the winter season.

The spellbinder of the striped pole was thirsty. He'd gone some two miles from Bill Thompson's ranch, and although he'd seen what he was certain were fresh tracks and other sign of elk, he was sure he hadn't spooked any out of their beds. Pausing now in the shadows of the timber, he surveyed the spring-fed pool in the grassy park ahead.

Half a mile or so down the mountain below him the Forest Service had a plot with a high pole fence around it. The study of growth and general health of the infant spruce enclosed in this acre of reforestation had pleased the ranger in charge. The ranger hadn't yet found where an old-age pensioner pine in its second childhood had given up the ghost, but Bill Thompson's pet moose had discovered it. In falling, the huge tree had chosen to rest among the young spruce. Nosy had sneaked through the wrecked section of fence, and was gaily lunching on the tender crowns of the defenseless baby trees, when the shifting wind down the mountain wafted the delicious odor of U2 across his busy snout.

The druggist friend of the great Shakespearean actor was also the perfume supplier of most of Roaring River's elite. To give more authority to the trimmer's hair restorer, the astute pill roller had included some of the same scent that Minnie the schoolmarm used. Indecision wasn't a curse to the calf moose. When he got the message he suddenly deserted his salad buffet. He was now in a gallant trot up the mountain train, his anxious kisser wrinkling in happy anticipation.

———————

Tom Worden, a former rancher with a natural flair for figures, including his wife's, had gotten into the banking business via her inherited cash and acquired culture. He could take the cash and let the credit go, that is when Esmeralda wasn't around. She had the curves, but Tom could pitch one when he had to. Since his wife had become the big shot in the Little Theater Group the banker loved to tease her with what he called *poetry*, but she sniffed it off as "sage brush vulgarity."

Mrs. Worden, looking for new worlds to conquer, decided it

would be fashionable to be a sportswoman. To set the pace for her followers, she had acquired, "foah rathuh a neat sum," as she put it, several distinguished outfits. "A hell of a lotta cash for queer duds," Worden called it. When his wife proudly paraded one of her more quiet outfits for the startled banker, he turned loose what he termed a real prize:

"O them skin tight britches
      An' real high boots
Don't b'long in ditches
      Ner ol' tree roots.
A plumb red shirt
      An' a real green collar —
I wouldn't kiss that flirt
      Fer a whole half dollar."

When hunting season arrived, it didn't take much persuasion to induce the banker to go big game hunting. In his time Worden had done a lot of it. And secretly it amused him to suspect that Esmeralda was disappointed when he agreed to go elk hunting. Tom was no armchair sport but he knew an actress when he saw one.

They parked their car and horse trailer at Bill Thompson's ranch. They'd have stopped to visit, since Bill was a long time friend of Tom's, but nobody was home. So now they were riding up the timbered trail looking for signs of game. Esmeralda spent so much time admiring her shadow as she rode along that she was nearly beheaded by low limbs. About the third time, Tom Worden couldn't resist a new one. He said,

"If too much tuh eat
      Is a plumb holy sin —
Then thuh low limbs'll beat
      On that ol' double chin."

Mrs. Worden was about half mad at this crack and of a notion to quit hunting, when a bull elk bugled in some close-by jungle. The banker beckoned wildly to his pouting wife, stepped off his horse, and started to tie him to a tree. He was pulling his rifle from the scabbard when a big-headed old bull came charging out into the small park. Esmeralda had gone deep into a dream of playing the part of Diana the huntress when she was suddenly spun into sad reality. Her old buckskin horse stampeded into the thick timber fringing the park. The amorous bull had been hearing the thumping hoofbeats and the stagestruck twittering of the huntress, so he decided that here might be an orphaned harem. But he plowed

84

to a disillusioned stop between the two hunters. Old Tom had his rifle up and was about to pull trigger when he heard his wife holler and tough branches crack.

The banker was thankful, to say the least, when he found he'd forgotten to thumb the safety off. The bull whirled and escaped into the green jungle, and Tom discovered he was aiming his blunderbuss at the middle-aged spread of his screaming pardner. Her straining horse was wedged tightly between two trees, and Diana the H. held her arms high in the air, with the ends of the reins clutched tightly in her frantic fingers.

Later on, as they were riding farther on up the mountain, Worden couldn't resist saying what he claimed was an old mountain ryhme:

"When yuh're a-ridin' in thuh timber
Yuh gotta watch them knobby knees;
Sure you gotta be plumb limber
Or yuh'll knock down all thuh trees."

All he got was a dirty look from his Diana.

Just over a small ridge from where Tom and Esmeralda were hunting, the barber started to lean his rifle against a log and go over to the pond to get a drink, when he had a lucky thought. "Things could happen in a hurry," he mumbled. "I'd better cock this rifle to be ready." Harry had an uneasy feeling. He thought he'd seen a bear track close to the swampy spring. He pulled the hammer back on his rifle and leaned it against a fallen tree. He walked the few feet over to the swampy pool, then got down on all fours. He was leaning over to get a few swigs of mountain dew when he heard the long-drawn whines of some animal. "By golly, by dam, that's a bull elk a long way off."

The eager Clipper sat down in the tall grass and fished his new whistle out of his pants. "I'll just bugle him up and give him the medicine—if he's big enough." Harry tootled a few screechy calls and threw in some heavy Barrymore grunts for good measure. He listened some more. Sure that he heard some distant and stealthy sounds of approach, he was about to creep over and get hold of his ready rifle leaning on the deadfall, when he heard a disgusted grunt behind him and received a contemptuous bunt which tossed him head first into the mucky pool.

The banker's bull had forgotten the sashay with the two city slickers, and was busy venting his spleen on a small green spruce when he half heard the barber's hopeful tootling. Old Big Head left off slashing the tree, shook the sticky shreds of bark off his massive rack, and started trotting through the timber towards the distant sounds. No tin horn could make sport of him, not the way he felt just now. An upstart younger bull with fancier footwork and some lucky jabs had run him out of the Buckskin Ladies Society a few hours ago, and here was some pipsqueak giving him the giggle.

When the big elk ran out of the timber into the park, hellbent for election, he didn't see the running gear and hind end of Harry, struggling in the boggy pond. In his frustrated fury, all he could see was the disappointed little moose, walking away from the waterhole. "That's good enough," the old bull grunted. "No dern bog-trotter can make fun of me." Nosy just barely kept from sharing a muddy bath with Harry Clipper. He jumped over the fallen log just in time to dodge the charging elk. The calf's hind foot struck the barber's rifle, and when the gun went off KA-BOOM, that settled it. Nosy took off down the mountain in a frantic hurry. He didn't know that he was the only moose on Roaring River ever to shoot an elk in self defense.

Nosy was halfway to Thompson's ranch when the barber drug his miserable carcass out of the slimy water hole, to shiver and drip and stare at the last shudders of the bull elk's departure to the land of his fathers. Harry hadn't seen the pet moose and didn't know the bifurcated truth. So now he was forcing himself to believe that he had shot the bull before he had been shoved — fallen? — into the pond. Yes, sir, it just had to be that way? No bull. Oh, what a story to tell the boys. A sudden thought struck the barber, no bull? He ran over to the huge body of the fallen monarch draped across the deadfall. He kicked around in the broken and bloody branches and finally found his rifle. It was scratched up, but OK, with an empty shell in the chamber. Yes, he had shot the bull, no bull.

The exultant barber piled up some red-needled branches, fumbled around in his soggy britches for his waterproof matches, and soon had a fire going. After he had dressed out his elk and was more comfortable, he suddenly felt that he was the noblest Roman of them all, and that a speech was in order.

Esmeralda and Tom Worden heard the shot that killed the bull but couldn't tell the direction the sound came from. They had jumped a few elk but hadn't got a shot. Riding through some open timber, Tom, in front, reined his horse up short and growled, "Oh, that damned barber." He had once suffered a long bear story with a duck-tail haircut from Harry. The banker had a low opinion of Clipper, and what he saw now made him want to cry. The director of the dramatic society crowded her horse up close to Tom's when she heard him cuss.

The two elk hunters, looking past some tree trunks down into a small park, saw the mud-covered barber, facing away from them, standing with one foot on the bull elk's neck. He had his rifle lifted high in the air, and was declaiming to the sky.

While the astounded pair stared down at the barber, they heard him chant in a loud voice:

"Then out spoke brave old Harry,
  The captain of his soul:
'Death cometh sooner, but barely,
  To this elk of Jackson Hole.
But how can this bull die better
  Than facing my fearless odds
For the ashes of his fathers
  Amidst the temples of his gods?'
Mumble, mumble, mumble . . Lessee, now . . YEAH! this might fit—
What is there out beyond his grassy parks,
  His yonder mountains with the snowy peaks?
O Bull, you've gone up your last trail,
  Your pretty cows you've left behind,
I'll drink to you with that good old ale,
  And hope you've joined up with your own kind."

A hungry horse fly lit on Worden's squirming neck and broke the spell up in the balcony. Tom slapped the pest away and happened to look over at his wife. Esmeralda, leaning forward in her saddle, was gazing raptly down at the orator, still waving his rifle and spouting to the universe.

Not to be outdone, the banker scratched at the flybite and came up with:

"He's noculated with uh phonygraph needle,
  That barber is a plumb crazy fool.
Probly et uh rotten ol' beetle
  Outa his musty ol' barber stool."

The entranced dramatic director didn't hear a word he said. She was still gazing awestruck at Clipper. So Tom reached over, pulled the horse's reins out of Esmeralda's unresisting hands, and rode off, leading the buckskin down through the aisles of timber. Diana hung onto the horn with both hands. But the show wasn't over, for Tom was mumbling to himself:

87

He was declaiming to the sky.

"C'mon, let's go,
  Get away from here.
First thing yuh know
  I'll shed uh tear.
C'mon, let's go.
  We need some air.
Next thing yuh know
  He'll kill uh bear."

It was getting along towards sundown as the banker and his wife rode down off Bull Ridge to Thompson's ranch. The Thompsons hadn't got home yet, but Nosy was there. When the hunters rode over to the horse trailer and car, they saw the little elk killer up in the horse trailer. He was licking at a lump of salt in a feed box. He got peeved when Tom drove him out to make way for their saddle horses.

"Oh, Tom, don't shove him," Esmeralda cried. "He's so innocent and bizarre."

"Bizarre, hell," Worden grunted. Then he turned loose with:
"O little moose,
  Don't look so sad.
It ain't no use
  To be so mad.
Take out that snoot,
  Go on, now git!
Or you'll have my boot
  Right where yuh sit."

No Moose

Nosy's visits to the ranch in the next couple of years were rare. The only way you could tell him now from other bull moose was some deep scars on both front legs from a ruckus with a barbed wire fence. He was nearly forgotten now, except for occasional wise-cracks aimed in Bill's direction by Velma or Tony when any moose were noticed close to the ranch.

This fall Thompson's hunting camp operated to full capacity, with Bill, Tony, and two other guides doing the work. Now the season was about over, the happy hunters departed with their trophies, and extra guides left for home. Old Bill and Tony were at the job of packing in some elk meat and gradually getting the camp back in to the ranch for the winter.

While Bill was arranging the sling rope on a pack horse, he noticed the wrangler. Tony was just leading a pack horse up to start loading some front quarters of elk. He stopped dead still and was looking at a mess of fallen timber close to the big swamp.

Thompson looked over the top of the pack-saddle. "What're you lookin' at, Tony, a grizzly?" Tony sniffed, "Naw, but I'll swear some silly ol' moose is followin' this pack outfit."

"Haw, haw, I'll bet it's that ol' gray moose that treed you. Prob'ly wants' t' return th' bridle she stole offa that buckskin horse you rode yesterday."

"Aw, go jump in the crick, yuh ol' moose lover." Tony glared around his droopy cigarette, and tied the pack horse up to a tree. "If y' wanta talk about moose, talk about 'em t'yourself, not t' me."

Just the day before, Tony had drowsed off to sleep while riding down the trail, having spent half the night looking for a lost horse. ("How did I know that nutty ol' buckskin would go right between a cow and her calf? Crazy damn moose!") His saddle horse stopped to graze. He wandered off the trail to work on some tasty grass in the fringe of heavy timber. What woke up the tired wrangler and the hungry horse was the furious mama. Maw had one front leg over Buck's mane in front of the saddle, and was coughing her snootful of slimy lily roots right in Tony's face. Her other front leg was twisted up in the bridle reins. The tangle of low tree limbs this affectionate meeting took place under sure saved his life, according to cowboy Tony. "When that ol' fool horse started t'back up, I saw my chance and crawled up in that tangle o' branches. Ol' Buck let the moose have the bridle she'd pulled off, and went hellity larrup right back t'camp. Well, I stayed 'up there awhile after that dang crazy thing took off with her calf. Good thing camp wasn't far off. Tore a hole in my hat, an' my coat sleeve is ruined. Damn moose anyhow."

Bill rubbed some bloody scraps of elk meat on the bronc's nose. "There, that'll take th' scare outa him, and I'll betcha we don't even hafta tie a hind leg up."

The job was to pack out three bull elk that their hunters had killed the day before. The two gentlest horses were loaded by now with the bull Tony's hunter had got on a rough timber-covered hillside a mile above this big open park where the last two had been killed.

"Good thing it's level down here, an' easy footin," Tony said. "This wet snow is sure slippery."

"Don't look like these ponies ever been packed before." Bill Thompson had traded for these last four horses just a few weeks back. They seemed fairly well halter broke, and their saddle marks showed they'd been ridden.

After a lot of trouble Tony and Bill had three horses packed solid, with good diamond hitches pulled down hard on each one. Thompson was pulling the sling ropes tight on the last one. He didn't make a move till the wind came up. Then he got a whiff of the strong bull elk scent from the quarters he was loaded with. That bay rared straight up in the air, busting some branches on the tree he was tied to, then he fell down, got up, and tried to buck the pack off. He was cussing with bawling snorts and weird grunts. "Looks like he done lost his religion," says Tony.

The two packers were finally ready to go. They had tailed each horse to another's halter rope. These ponies would scatter their loads all over the mountains if turned loose to drive. "If you wanta go ahead," says Tony, "leadin' them two we packed first, Bill, I'll follow you. I'll show these four onery so-and-sos who's boss. I'm onery, too. If I git in a jackpot, I'll holler."

Bill was on his big black saddle horse, leading his two meat horses. They were tied head to tail and were gentle. "Good thing it ain't far t' th' ranch, with this setup. I'll travel up ahead aways,

Buck let the moose have the bridle.

an' if I hear any hollerin' I'll come help yuh, Tony. I'll keep any moose outa yer way, mebbe!"

Bill looked back after they'd lined out on the trail. Tony rode along, with all four meat horses walking head to tail and acting like old timers at the game. After about four miles of easy going in open timber, it started snowing hard. Bill's horses were traveling right along, so he pulled up until Tony, with his string, showed up.

"We're doin' OK, Bill." Tony was having trouble rolling a dry smoke in the gusty snow. "These here four broncs act like old hands."

Bill looked at the sidehill ahead and said, "I'll wait for you at the top of the clay slide, Tony. This wet snow ain't goin' to help the footin' on this greasy trail." Tony waved a wet glove, so Bill rode up ahead with his two pack horses.

The tromped-down trail that led up the clay hillside was a soggy mess of slippery horse tracks. There were lots of badger holes along the steep side. Up above the clay slide was a fringe of heavy timber. Down below, where the old clay slide had stopped, the timber and big rocks along the Shoshoni River was a jumbled-up bad dream of huge tree roots and snaggy poles all mushroomed together.

Just as Bill's outfit topped the trail and was heading into the timber he heard a big yell. It was from Tony. His outfit was about half way up the slippery trail and he was in trouble. Bill knew there was no room for his horse on that narrow trail, so he jumped off and tied the string of three to a tree. As he started running down towards Tony a bull moose trotted past him and disappeared into the spruce jungle. He was grunting his love call but Bill didn't appreciate it. Slipping and sliding, he passed Tony's saddle horse, who was just about pulled off the trail. This snorting and heaving tailed-up string of struggling horses was a soggy sight. The wrangler and his saddle horse were both trapped by his lead rope. It was clamped down under his horse's tail and tied to the string of pack horses behind him.

A horse packed with hind quarters of elk had slipped off the trail and was pulling the horse he was tailed to off with him. The meat horse behind him was braced stiff-legged in the trail, head and neck stretched out like a giraffe. The whole outfit was having a ring-tailed fit. Tony was so busy he could only grunt and cuss.

Bill climbed up opposite the helpless pack horse in the middle. He pulled out his hunting knife and whacked off the lead rope and then the tail rope. The freed pack horse went rolling and plowing down the steep hillside toward the jumble of big rocks and crazy upended tree roots at the bottom. Bill could hear his despairing grunts and crunchy thuds. Looking up the trail, Ol' Bill saw that Tony had come out of his jackpot and was OK. The last two pack horses hadn't made a move. Bill led them, walking behind Tony and his lead horse up the hill.

After they'd tied up the horses to trees alongside Bill's at the top of the trail, they floundered down afoot through the heavy timber fringing the clay slide. Bill said, "If this horse is still in one piece after this trip, he's a tough one." There was the pack horse at the bottom, a-laying on his pack of elk meat. His feet were trapped in a tangled up mess of roots and broken off stumps of upended spruce. This muggy dish was garnished with big blobs of snowy clay and chunks of shale.

"He ain't dead," Tony said, "but how in the devil are we goin' ta get him outa here?"

"We can cut the latigoes and lash ropes." Bill got out his knife and started in. The horse of many brands rolled free and staggered to his feet, trembling and heaving. "I'm goin' t'call him Lucky." The horse wrangler led the bruised-up horse over to the timber edge. "By golly, Bill, he's jist as spooky as ever, don't hardly even limp. Tougher'n a moose, he is. Dang ol' fool, I'm bunged up worse'n he is." Tony led him over to a tree and tied him up. "Musta been protected by all them brands he's plastered with."

"Or that tough ol' bull elk he was surrounded with," Bill put in. When the packers looked over the wreck, all that was busted up was the pack saddle. The heavy saddle pads, the elk meat, the cape, and the canvas pack cover had cushioned the rolling horse. Tony got out his tobacco and rolled a smoke, while Bill looked up the trail the horse had left when he rolled. "Them churned up furrows of mud an' rocks looks like a drunk bull-dozer went on a spree."

With one thing and another, Bill and Tony finally got the meat outfit in to the ranch. That night, Bill asked, "What caused all the ruckus, Tony? Don't tell me a moose done it."

"It's a short story," said Tony. "Th' truth is, it was my own damn fault. I just had t'have a smoke. In tryin' t'find a dry match, I needed both hands. So I thinks, everything is goin' fine, we ain't far from camp. So I *looped* the lead rope t'my saddle horn, and found *two* dry matches stuck together at the tip. When I scratched 'em on the brass screw on top o' my saddle horn, they sounded like Custer's last stand. It spooked that wringtail I was ridin'. He jumped, clamped his tail on th' rope, an' bogged his head t'buck. About that time I

94

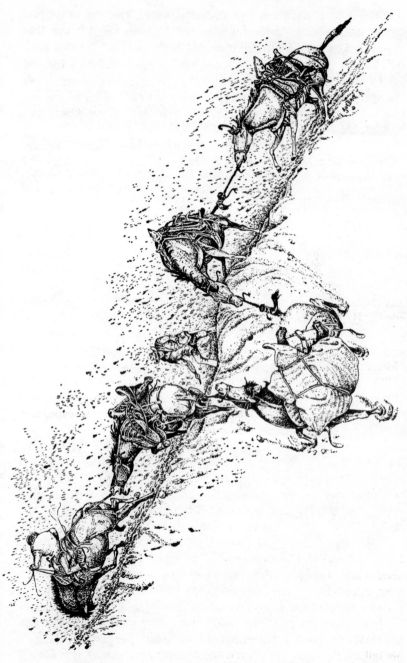

Bill climbed up opposite the helpless pack horse.

was kinda busy, but I can figger what happened (hell, no, I couldn't look). My buckskin horse musta crowded my lead pack horse, who musta kicked th'horse tailed t'him. That's ol' Lucky. The horse tailed t'him musta got bit by the horse he was tailed to. Then ol' Lucky many Brands, with no other place t'go, plunged off the trail and you seen th'rest. I gotta admit it for once. It wasn't no moose. It was me. An', Bill, from now on, I ain't loopin' no lead rope over anybody's saddle horn. Not after this!"

Bill Thompson looked at Tony Belknap a long minute. Finally, "Tony, if I hadn't seen jist about th'whole deal, I'd a believed you read it in one a them dang magazines yuh pack around."

Old Gray Moose

Tony was a terrified ten feet up in the snaggy dead tree before a limb stopped him. The roaring grunt that lit his short fuse was coming from the same big moose he'd put his hard twist necklace on an hour before. When she rared up and clawed at the tree trunk with her sharp toes, the scared horse wrangler tried to climb higher, but a sharp snag spearing through his mackinaw pocket stopped that.

When Tony Belknap broke off branches and threw them at the glary-eyed moose, she didn't scare a durned bit. The bog trotter would just bunt at the tree, then strike at it with her strong front feet. Every time she would paw at his roost, the tall tree would sway like the town drunk. The wrangler suddenly decided to quit throwing limbs—he realized that sometimes tree roots have trench mouth; but that big-nosed devil didn't look like any dentist he'd ever come across.

The big gray cow was at the end of Tony's own rope. He could even see the stub of the corral post, with the spiked ends of broken poles, snubbed tight in a huge willow clump. But she had slack enough to give her treed friend the shivering tantrums. Tony figured that if he did sneak down, the foot-deep crusty snow wouldn't allow any quarter-horse speed, and his snooty jailer would stomp him in a hurry.

She stood quiet for a while, then she remembered past wrongs and glared up at him and stomped at the tree. She found the gunnysack with the horse bait close by the tree hole. She rared up and pounded it to shreds in a squealing rage. Her shivering prisoner realized that the passionate regard she had for him wasn't the kind of affection he cared for, so he hung on to his splintery snags a little tighter. I sure wish I'd opened the gate 'n' let 'er out 'steada ropin' th' damn thing," Tony chattered to himself. "Looks now like the best I kin git outa this deal is th' worst of it."

When the horse wrangler had found the cow moose in the old horse corral, he knew she'd jumped in over the top to get at the little pile of native hay he'd put in for his wrangle horse. Bill Thompson wouldn't be back to the ranch till night with the elk meat he was going to pack in. With the boss gone, Belknap figured it was up to him to teach one old swamp angel a thing or two. He tied the end of his saddle rope to the top of a corral post, got up on the top pole where he could make

97

a good cast, and throwed a big loop. Tony caught the moose right snug around her short neck. When she hit the end of the hard twist rope, the post busted off at the ground, and that part of the old corral caved in.

He got back out of the way of the stampeding moose all right, but he sure was mad when his forgotten wrangle horse ran out of the connecting corral and followed the cow moose. The wheezing bog trotter was making good time down through the willow swamp. The corral post stub with a couple broken pole ends attached would hit in the crusty snow, then fly high in the air. The big black horse veered off down through the timber one way, and the moose kept a snow-clouded fast gait the other, squealing every jump.

The cursing rope-happy gent realized he was afoot, the horse bunch was three or four miles down the river, and a foot of crusted snow to travel in. He darn well knew that when Bill rode in and found him afoot and what happened, that would be a fool thing that Tony would never live down. So he got a roped halter and threw it over his shoulder, threw a couple feeds of grain in a gunny sack, and started plunking off across the meadow. The wrangler figured he'd find the horses and oats-talk some pony up to easy reach, then drive the horse bunch in bareback.

Tony mumbled a couple of stumbling miles crunching down through the timbered parks, and now he could hear faint sounds of horse bells. He was just passing a big dead spruce in the middle of a willow park when it happened.

Tony didn't dare move. At least, he didn't think so. For when he even tried to shrug the cold off, the ancient spruce would sway a little, just a little. And the old swamp angel would come over, grunt a mean howdy, and paw at his roost if he made a small movement; that made the old spruce sway, too. The man in the tree house got cold. He got numb. Awful damn cold. His tight-fitting cowboy boots had overshoes, all right. "But did Admiral Byrd wear them things? Hell, no!" thinks Tony. "They ain't meant fer climbin' trees either, but here I am. Damn it. Damn all moose anyhow!" He thought, when the gray-coated bitch of a jailer lays down ta rest, he'd sneak down real easy, yeah, real quiet, then run like the devil.

Well, there she was, bogged down at the bole of the tree in her snowy bed, nodding her big dumb head. Tony's rope was even quiet. That manila collar he'd laid on her short hairy neck wasn't even moving. He waited, colder'n hell. He waited some more. Tony wondered if moose snore. Then she did. It was like a signal. Tony was ready to make the jailbreak. Just about that time here come three big blowzy ravens and lit on different limbs above him. Their beady eyes surveyed him, and one of the big birds said, "Caaw!" The snoring jailer whined up out of her sleep and lunged at the tree. Scared Tony into hollering. The dead tree weaved like a broken down ferris wheel, but Belknap didn't enjoy the circus, not that one. But those ravens did. They gave out with a lot of gurgling caw, caws. When they jumped off their snags at the top of the tree to flop on their way, the leverage they had at the crown made the wrangler hate roller coasters, too. Did that spruce weave then, and sway!

Mr. T. Belknap got so scared he got warm. Then Old Snouty walked over six or eight feet and lunched on some willows. As she flopped her big upper lip around the moose macaroni and snapped it off, she'd roll her eyes up at the wrangler and give a moany wheeze. The hard twist necklace made her fidgety as it got in her way. Tony knew by that time that moose have a single-track mind, and he was on the main line. Every time he'd move a numb foot or blink a cold eye, she'd stop crunching and look up at him and squeal. Just a little, but enough.

The horse wrangler had cooked himself sort of a skimpy breakfast. Velma Thompson had left the ranch right in the middle of hunting season to take care of her sick sister Minnie. Ol' Bill was a pretty good substitute cook, but now he was gone, too. Tony was feeling sort of empty, now, in more ways than one. The sun warmed him quite a bit. But now it started to cloud up a little. What sun he could see was on the opposite side of the tree from him; and he was a little leery of getting on the sunny side, because any movement enraged the moose and jittered the spruce. Tony said feebly, "Damn moose ta hell, anyhow!"

The sun came back and warmed him a little, but the breeze that came with it swayed his tree so much that Tony wished he'd gone to church that Sunday he'd been in town with the boys. He remembered that his mother had warned him long ago that little boys playing with ropes sometimes came to bad ends. Yes, that was long, long ago.

Mr. Belknap got so cold he got sleepy, but when he woke up with a moosemare, so did his snooty pardner. After she quit cussing him in her whiny language, Tony thought of the life jacket he had hung on his shivering withers. He slowly got the halter off his shoulder, and finally got its rope around the big tree trunk, and fumbled it around his body in a loose knot. "If I go to sleep or freeze, that moose won't git me," he whispered to himself. "If this blamed tree falls, I'll go down with the ship." His thoughts must have got to the cow, for she gave him a swampy sneer and the coarse hair of her mane stood up. She stomped on the snow, and her tongue ran in and out under that floppy nose.

The cold man in the tree had a glimmer of hope once. The bog trotter moved around to get some fresh willows. She twisted up the stiff saddle rope into a kink. It was wet and half frozen, and she mistook part of it for a willow stem, and flopped her lip around it. As she closed her jaws down, Tony, watching in frantic hope, thought, "This is it! She'll free herself now, and pull outa here." When his captor gave a disgusted grunt and spat the rope out unbroken, Tony B's heart nearly failed.

Time wore on. The moose laid down and chewed her cud. Then she got up and walked around in the hard-cased snow till she came to the end of Tony's best rope. Then she wheezed an angry squeal and glared up at the freezing wrangler. He said to himself, "When I die and go to"—he then remembered some of his past life—"well, wherever I go to, I sure hope there ain't no onery moose there."

Finally it got dark, and Tony figured maybe moose can't see at night. So he made some quiet and stealthy descending moves. He discovered that this one could see better at night than daytime. After the tree quit swaying and the swamp angel quit pawing it, the clouds moved over and let the moon come out. About that time some big whirring bird lit in the crown of Tony's private spruce, flopped its heavy wings, and called, "Who, wha, hoo."

The gray moose wheezed and crunched away from the tree a little. The big horned owl would peer down and holler, "Hoo, ha, hoo, hoo," then flap its wings and make the tree sway, just enough to give Tony the hooting d.t.'s.

Just about the time the miserable, half-frozen man decided he'd let go all holts and let the owl finish up what little the cow moose left on the ground, he heard some horse sounds from over in the dark timber toward the main trail. Tony took a chance that it was Bill coming back from camp. He yelled, the big gray jailer gave a coughing grunt and pawed the tree, and the big owl hoo-hooed the very idea.

It *was* Bill, and he hollered back and rode out into the moonlit park. The big gray moose got scared, and when she hit the end of Tony's rope, it broke where she'd chewed it, and she was gone, hellity lick, down through the black timber. Tony couldn't get down out of the tree, he was so cramped and numb. When Bill helped him down, Ol' Bill said, "If ya want me ta help git your big-eyed friend outa the top

She remembered past wrongs.

101

a your playhouse, you'll have ta wait till mornin'." The horned owl flapped his wings, the tree swayed, and both men crunched away from there fast. "Hoo, ha, hoo, hoo!"

The Ridin' Moose

The only thing that kept the pack horse from sinking deeper was the flat bottoms of the rawhide panniers slung under the top pack. Tony and Bill were in the process of getting the last of the pack and camp outfit back to the ranch when this had to happen.

"Ease up a bit on that rope, Tony, I gotta tie this pole under his tail ta hold him steady." Bill was spotted with blobs of slimy clay, and wet from his hips down to his boots, half sunk in the litter of broken up green spruce branches and splinters of shattered poles that used to bridge the boggy part of the trail crossing the moose swamp.

Tony jabbed lightly with his spurs. His apaloosie gingerly stepped up a few inches, his feet sinking in the blubbery mess of swamp grass on the edge of the dense timber. The wrangler kept his tight rope dallied around the saddle horn to keep the bogged pack horse from struggling deeper into a maybe grave. The mud-splattered packer cut the pack rope. He finally heaved, hauled, and slid the tent top pack and the grub-loaded panniers to safety on higher ground.

After the trail pardners drug the pack horse out and reloaded the cargo on the shivering animal, they stopped to take a rest. Tony licked a cigarette together, and let a couple dribbles of smoke out of his bony beak. "You shore don't look like any creasy pants dude I ever seen, Bill. Them spots of mud make you look like a messed-up apaloosie. My horse is gonta be jealous."

Bill was scraping the slimy mud off his mackinaw and leather chaps with the back side of his hunting knife. The rest of the loaded pack string and Bill's saddle horse, all tied to trees bordering the park, interrupted his answer to Tony's jibe by snorting and raring back on their halter ropes. Just about then a big cow moose, followed by her awkward knobby-legged offspring, trotted out of the timber.

The old mamma moose didn't look right or left. She just trotted right through the soggy hole recently inhabited by the pack horse, and was successfully followed by her offspring. They disappeared in the jungle of swamp-rooted trees. "That danged old bog trotter didn't even hesitate, Tony, and look at the hell me and that horse went through in that mudhole. Yeah, you helped, but that there horse and

103

The guide kept his tight rope dallied.

me shows who done the work. Now, like I've always said, we oughta ketch us a few moose, and break 'em ta ride 'n' pack."

"Yeah," said the horse wrangler with heavy sarcasm, "you showed your style of moose-ridin' last trip." Bill's hunter had apparently killed a big bull moose. The guide walked up to the huge prostrate body and prodded it with a long pole to see if life was extinct. He thought it was, so he leaned his rifle against an old deadfall, straddled the body, and was trying to pull it over on its back to start dressing it out. The hunter, meantime, was focussing his camera on Bill's struggle to get set. He was flabbergasted to see the big bull suddenly revive and carry Bill, riding backwards, off into the timber at a staggering run. When his guide came back out of the timber, ragged and skinned up, and wobbled over to the horses, he was in no mood to listen to the photographer's excited claims about the best action shots ever produced this side of Hollywood.

"That there ride was different," Bill protested. "That bull didn't know what he was doin'. I think if a feller would ketch 'em young and train 'em right, it could be done. If that pet Nosy had stuck around, I'd a tried it on him." Tony the moose hater snorted and half swallowed his cigarette. Between gulping coughs he got out, "Yeah. You and them funny ideas. That bear cub you tried t'teach how t'track elk last fall'll do me. The bacon grease you spilled on your britches dang near caused you t'be th'only one-legged bear trainer in Jackson Hole."

The guide knew that his horse-wrangler friend detested moose. After he'd been treed for five or six hours by a cow moose he had a healthy fear of them. Bill liked to dig him about his prejudices. They got on their horses and started to drive the pack string up the trail when Bill jabbed him again: "Tony, I was readin' a book the other night. A famous natcherlist claims that moose *have* been trained ta ride 'n' drive."

The wrangler spurred his horse into a trot to get ahead of the pack string. His parting jibe was, "If ya don't quit readin' them ol' books, ya'll git as loony as th'guy that wrote 'em."

Ol' Bill, back at the tail end of the bobbing string of pack horses, grinned to himself in the cold and growing darkness. He couldn't glimpse his jittery friend away up in the lead. The tree-lined trail twisted up the steep timber-covered mountain. But he caught a few stray whiffs from the wrangler's homemade cigarettes. "Ah ha," the guide thought, "Tony's smokin' t'keep himself company. Figgers th' dang smoke screen'll keep th' devils away, especially th' willow

Carried Bill, riding backwards.

crunchers." The clip-clop of iron shoes and an occasional snort as some low branch scraped on a pack cover was the only noise. Horses traveling mountain trails at night seem to forget grudges. They are luxuries for the daytime, but all enemies are friends in the dark. Going up the switchback trail, they jumped two or three elk, but had no trouble. As they came out into the parks below the ranch, two moose cows and a calf were feeding in a small beaver pond full of slough grass. Bill saw them outlined in the frosty moonlight, against the silvery aspen hillside above them. They just raised their long dripping snouts to watch, and never made a move.

The two men got their pack horses into the corral and went to unpacking. After Tony and Bill grained the horses, they saddled a couple of fresh ones and throwed the whole tired string down in the timbered parks to graze for the night. They put their wrangle horses in a small side corral, gave them hay for the night, and headed for the bunkhouse for supper. After Velma had left, Bill and Tony had sort of let things get cluttered up around the home cabin. So they had taken to using the old bunkhouse. Their domestic disorders were less easily detected and the housekeeping was simpler.

Tony was reading a dog-eared old pulp western, his big hat tipped over close to his long bony nose. He'd read this one five or six times, but it was his favorite. The rickety old bunkhouse had lost a lot of the clay daubing in between the logs, and Tony sat close to a crack you could throw a cat through. He was used to breezes so he was reading one.

His pardner Bill was hunched over a tattered old dictionary, propped up by a couple pieces of split pine stove wood laid on the shaky-legged board table. He detested the sight of the pile of gaudy western magazines stacked in the corner by the horse wrangler's bunk. Bill had to read the dictionary as this was the only other printed matter he could find. Reading can labels was out, he'd memorized all of them, from Alphabet Soup to Zedder's Baked Beans. Besides, he was finding words that would come in handy on onery horses and locoed horse wranglers.

Maybe that contrary college professor he guided on the last trip had done him a favor. This cubic foot of words might turn out to be the best tip he'd ever got from any egocentric big game hunter.

Tony was leaning over his tale in literary ecstacy. Just as Wild Bill Hiccups was drawing a bead on the last of the brawlin' Balton boys, the old pillow fell out of the busted window pane back of his tensed

107

head, and a long bulbous snout reached in to caress the black hat brim, and pushed it on to Tony's nose.

The startled cowboy came out of his dreams of the Hokay Corral, and turned to stare into the curious eyes of a maudlin moose. He fell over backwards with an uncowboyish squawk of terror, shoving the senile table against the serious Websterian scholar. Down went Ol' Bill on the floor with the wrecked table. The coal oil lamp lost its smoky glare of competence; and when the cork let go in the bowl, the flame joined forces with John D.'s product, and lit the little old log shack of intellect with a snaky blaze of fiery exuberance.

Bill's hairy paw clutched the professor's wordy book for a new slant on education. He got up in a singed rush and made for the door. He put one shoe-pack on the prostrate wrangler's belly in his stampede, but got the door open, and galloped out of the lit-up house of learning. He grabbed a shovel leaning up against the cabin, and began throwing snow inside to douse the fire. The first shovelful hit Tony in the face, ker-whunch, as Tony groaned to his feet. The next few cooled the fire, but met obstacles being thrown out of the cabin. Tony was bent on saving the Balton Boys and all their enemies from the flames.

Finally the fire sizzled out. The two tired students got another lamp from the cabin behind the bunkhouse. Bill found his dictionary in the snowbank just outside the door. But poor Tony found his best magazines in a pulpy mess, half burned and half soaked, where Bill's shovel had ricocheted them back into the fire.

The men straightened up the wrecked table and battered chairs. Tony examined what was left of his library.

"Bill, you musta been th' star batter when you was a kid. Yuh batted my readin' right back inta the fire when I was a-tryin' t'save some o' the best."

"Now that there is gratitude fer yuh!" Bill snorts as he is sweeping up the glassy wreckage off the singed floor. "Save your life, and you kickin' about them dog-eared old westerns."

Tony piled the remains of his classics into a safe corner and helped clean up the mess. Then they decided to hit the hay, the class was over. Bill's bunkful of blankets had escaped the soggy snow. Tony shook out his wet blankets and finally crawled into his damp bed. He groaned all night. His belly hurt where the bowlegged fireman had stomped, and from the loss of Gray Zane's best. The triumphant fireman slept good. He had his dictionary safe under a dry pillow. Bill woke up just once. That was when poor Tony was having a wild dream about a moose that was chewing on some of his pulpy literature.

Before sunup next morning Bill heard Tony outside the bunkhouse mumbling to himself. He remembered the ruckus last night, and figured Tony hadn't had too good a sleep. He dressed and popped his head out the door. There was Tony, moon-eyed and grumpy from a poor snooze. He had one end of a saddle rope tied to a tree about seven feet up, and was just jerking the rope tight to another one about thirty feet away. "Gotta dry them blankets out. That snow you throwed on 'em last night wet 'em up. I'll hang 'em up after we wrangle horses."

"Man, I'm glad yuh put that rope high enough so it don't ketch a feller under the chin," says Bill, buckling his chaps on. "I knew a gent once who was kinda in a hurry one night. He run his horse under a clothes line. It caught him in the Adam's apple. And bein's that his boots hung up in the stirrups, that bird's career is now bein' pursued down yander. Knowin' this guy pretty well, it's a cinch he ain't up above."

It was getting a little lighter in the sky by the time they ran the horses in from the grassy parks below the cabins. Bill shut the corral gate on the last of them. Tony, still groggy from his dreams, stepped off his mount. He uncinched his horse and was looping the latigo up on the rigging ring, when Bill hollered. The horses were all running frantically around the corral, trying to get away from something black moving along in their midst.

Tony forgot his dangling cinch and stepped up on his horse to get a higher look-see at what all the commotion was about.

Bill was on his own horse. He yelled, "There's a dang ol' moose in there. I'll open th'gate 'n' let 'em all out. We c'n git rid o' th'moose 'n' run th'horses back in!" He leaned from his pony, slid the pole lock back, and swung the gate open. The nervous bunch of snorting horses streamed out of the gate, with a big bull moose following at a grumpy trot, his long bell swinging sidewise, with angry flourishes. Not wanting any more close association with a moose, Tony reined his high-withered nag around, and loped him off to one side, out of the way of the fast-running horses.

Bill galloped his horse up through the willows and bent the horses around to head them back to the corral—minus the moose, who faded away in the timber. It was light now. As Bill hollered at the reluctant horses he could see the horse wrangler riding fast on the far side of the loose bunch. He was just going through some high willows.

The thick mat of willows hid a trail through the bog. Tony was riding hell for leather to get around some loose horses. He was mak-

He automatically reached for a mane holt.

ing good time when his horse stopped short. The amazed wrangler lost his reins and grabbed the saddle horn with both hands. He sailed through the air, his cinch popping against his heavy chaps. When he lit, he found himself *still* in the saddle, and *still* going like hell. But it wasn't old Brownie he was on. From the squealing coughs and startled grunts, he knew dang well this must be a dream. He shut his eyes and hung on for dear life.

Those popping snores couldn't be Ol' Bill over in his bunk. It didn't smell like Bill, either. When the wrangler felt his saddle slip, he automatically, dream or no dream, reached for a mane holt. That's what woke him up. When his clutching fingers grabbed a handful of stiff, bushy hair, he woke up. Then what he saw made him shut his eyes plumb tight. "Ride 'er, kid. Ride 'er! Whoopee!"—Tony dimly hears Bill holler with wild enthusiasm. "Yuh made a good trade. Stay with 'er, Tony!"

"Oh, no! Traded ol' Brownie fer a moose?" Tony fearsomely opened one eye, then shut it quick. A moosemare for sure. The wind whipping past his dizzy head brought the bitter and musky smell of his fast-moving mount. He wanted to pinch his nose, but didn't dare let loose of her mane or the saddlehorn.

Tony was thankful he'd taken off his spurs last night. He was going to hell fast enough. About the time poor Tony was wishing he'd led a better life, he felt a terrible jerk on his brisket. He knew for sure it was the top pole of the Hokay Corral he'd hit. Then the lights went out.

Now Tony was afraid he was going to live. He was coming to. The wrangler's hand clutched the broken clothes line. He moved, then knew his back wasn't broke. He was still in the saddle, his other hand on the horn. . . . He felt a boot in the stirrup, oh, why was he born? . . . "Damn all moose, anyhow," Tony started to sneeze. . . . He lay back on the snowy ground, and felt the big breeze. . . . He stared up at Ol' Bill who knelt on his knees. . . . He was fanning the reclining wrangler with the professor's dictionary.

As the dazed wrangler sat up, close to the bunkhouse, he realized what had happened. "Yuh was doin' fine, Tony," says Bill, helping Tony get unscrambled from the saddle. "You ain't defunct, but yer deceleration was too durned expeditious."

Tony got up then, and muttered to his grinning nurse, "Aw, hell, take that damn dickshunary, an' go t'college!"

The Perfessor

For several winters a family or two of moose had wintered below town a few miles. There were some extensive willow flats along the river, and the snow didn't pile up enough to bother them. One cantankerous cow moose lost her bearings on her way to these winter quarters, and was hung up temporarily in a dense patch of willows and cottonwood trees just behind Minnie's house on the outskirts of Roaring River.

This long-nosed crosspatch was extra irritable because some boys had sicked their dogs on her the evening before, at a ranch above town. She had just about regained a full belly and enough aplomb to make a detour and continue her journey, when the retired schoolmarm came crashing through the tall willows. Old Minn was searching for Algernon, her Pomeranian pup. He was asleep in a safe corner of her back porch, but she didn't know it. She was in a hurry to shut him up so she could go shopping with her sister, Velma Thompson, and a friend.

The pup's scent on Minn's coat set the moose into a swampy rage. When the two crusty old maids met face to face in the willow clump, the one in the red coat gave an eighth grade screech and lit out for home. The longer-nosed one in the gray coat wasn't about to take any such mean remarks, so she started blowing snuffy insults right back and fell in behind. The school marm forgot all about the desk-bound arthritis in her joints when she came to the barbed wire fence she'd laboriously crawled through a few minutes ago. She went under the wire like a squatting thoroughbred. Minnie thought she'd won the race, until she heard her cantankerous contemporary bust through the barbed handicap and start to close up the snorting and breathless gap in between.

Just about to be overtaken, the ex-dictator of county education suddenly ripped off her crimson jacket. She threw it in the path of her opponent, who seemed about to win the election. This was no fixed race, but the cow moose suddenly plowed to a stop, and started to stomp on Minnie's jacket with her long front feet. Snuffy knew if she got the hide first, the carcass would come later.

Back at Minnie's house, Velma Thompson and her friend were still waiting. The friend spied the old maid windmilling along in the distance. "Isn't that Minnie," she asked, "running over there?" Velma looked out the window. "Oh, no, that isn't her. Min can't go that fast."

The frantic woman was running to the nearest haven, her neighbor's house. They were just about to get into their car in the driveway, when Minnie came spurting around the corner and tripped over the man's legs. The heaving bundle of petticoats and old fashioned education banging up against his legs threw him in the open car door and against the horn button. The moose came pounding around the house at full speed, but was turned by the blaring horn and the screams of the two women.

The cow moose was back down in the safer willow clumps along the river. Minnie and her neighbors were inspecting the wreckage of the two moose-made gaps in the freshly painted picket fence enclosing the garden. The old maid had been revived to her usual vinegary humor, and she was now vowing that she was going to have vengeance on that cow moose, even if she had to use up all the wardens in the whole game department.

The new game warden had only been on the job a short while, but he had already been dubbed "The Perfessor." His talk of scientific game management, and his badge-heavy manner hadn't won him any trust or affection. Minn, hurrying up the main street of Roaring River next morning, nearly ran over the warden. He was adjusting his large hat in the reflection of the windshield of his new pickup parked in front of the post office. The post office door was open, and Minnie stuck her tongue out at the postmaster slyly peering out through his bars. These two old people had feuded ever since he had first pulled her braids in school. Then the schoolmarm crowded right up to the game warden and said, "Young man, I want you to do something about that mean moose in my back yard."

"Just what are you talking about, madam?" The perfessor gave her a quick once-over. He felt of his manly chin and straightened the collar of his well tailored red shirt. The sight of that red shirt made Minnie remember her own moosed-up coat. It got her dander up. "Now you listen to me, young man," Minn had her best long finger waving in front of the tall warden, "The cow moose that chased me through my own fence and wrecked my neighbor's fence has got to be dealt with."

A man in an old faded shirt and worn levis paused in the post office doorway with one scuffed boot on the threshold. He was intently

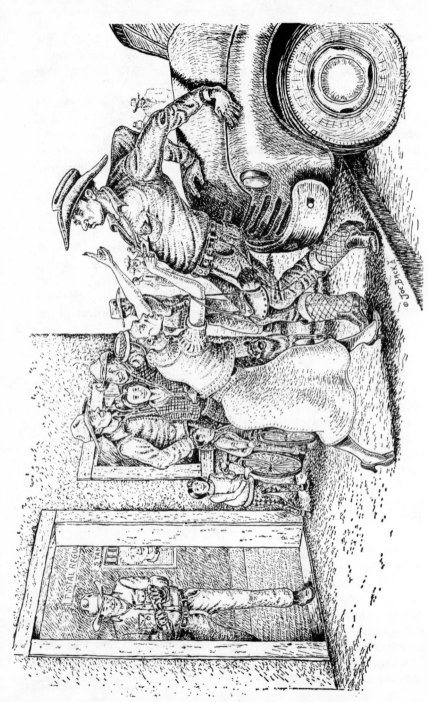

You know all the answers—YOU JUST DON'T UNDERSTAND THE QUESTIONS.

114

studying the wrapper on a tightly rolled newspaper, and appeared to be in a pleased dreamy trance. The bored game man yawned and started studying his highly polished fingernails. "What moose, lady?" A couple of kids parked their bicycles squarely in the center of the sidewalk and were listening with knowing grins, as Minnie, striving for control, got to going on her description of the happenings. Her voice got louder and louder. Now, other townspeople, young and old, most of whom well knew the old school superintendent, casually strolled by, or stood and studiously gazed up at Old Baldy, back above town.

The seething old maid finally got her story told to the disdainful game expert. When she had finished, he suddenly leaned forward, stuck both hands in his hip pockets, pushed out his well rehearsed jaw, and said, *"Who* do you think you're kidding, lady? Moose don't do *that!"*

"Don't *you* tell *me* what moose don't do." Minnie was now tapping her veteran finger on the shiny badge. The startled man was backed up against the hood of his official pickup. "I've seen hundreds of your kind. The back of your books are all worn out before you've ever seen the front. You *know* all the *answers*—but you JUST DON'T UNDERSTAND THE QUESTIONS!"

The game warden for once in his life absolutely didn't know what to do or say. The old school mom, who loved infighting, saw that she had the Perfessor punchy. The audience gathered around, enjoying the show, waited for the climax. So she gave him the old one-two. "Young man, you can keep your *degree,* but if *you* don't *do* something about that *moose,"* she had her jaw synchronized with her finger, "I'll have your badge pinned on *somebody* that's got more between the ears than *you'll* ever have!"

The old school supe punched a final period on his badge, shook her digit under the man's flustered nose, and marched into the post office. She glared at her schoolmate behind the bars, got her mail, and made a triumphant Carrie Nation march back to her home among the cottonwoods.

Minn learned from her neighbors that the warden spent the next day or so combing the willow clumps along the river back of their houses. The old cow moose had moved on, for the Perfessor hadn't contacted her or any of her kind, one neighbor reported.

The warden must have found out Minnie's relationship to Velma and Bill, and something about the pet moose. Velma told her sister that the game man was evidently very much offended at the public lecture administered by Minn. He drove up to the Thompson ranch and accused Bill of keeping a game animal in captivity. And that, he reminded Bill, was against a state law.

"If you're thinkin' about that pet moose Nosy, mister, yuh've got another think comin'." Bill had heard about the new warden and wasn't impressed. "He ain't in captivity an' never was. Only time we ever see him any more is when he gets a notion to board off us for awhile. The game department owes me plenty for moose-boarding, if that makes yuh feel any better."

"Well, I've heard of you, Thompson, you and your pets," the Perfessor was miffed at Bill's lack of reverence. "I'll have you know I've got my eye on you."

The old guide had to laugh at that crack. "Well, well, warden, yuh *shore* make me jealous. Why, hell, man, *everybody's* got their eye on *you!*"

The Perfessor gave Bill his most scientific glare. Then he stalked over to his pickup and drove back down the road. Thompson soon got word on the grapevine that the expert had got his F.B.I. instincts aroused, and had confided to admirers that he was onto Old Bill. And that he was going to get evidence to cinch Bill's hide to the Game Department fence.

Nosy, off on some trip of his own, hadn't been around the ranch for quite a while. Velma tried to check up on him with Bill's binoculars. She reported that several times she'd seen a gaunt old cow moose with a pair of twin calves, hanging around up in the swamps above the ranch. "Those calves are sure cute, Bill," Velma said. "They're so fat, no wonder the old lady is so skinny. Once, I *think* I saw Nosy, trying to cut one out of the bunch."

Awhile later the rancher was up on the hillside above the buildings, checking on his water system. He cleaned some moss out of the spring. Now he was looking for a stick to scrape mud off the shovel. Seeing movement over in some close timber, he located two men walking through the trees. Their manner and gestures seemed furtive to Ol' Bill, so he walked over to stand behind the huge trunks of spruce trees for a closer look-see.

The old hillbilly soon recognized the men as the game expert and a man new to the country, who had started a gun and sporting goods shop a short time ago in Roaring River. The big game warden had a pair of field glasses slung around his neck by a long strap. He carried a large camera in one hand, and the other hand and arm were pointed down at the Thompson ranch buildings below them. The

116

short four-eyed gent had a large long-snouted movie camera focussed down on the buildings. Bill could even hear the whirring clicks as the machine was turned slowly around. This man's pot belly was encircled by a wide, well-filled cartridge belt. From it a long barreled hog leg dangled in a huge holster.

Ol' Bill got kind of ringy at their sneaky actions. But he got so tickled he nearly gave himself away when the camera man fell down, tripped by his own heavy artillery. The Perfessor was directing the documentary film, and had his red clad official arm pointing down towards the ranch when the camera man tripped. Hollywood was trying to get to his feet from the mixture of swamp grass and tree limbs, when Bill saw two moose calves rise up out of the hiding place where maw had planted them. They were halfway between the two detectives, who hadn't been aware of them; but their mother was, and when she heard their moggy whines she nearly ruined Bill's new underwear. He hadn't seen her, nor did she see him, as she roared down past the big spruce Ol' Bill was so affectionately behind.

From her root-chewing station in the hidden bog above the spring, her snot-blowing whuffy charge brought maw moose dang near on top of the warden's head camera man. The only thing that saved him was the still whirring movie camera upended in the grass. As he dived under a snaggy deadfall near by, the infuriated moose started to stomp and pound Mr. Bell and Howell into a conglomerate mess of worthless evidence.

The Perfessor had been so fast getting up in the tree that the interested spectator peeking from behind the big spruce saw only a blur of red. But the movement had attracted maw even if she couldn't tell time. Like most people on their way up, the game warden had left something behind. It was his own private camera; and while it did save his life, he lost some skin where his hip pockets had been. The big cow was viciously clawing and spearing her front toes into the warden's camera, while he was vainly trying to climb higher up in the limby dead tree. The strong strap looped over his neck held his wildlife special binoculars tight under his pugnacious chin, while the encircling strap was hooked to a snag on the tree trunk. The cow moose got over her photogenic craze, and now turned her attentions to the struggling Perfessor. She had shoplifted one hip pocket with some epidermistic interest, and had inserted a slashing toe into the other, when the problem was solved by the breaking strap.

While the big bog trotter was settling her maternal difficulties with the game department, the bowlegged witness behind the tree enjoyed the proceeding and judged it a smashing success. Every time the game expert up the tree hollered to the picture expert under the tree to get his cannon and kill old Snuffy, the camera man would make an effort to crawl out to look for his lost six-shooter. The moose calves hadn't moved out of their tracks during the whole ruckus as maw hadn't told them to, yet. Whenever Hollywood made a move the kids told on him, being close by and squealers by nature. Maw spent the next few minutes commuting from tree to tree, until Nosy showed up and tried to make friends with the twins. That settled it. The snooty old female couldn't stand the idea of any delinquent contaminating *her* kids, so she run Nosy off down the mountain, and was soon leading her long-legged offspring out of such a gossipy and troublesome neighborhood.

Thinking that the show was over, and sure that neither of the treed men was hurt, Thompon was about to slip back unobserved down to the ranch buildings, when he heard some range cows bawling and some loud shouting. On the other side of the still waiting pair of treed men, a couple of unwilling white face cows and a calf came into sight. Through the open timber on the trail leading down the mountain, Bill could see his friend Tony Belknap riding along, hazing the range cows. Ol' Bill could see that the game warden and the camera operator were hiding from Tony, now. They were sure the cow moose had departed, but didn't want the cowboy to catch them in such tale telling circumstances.

One of the cows tried to break back up the country, but Tony spurred his horse and bent her back down the trail. The red shirt of the Perfessor up the tree must have caught the cowhand's eye, for he rode up for a closer look. He darned near got thrown off his startled horse when Hollywood crawled out from under his snaggy shelter to shake the kinks out of his carcass.

The hidden hillbilly saw Tony's mouth open as he held in his plunging horse. The cowboy finally took the picture in and got his wits about him. "Say, warden, mebbe it ain't any o' my business," Tony said, "an' yuh don't hafta tell me if yuh don't wanta, but what in hell are yuh a-doin' up that tree?"

As Belknap looked from one to the other of the strangely silent men, Hollywood got uneasy. He figured that the Perfessor was the cause of it all and knew all the answers, and should understand the question. He was just as dumfounded as the cowboy at the long pause.

"Yes, by George, *what am I* doing up this tree?" The Perfessor was staring down at the two men down below him. "*Me,* with my *education!* By golly, I quit!"

Bill Thompson had a silly grin on his face as he turned around and sneaked back down to the ranch house.

Washday Moose

Velma's numbed fingers fumbling a clothespin over a shirt were nearly torn off by the clanging wire. Looked along the jumping jacks of her freezing wash, she saw the huge maw crunch down on Bill's new levis. Turning in frantic haste to run towards the cabin, she caught up the big clothespin pail and took off down the shoveled path.

The bull moose spat out his fresh chew, plunged around the rattling clothes and trotted easily through the snow in her wake. Velma, out of breath and overtaken, suddenly jumped into a deep snowdrift and instinctively pulled the pail over her head. Puzzled at the disappearance of his quarry, the bull plowed to a stop, took a good look at the pail bottomside up; and he reached his big smeller over to nose at the shaking metal. The freezing prisoner in the tin hat, hearing the breath of doom, gave a nervous sneeze and shoved the pail up in a desperate attempt at escape.

Down in the corral, Bill had just pitched some hay to his horses when he heard a loud grunting SPANG and Velma's scream of anguish. The startled bog trotter, his bruised kisser high in the air, had run slam bang into the loaded clothes wire, stuck his toes into Velma's waiting clothesbasket, and turned an undignified wintersault up against a tree trunk.

The freezing washerwoman, hip deep in her private snow bank, turned loose a screechy yell of agony at the garment-and-wire-enshrouded villain who had now regained his feet. Velma's wails started the dazed bull into motion. Like most of his curious kind, he lumbered off in the direction he happened to be headed, which was around the cabin toward the barn. Ol' Bill, at a wheezing lope, was halfway up the shoveled path, when the bull, his horny umbrella festooned with laundry, snorted around the cabin with the clothes line and the frozen clothes trailing along behind him. He took one look at the puffing hillbilly, and mooselike, decided this was all Bill's fault. Old Snooty had a towel hanging on a lifter horn, and could only see out of one eye, but that was good enough. He lunged at Bill. He was brought up short by some of the clothes and wire snagging on the corner logs of the cabin.

This was only a slowed down interval. The irate washerwoman now

120

He reached his big smeller over.

had her second wind, and came up just in time to see the singing wire snag her best clothes on the log ends. Velma let out a frustrated scream whose velocity so jolted the big-nosed animal that he forgot poor Bill. He gave a worried squeal and trotted down the path. The wad of clothes sprung off the log ends at the impact of his weight. The wire whipped along behind with a gleeful hissing through the snow.

"Lookout, Bill, oh, that wire! Oh, Bill!" The jittery Bill was a little late. He jumped to one side, but it was the wrong one. The speeding lumps of clothes jerked him off his feet and trapped him in the kinky loops of wire. He was snaked along at a fast clip, with Velma screaming along in the rear, her speed slowed down by stray lumps of frozen clothing. The two work horses, hearing the hullaballoo and seeing the grunting apparition trotting towards them, ran frenzied around the corral in a race of their own. The flag waving moose burst into the open gate, the horses dashed past him and nearly ran over the snow-clouded procession behind. Old Big Nose gave a whining squeal when he came up to the high corral poles, but he didn't hesitate at a little thing like that, not with the following he had. He rared up in an ungainly leap and crashed over the corral. The clothesline, having suffered all the foolishness it could stand, kinked up and broke off in the noisy mess of splintered poles.

That bull moose was thrifty. He'd made a deposit on the manure pile and Bill was it. Velma couldn't stop now for hell or high water. She lit right on top of Bill, and he sank a foot deeper into his providential cushion.

The washerwoman jumped up to pull Bill out of his warm bed. When she saw that he was unhurt, she broke into tears of relief. The numbed victim tried to see where he was. What he heard was, "Well, this is *the absolute end*. I am going to renew my teacher's certificate, if we don't start wearing moosehide clothes!"

Bill sat up in bed, rubbed his face clear, and mumbled, "You thaid a mooseful!"

The Alcoholic

The ways of women and moose are strange, Bill thought as he hung out the re-washed clothes the next morning. "Here I am, an innocent bystander caught in the web. Innocent, hell, come to think it over, I shouldn'ta even seen the calf that spring, a-whinin' an' lookin' so needful of a friend. An' I thought *he* was innocent." Ol' Bill had one eye on the snowy timbered hillside above him, and the other towards the window where Velma was looking over the picture collection of her college days. The wind came up as Bill was hanging a heavy, fast freezing shirt on the sticky wire. An arm whipped up and the sleeve cuff whopped him square in his moose-watching eye. "By the Judas, even my own shirt's against me. Dang near got an eye out from that button. An' who'd think the skin'd come off, touchin' a bare wire with a wet hand. Why dang them clothespins. Bust up easy. Blame companies sure make things cheap nowadays. Thinkin' it over, I was sure lucky findin' all the clothes that blame moose drug around yesterday. Didn't seem ta hurt 'em much, either. Funny. Musta been th' heavy snow saved 'em—an' me—*and* Velma!"

Bill grinned to himself, thinking how angry Velma had been when she told about hiding under the pail. "Haw, woulda sure like t'of seen that, hidin' under a little pail. Thinkin' it over, though, she sure coulda been hurt bad from that moose. Damn him. Sure glad I only got a few more t'hang up, fingers a-freezin'. By George, I see now what a woman's got t'put up with, a-hangin' out clothes. Specially in winter." The wind had really got to blowing by now, and freezing clothes popped against each other. Bill blew on his fingers. His grin turned into a frustrated pucker as he worked on down the line. "Wouldncha know, everything come at once? First Moocher gets kicked an' his leg broke—hell, no, that was good luck, come t'think of it. If he hadn't been down t'town t'the vet's, mighta complicated this moose deal, seein' how he don't like moose. Well, then, the moose an' the manure pile—that was lucky, too, only Velma don't believe it. An' the radiator hoze on the buzz saw engine sprung a big leak 'n' I had t'saw wood by hand. Then last night Velma gets a toothache. Sure scared me, middle o' th'night. Wisdom tooth, she says. Better this mornin'. Then th'washin' machine engine breaks down. Velma doesn't say a word, just hums college tunes 'n' plays them high-toned records on th'music box. Well, I sure was glad t'find that ol' scrubbin' board in th'bunkhouse. Washin' clothes by hand ain't no picnic, I'll tell a man. By damn, women do have it hard, when ya come t'think of it. I sure hope that hummin' 'n' talkin' about a teacher's certificate ain't serious. I wouldn't be able t'stand that."

On the porch, Bill rubbed his freezing fingers together and grabbed a broom to sweep the snow off his shoepacks. He was still talking to himself. "Damned if I'll ever have a pet moose again. By hell, she's still a-playin' them hi-flyin' records. I c'n see where she's scraped the frost off a window ta see if a moose scared me off. Why, damn th'things anyhow. No more pets for me—why, damn me fer a sap anyhow. That blame calf a-layin' there in th'willows that spring—innocent, hell, I was the innocent one. Sucker, hell, yes, sucker. That's me, might as well admit it. Dammit.

"Looks like we gotta go t'town now, an' th' snow too deep fer th' pickup. Dang th' early winter anyhow. Take Velma in t'git her tooth fixed—hope th'poor kid c'n stand th'snowshoe trip."

Bill stamped his way in the door, still mumbling, "Gotta fix up a list, le's see, yeah: Lower hose f'r buzz saw radiator. More anti-freeze alkyhaul—lost some before I got it drained. See Moocher at ol' Doc Frazier's—better not try t'bring him home, deep snow, cast on his leg. Spark plug 'n' condenser for washing machine. Damn moose anyhow. I know dern well this washday moose couldn'ta been Nosy. Naw, he wouldn't do a thing like that. Well, now, thinkin' it over—it just coulda been. A pet! A damned pet!"

Nosy the pet moose had gone back to his own kind two or three years ago, and since that time Bill had made no more pets out of lost mountain children. Bill found out he could get away with an occasional damn around the house, but moose was a bad word. He'd found that out the hard way.

Velma and Bill had a few visits from Nosy during the last two or three winters. The only way they could tell him from other moose was from the barbed wire cuts he'd suffered on his lower front legs. He would come in February or March after he'd shed his horns, so the scars were his only trademark. The dimly remembered handouts made him comically dangerous. But he stayed away after a few lumps were hammered on him in the hay corral. Velma swore Nosy was the laundry moose, but Bill wasn't sure. He hadn't really checked those front legs yesterday.

"If we can make it down to Murphy's ranch, we can get Johnny to

124

take us to town," Bill said as he was strapping Velma into her snow-shoes. "We ought to make the six miles easy enough. All downhill. Here, wrap that scarf up tight around your jaw." Velma doggedly plunked along in Bill's big tracks, bracing herself with a pole Bill gave here. The heavy snow on the old crust was hard traveling in, and she could barely see the wind-whipped trail ahead through the peephole above her scarf. That wisdom tooth in her swollen jaw ached from the knifing blasts.

Breaking trail about 40 feet ahead, Bill kept looking back anxiously at Velma. There were a few scattered moose feeding in the willow clumps along the river bottom below the road. They seemed to be minding their own business, so Bill gave them no more thought. The two travelers hit their stride and were making good time. Three miles to go, and the snow got thinner and easier to travel in.

Crunching along behind, intent on her painful problem, Velma suddenly had a new one. And wouldn't you know, it was moose. She heard a pleased grunt and a muffled yell. Stopped short, she saw a huge horned bull right in front of her. Bill was humped over sideways with one snowshoe waving in the air. The moose had his long snoot rammed in Bill's shoulder pack and was rooting around for a handout.

About that time, the grownup grafter found out never to fool around with a bad wisdom tooth. Bill was lucky again, even if Nosy did have one scarred foot punched through the rawhide filling of Bill's long-tailed web. Instincts had flared up from Velma's sea-faring an-cestors, for Velma viciously harpooned the bull moose with her pole and then started hammering him on the stern. The bog trotter tried to match the mad woman's snarls, but when her pole broke across his suffering rump, he gave a choky whine and plunged off up the moun-tainside. He had a paper-wrapped lunch in his mouth and Bill's snow-shoe above his knee. Every time he sank through the snow crust the web worked higher.

Velma had forgotten all about her tooth during the mixup with the grownup delinquent. Bill struggled up the hill above them and re-covered the punctured web where Nosy had shed it. He found he could patch it up fair enough to hobble along on, and nothing else seemed to be damaged except frayed tempers.

About the time her wisdom tooth forgot the excitement and started throbbing again, Velma heard Bill give a big holler and saw him wave at a pickup away down on the snow-cleared county road far below them. It was Johnny Murphy and he was tooting the horn.

A few hours afterward Velma was safe at her sister Minnie's house

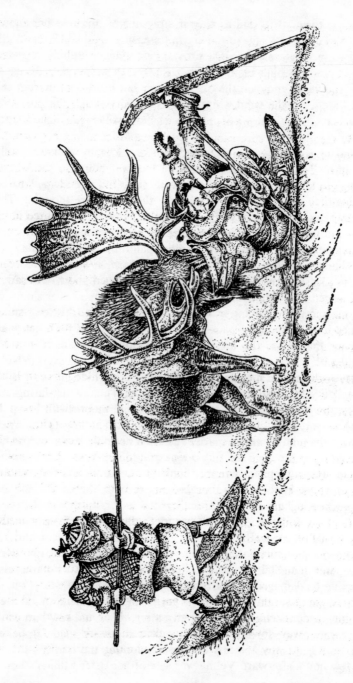

Velma harpooned the bull moose.

in town. Seemed the dentist was gone on a trip down to the county seat. Moocher was doing pretty good on three legs and a cast, and Minnie acted like she thought she could get along with him, too. But she didn't put out any objections when Bill said he had to get back to look after the milk cow and chickens, and run his line of marten and coyote traps. While Bill was filling up his knapsack in the store, John Murphy was busy loading his pickup with supplies for his own family.

"By George, you sure shoulda stuck your foot in my big mouth," Johnny Murphy looked at Bill with a grin. "That word *moose* must be a dirty one in your family." Johnny kidding about the lunch-stealing ruckus hadn't been funny to Velma. Now Bill added the story of the washday moose.

"Well, I reckon you're lucky at that, Bill. If that'd happened at my place I'd have had to wash all our clothes from now on. And we've got five kids."

"You know, Johnny, it's close to Christmas, and I've decided to give Velma a present she'll like. A resolution that I won't adopt any more pets."

Johnny, knowing Bill, says with a snicker, "Well, maybe not moose ones, anyhow. When things get dull down to my place, Bill, I'm going to come up and pay you a visit. You folks never seem to have a dull moment."

"By gosh, you do that, Johnny. We'll have everything except moose meat. I wouldn't eat that stuff on a bet."

Murphy hauled Bill and his plunder as far as he could, after he failed to persuade him to stay the night at his ranch. That was a couple of dark hours ago. The hillbilly was all worn out as he clunked up to his shadowy and snow-covered buildings. Last summer he had added a roof to connect his home cabin with the storehouse behind. Now the snow had drifted in on both sides. Ol' Bill unstrapped his snowshoes and stuck them tail down, upright in the snow. He fumbled with his pack straps and finally got his heavily loaded pack board off his weary shoulders.

After he slid down into the area-way to get his load into the storehouse, Bill thought he heard stealthy crunches in the rock-hard snow, banked eye level above him. He remembered willow crunching thieves and thought about the apples in his pack sack, but there were no more sounds out of the night. He leaned over to hang his pack on a nail until he could open the door, and stumbled and stuck a shoe pack into a washtub half full of the anti-freeze he had drained from his buzz saw engine.

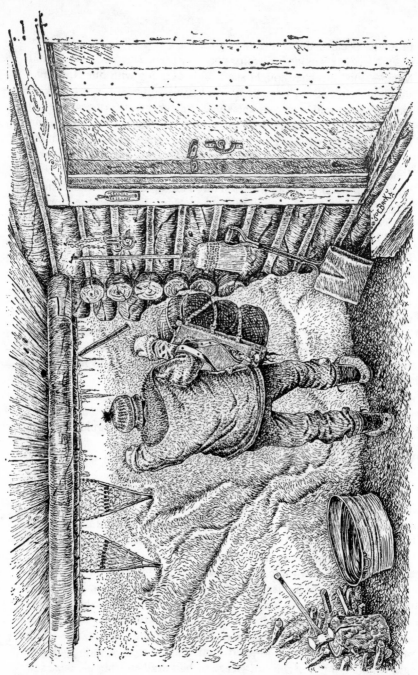

Bill thought he heard stealthy crunches.

Nosy couldn't stand it any more, he'd smelled apples for a mile, and here it was just about Christmas. So he took a chance and down he came. The soggy-footed rancher had just pried the frost-locked door open, when a thousand pounds of hairy Christmas resolution fell down against his weary carcass and shot him through the door right onto a pile of sacked oats. Ol' Bill was in but he was out.

The white-footed mouse had found it a tight squeeze through the knothole in the floor. She got her belly full, then she started back and forth, packing oats down under the floor boards. It looked like a long cold winter ahead, and sometimes hillbillies patch up knotholes. Mice, like men, know straight lines are the shortest, so Bill was brought to by strayed oats spilling down his open mouth. Strangled, he sat up and coughed out the grains. He lay back a minute listening to kicking thumps and unearthly groans. With a start he realized that he wasn't asleep at all. He fumbled under his heavy coat to the matches in his shirt pocket. He lit one and then limped over to the door, but the cold breeze flickered the small flame out. Just as Bill started to figure what had happened a thrashing hind foot of the trapped bog trotter caught him on his bruised hip and knocked him up against a cupboard. It crashed down on top of him. As he fell, he could hear Velma's new china set, as yet unused, get a breaking in that was going to be hard to explain.

It was dark again, but Bill's memory was afire and that kind of heat was uncomfortable in the frigid storehouse. Bill got up in a hurry, though, when he heard the gurgling and thumping sounds that finally died down to an uneasy silence. Reminded Bill of a drunken fight he'd seen once.

After that last gargling sigh in the area way, there wasn't a sound. Bill mustered up enough strength to stand up. He fumbled around in the dark and finally found another match. He remembered an old kerosene lantern hanging on a rafter nail above him. He got the lantern lit, and wobbled over to the open door to see the sights.

There was a huge bull moose lying belly side up with his head turned sharply to one side. He filled the whole space with his dark roan carcass. There were deep scars on the limp gray legs. It was Nosy come home to roost. Bill Thompson could see that the moose was defunct, and for once he was thankful. For that anyhow.

Nosy's magnificent set of horns had caught in a stack of split wood piled against the log wall, and his head was twisted at a grotesque angle, with his long snoot stuck into the washtub full of antifreeze.

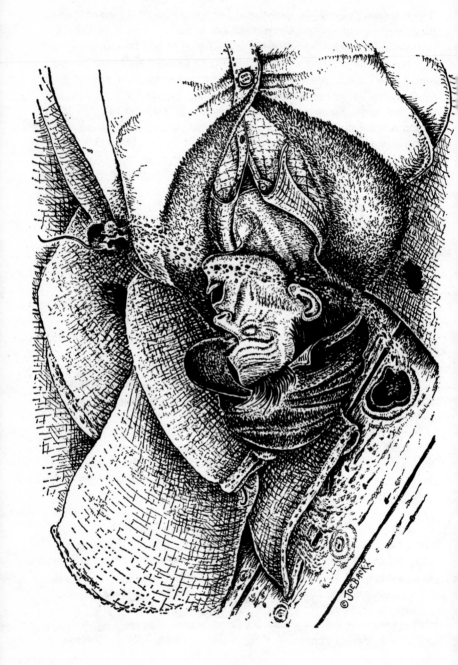

Some apples from Bill's knocked-down pack floated around in the beverage.

Holding the flickering lantern high above him, Bill began to realize that Nosy really must have acquired bad habits out there in the wild blue yonder. The moose had died a drunk. Ol' Bill put his soaked shoepack up on the short-tailed burglar's limp carcass with a last fare-well. He looked at his grownup pet and sadly said to himself: "Yessir, a plumb alcoholic. Too late now to join the alcoholic non-a-moose."

Bill was a teetotaler himself.

THE
SUCKER'S
TEETH

A Foreword About Tusk Hunters

One of the last wild refuges of the American elk is away up high in northwestern Wyoming, a strange and wonderful upland called the Buffalo Plateau. This massive upthrust is over eleven thousand feet high, and large enough to affect the weather. It rears up and splits the storms, so that Wind River Valley southeast of it enjoys a relatively mild climate. It's wild, cliffy, and untamed, yet it contains many peaceful meadows, with great sweeps of timber following down the network of streams rushing from the enormous arctic uplands. After calving in the valleys below, many families of elk head for this lush paradise, there to stay until late fall and early winter storms force them to the lower valleys.

This is horse country—no roads, no jeeps—and hard to get into. Winter snows pile up from ten to fifteen feet. Streams radiate from it to water much of our continent: the Buffalo Forks to the Snake, to the Columbia, to the Pacific; and the Yellowstone, Shoshone, and Wind Rivers by way of the Missouri and Mississippi to the Gulf of Mexico.

Stangely enough, you can't see this magnificent plateau. Nowhere, away from it, does it dominate the skyline. It is not celebrated in song or story. It is a strong and secret refuge in the hearts of those who know it, and knowledge of it forms a bond between strangers.

Most of the story in *The Sucker's Teeth* is based in the lower reaches of the Buffalo Forks of the Snake River: South Fork, Soda Fork, and North Fork. As this story is twisted up with people versus teeth and a few other things, I think some explanations are needed about the trouble a lot of elk had with some of their teeth, and *this* is not fiction.

Some folks say that a scamp, a scalawag, and a scoundrel are three stages of the same thing, and that the latter had to start in on the ground floor to attain the final qualifications. But it seems in most of the professional tusk hunters of Jackson Hole had graduated at the head of their class without any first grade preliminaries.

There wasn't very many of these corrupt sinners or we wouldn't have any elk left now. You'd think that anyone who would kill a wapiti or American elk for just two of his teeth had sold his soul to the devil. For in the days before the turn of the century, and for some years afterwards, a fine pair of bull elk tusks would bring as much as fifty dollars, and that wasn't hay—not in those days.

The B.P.O.E., or Elks Lodge, was organized in 1868, and eventually the canine teeth of the wapiti became just about the most official emblem. Both sexes have these canines, the big bull teeth the most valuable and wanted. Cow teeth are smaller and brought lower prices. The teeth of the spike bulls, being immature, are hollow and of little value. For centuries, elk teeth have been collected, treasured, traded, and used, by most of the Indian tribes, for buttons, necklaces, charms, and adornments. Some tribes could get their own supplies, others traded for them.

The Indian market was small, but was added to by other collectors, and the supply came unequal to the demand. The tusks are stunning jewel-like adornments, and are of natural ivory, the same as elephant, narwhal, walrus, and fossil mastodon tusks. The noble elk, endowed by nature with the tastiest of meat, a beautiful hide, the males with magnificent antlers and the most melodious and articulate voice in the mountains, was nearly damned to extinction by also possessing these two small bits of ivory.

By the nineties the buffalo had been about all killed off. The elk, deer, antelope, and mountain sheep were going the same way. Most of the mountain states were just emerging from territories. Laws and regulations were coming into being, to govern and protect the citizens and the natural resources.

Jackson Hole and Yellowstone Park and the mountains around them were nearly the last refuge of the wapiti or American elk, and this country was beginning to get settled. By 1900 the game laws were just starting to take effect. This immense and broken-up, timbered and mountainous game paradise was hard to police with the few game wardens alotted to these parts. The wardens, the more alert settlers, and others were becoming alarmed by the startling decrease in the elk population. It was no longer a matter of occasionally finding an elk carcass with nothing taken but the tusks. The situation had exploded into the finding of bunches of hundreds of elk carcasses, those two ivory tusks the only part missing from each killed animal.

In 1906, D.C. Nowlin, an able state game warden, from 1902 until about 1910, wrote a very angry and vociferous report, in which he condemned the use of elk tusks as emblems and trophies for the members of the Elks Lodge, which was causing the extermination of many hundreds of elks.

This strong report did its job. The B.P.O.E. outlawed the elk tooth as official insignia. The loss of this enormous market, plus the stronger enforcement of game laws and the aroused anger and apprehension of most of the residents of Jackson Hole, practically stopped the wholesale killing of elk for teeth. In 1907, the legislature made killing big game for heads, antlers, and tusks a felony, punishable by a prison term of up to five years.

Elk teeth are still prized trophies, but most of them come from elk legally killed in season, from winter killed carcasses, or from animals found dead from natural causes. By 1909 or 1910, tusk hunting was pretty much a thing of the past, though isolated cases were found occasionally. Some few caught in the act had silencers on their rifles, which made this crime even a more serious offense.

My friend of many years, Cecil Lawrence of Moran, Wyoming, has kindly let me have access to his many records, relics, and photographs concerning these tusk hunters. This famous historian and his wife, who also is an authority on Jackson Hold, have traveled many miles and many years, afoot and horseback, to ferret out the remains of hide-outs built by these tooth pirates. Located away from water, hidden in nearly inaccessible places, these stealthy habitations must have taxed the homing abilities of even those elk killers.

The records state that the tuskers were very active in the years 1904, 1905, and 1906. Five or six men made a ring that did most of the killing. Some were caught but were turned loose for insufficient evidence. One was sent to jail for a year and fined. On May 3, 1907, Charles _____ and William _____, formerly of Uinta County, were fined $200 each and imprisoned, by U.S. District Court, Boise, Idaho. They had been caught with the goods, having killed elk for their teeth in Yellowstone Park and in the U.S. Forest in Uinta County. A few of those caught returned, after serving out their terms, to resume their old trade.

Most of the professional tusk-hunters no doubt had evolved from former trappers and market hunters. Unable and unwilling to adjust to the new way of life as settlers under laws and regulations, these men had led wolfish lives and become like wolves themselves. These wild and exultant freebooters of the wilderness had become vicious pirates, the elk their victims and money their god. Life wasn't easy then, and this butchery was the quickest money in the mountains.

The elk have survived the tusk hunting massacres, many hard winters, game hog firing lines, and careless protection; and they still summer in most of their old mountain retreats. But their most secure and safest refuge is in the area of the Buffalo Plateau.

In 1926, I was a horse wrangler for a hunting outfit, making my first trip into this part of Jackson Hole. Many times since then I've worked for different outfits, traveling through this section. I hope my last trip is still ahead of me. In this story of *The Sucker's Teeth*, the characters are suggested by people I know now or knew then. All names are fictitious and the plot is pure fiction. The country and the life are real.

My friend, if you would like to join Shorty Beel and Buck Bruen's club, just keep turning the pages.

Yours truly,

Joe Back
Dubois, Wyoming

Chapter One

Vince saddled up and rode out early that morning to hunt the horses. The big spruce had wrecked two or three sections of buck fence when it fell over dead, and the horses found the hole before we did. I had just got the last poles spiked tight on the repair job when I heard Pete's Democrats set up an infernal braying. It was a half mile up to the corrals, but the racket sure carried through the timber. When I heard the story of my wife, Velma's troubles at the ranch, I knew those mules must be psychic.

Vel was just stoking up the kitchen range to start dinner when she saw a car drive up in front of the bunkhouse. A thickset man got out, and as he looked around, Vel thought she recognized him as a deputy sheriff from the county seat 75 miles below Roaring River. When she opened the kitchen door, the man with the badge and the big hat saw her and said, "Hi, Mrs. Thompson." Just then the wrangler rode into sight, driving some loose horses ahead of him toward the open gate of the corral.

"Before I could say a word, the sheriff said, 'Excuse me a minute,' and took off toward the corrals. Pretty soon he came back into sight, with Vince walking alongside. He was waving his hands around talking, and the sheriff was shaking his head." It wasn't an election year, and Velma said she couldn't figure it out. "Vince went into the bunkhouse, and the deputy came over and started explaining. 'Sorry, but I've gotta take Vince with me, Mrs. Thompson.' He waved a folded paper at me. He said, 'I've known Vince since he was a kid. Good boy, except he goes on a binge once in a while. Coupla months ago he went on a party. When he come outa' th' haze and found he was married to a tramp, he took a look around an' pulled out.' He shook his head and waved the paper. 'She got out a warrant for wife desertion, and poor Vince has gotta face th' music.' When Vince came out of the bunkhouse with his bedroll, he came over to say goodbye, and *then* those darned mules started up the darndest hullaballoo I ever heard.

"After the sheriff left with Vince," Velma said, "I was just dishing up for a lonely dinner when you showed up, Bill, just in time for the bad news. No, the sheriff wouldn't stay for dinner. He said he and

Vince would eat in Roaring River." Velma went over to the stove to dish up more food. "Vince asked me to tell you he was sorry to put you in the hole, to have to get another horse wrangler. Well, I gave poor Vince a check for the time he had coming, so I guess that's that."

While we finished dinner, we were wondering how Pete Elaby was doing with his ulcerated tooth. This was the visiting dentist's day in Roaring River. "He should be back tonight," Velma said, "Hope he gets over to the store. I gave him a big list of stuff we need." We got up from the table, and were still talking about where could we locate another good horse wrangler, when those jacks down to the corral started to bray. Velma went over to a kitchen window. "Maybe that's Pete now. Hope it's not another sheriff," she was saying, when Moocher the collie started up a frenzied barking out in front of the ranch house. A loud car horn started to compete with the mules and the dog, so Vel and I hurried to the front door. As I opened the door, I could see that the driver's brains didn't match none with his big car. The shiny new car, close to the front porch, was gouged into the fringe of Velma's delphiniums she had worked so hard on. The fat man behind the wheel stopped blaring the horn when he saw us come out on the porch. I shushed Moocher under the porch, but those angry growls should have warned me. The dog had a dang sight more insight than I ever will.

As the portly figure grunted out of the car, Velma noticed the *Kansas* on the front license plate, and figured out just who this was. "By gravy, if I'd known what a crummy lookin' outfit. . ." He stopped short when I waltzed over. "If you don't like what you. . ." I was just about to go whole hog when Vel jabbed me in the ribs with a "Sh! Sh! Take it easy, Bill." Then I remembered who this rhino could be. O yeah, the hunter list. Big wheat farmer—biggest, he wrote. More subsidy than any other in Kansas—big talk—lotsa letters. Paid only part of the earnest money down. O yeah—wait 'n' see—yeah. Well, the loud-talking hunter finally got settled in our strongest chair at the dining table. While he was cramming down Vel's fine vittles he kept rolling his eyes at the trophies I had hung on the log walls. As he puffed and panted his food down, he kept mumbling comments under his breath.

Every once in a while he would shift his weight around and adjust the long, bayonet-sized hunting knife attached to the straining belt of the barrel-sized middle. While I sat in a chair waiting for the man to finish his meal. I noticed the wheat baron suspiciously examined each dish Velma set before him. Finally he heaved to his feet.

"Well, Thompson, I come early, I admit, I sorta wanted ta see what I was gettin' inta. An' now that I'm here I might as well go through with th' hunt. Your rates are O.K., and I would. . ." I had to interrupt him. "I can't take you out to camp for a few days. Guides won't be here for a coupla days. Be tomorrow or next day." I told Kansas we could put him in a cabin and feed him till then.

After he drove his car around to a newly built cabin, I helped the fussy guy unload enough equipment for six hunters. Just as I stacked his last three heavy gun cases in a corner. I saw this lovable character turn back Velma's prized Hudson Bay blankets. He was thumping the new mattress and springs on the rustic bed frame. The fire I'd built in the stove was starting to warm up the cabin, so I figured the mighty hunter was settled. "Mr. Long," I says, just recollecting his name, "supper is at six and breakfast is at seven o'clock. In the meantime, if you need anything, just holler."

Long hadn't heard me. He was busy rubbing at a label that had been left on a window frame, and was mumbling half to himself, "By gravy, if I had this place I'd. . . Oh, yes, Thompson, I think I'll make out. Uh, thanks."

Well, I was sure glad to be leaving, so I grabbed the door knob and started out. Velma dang near ran over me as she came in, kinda red-faced, with a mop and a dustpan. "Oh, Bill, I haven't yet had time to get the shavings and sawdust cleaned up. If you'll show Mr. Long around the ranch, I'll tidy up the cabin." As we left the cabin, and Velma started to lift a heavy leather bag out of her way, I saw Long give her a suspicious look.

We were just starting down toward the corrals when Pete Elaby drove up in the pickup. After Pete got out I introduced him to Long. The grinning packer stuck his hand out to the reluctant farmer. "Glad t'uh know yuh, Mr. Long!" Long quickly dropped Pete's hand, and peered up at the black eye and swollen jaw. So I put in my two cents' worth. "Didja get it pulled, Pete, or who hit yuh? A bad tooth is no cinch in this frosty weather."

Pete rubbed his face and grinned, "That dentist pulled it, Bill. Now mebbe we can git some work done." When Long heard that, he mumbled something about going back up to his cabin for a camera, so Pete and I kept on walking down toward the corral.

We worked till dark stopped us. We turned out the horses and mules, and kept the bell mare and couple of wrangle horses on hay in the corral for the night. I'd forgotten about the grumpy hunter till we went past his lighted cabin on our way to the ranch. "Looks like your friend knows how to operate a gas lamp," Pete says. "I'll bet he had t'find out from Velma." I wasn't very happy about this bird, anyhow. By the time we had stoked up and were feeling spry, Vel told us that Mr. Long had eaten supper with very little comment and gone back to his cabin.

Moocher started to bark outside as a car drove in and stopped at the back porch. When we heard voices and a knock at the kitchen door, Velma cried, "It's Sally! I'm sure glad she could come," and opened the door."Oh, Sally, I'm sure happy you could get off the job to help us for hunting season."

Sally Sublette and her brother-in-law, Tom Hoster, ate supper, while we sat around and jawed about all the news down on the reservation. They were Shoshone friends of ours. Sally, a small, pert Indian girl, had worked for Velma several summers. Last spring she graduated from college. Now she was working in the office at the post. While Sally and Vel washed up the dishes and got all the women-jabber outa their systems, we got Sally's bags outa Tom's car. Tried to get Tom to stay all night. But he said he was right in the middle of haying and had to git back to the ranch.

Sally Sublette was serving breakfast to Long the next morning. He got up late, and his sulky manners irritated the sweet-tempered Shoshone. Pete and I ate early and were down at the corrals. Pete was shoeing one of his mules and I was squatted down in the saddle shed fixing a latigo on a pack saddle when Velma squeaked open the corral gate. "If you don't take that . . . that . . ." she looked at the mule tied to a corral pole, "that jackass hunter out to camp or run him off the place," she was shaking, "I'll . . . c-crown him with my worst frying pan.

"This . . . this Long character told Sally to take back that ham and eggs and serve him something fit to eat." Vel was livid with rage. "He said he didn't like foreigners to be cooking his food anyway!" I throwed that good pack saddle down and stomped out of the corral. I could hear Vel panting along behind me. I heard Pete shut the gate I forgot, and by the time I got up to the big subsidy standing by his car, dang if one of them jacks didn't start to hee-haw.

Maybe there's no money in getting peeved, but I wasn't that broke when I whirled the wheat man around and grabbed him by the wrist. "Look here, you fat farmer, if you don't go an' apologize t' Sally, I'll beat your dumb head off." He had his expensive rump backed up against that car, and was bulging his eyes at me. I could hear Vel behind me swearing college words under her breath. I hadda notion to bust him one anyhow, and then he got to stuttering, "Wa-wa-wait a minute, Mr. Thompson. I uh, I uh, I can see I was in th' wrong. I uh, I uh, wasn't feeling too good this morning."

Well, Long waddled over to the kitchen, with us right behind him. He made his apologies to Sally, adding, "To be truthful, Miss Sublette, that was the finest breakfast I've had in a long time." His ruddy face flushed some more and he stammered, "Yuh know, I-I, haven't been well, and I uh, I been outa sorts lately."

Well, I thought, this oughta be tailgate for this hunter, but he went over to his cabin and didn't show any sign of pulling his freight, so I figgered his hide was thicker'n any moose I ever skinned. Later on, Pete and I came up for coffee. Velma was checking over the camp lists and Sally was kneading up a big batch of bread dough in a dish pan. They stopped and had a mug with us.

The packer sipped some coffee and said, "Bill, I figgered when I was sittin' on the corral pole watchin' th' show, I'd get to see guide hide an' wheat grains scattered all over th' landscape, but I got fooled." Pete reached over to pinch off a piece of dough, and Sally turned a worried eye on him. He started to chew it, rolling his eyes at the roof logs. "Nope, it's O.K., Sally. If it was his wheat it couldn't taste that good."

Well, that crack cleared the air. I asked Sally, "Heard from Johnnie lately?" She looked pleased. "Sure have, Bill. John writes me a letter nearly every month. Sometimes two." Pete, his face still swelled, looked like he was having a hard time swallowing his coffee. "Shorty told me, out at camp, that that boy Johnnie'll be the best dentist Roaring River ever saw, when he sets up his office next year. Even if he is Shorty's nephew, I wish he coulda fixed this tooth."

We went down to the corrals, and passing Long's cabin I told Pete, "I gotta notion ta run that sap head off th' place. If I hadn't made a deal for that land down below, I wouldn't need cash that bad." Elaby opened the gate and grinned. "Sometimes, Bill, yuh gotta take th' bitter with th' sweet. Winter's a comin'." "Yeah, sure is, Pete." I was still sore about the wheat magnate. "Callin' Sally uh foreigner! Why, hell, Pete, th' Indians was in the mountains thousands a years before the whites stole 'em from 'em. We're th' foreigners, and that subsidy-grabbin' jackass is the worst of us." That packer put his paw on my shoulder, he says, "Look here, pardner, *don't* insult my mules."

Velma and Sally were busy packing panniers full of food and other supplies. The list that Shorty, out at camp, had made was a big one. In the next two or three days another guide or two were due, besides, three more hunters were due in. Elaby and yours truly were busy getting his mules and the ranch horses shod up and figured out. The barn and saddle shed was stacked with equipment. The log store house looked pretty empty. We had tents, tarps, and other gear strung around on the hitch rack and corral poles. Our fingers were sore from sewing rips and repairing holes left from last season's use.

Long showed up with a camera, and took a lot of pictures of the activity around the place. He made half-hearted friendly comments, and asked questions about the game conditions, and life in the surrounding mountains. He seemed to be most concerned about the camp, and especially the cook. I told him about Shorty.

Elaby grinned at my picture of Shorty. "By hell, Bill," he says when Long left, "if this grain king ever *does* get ta camp, ol' Shorty'll cut him down ta size. If he gets poppity with *that* cook, there'll be a lot less wheat raised in Kansas."

The rest of the busy day was pretty tranquil. The noon meal and supper seemed to agree with Long, and his friendly overtures were accepted in kind and returned by everybody. Nearly everybody. Sally said that evening, "I've noticed Mr. Long several times trying to pet Moocher. But you know that dog is smarter than I thought. He just isn't having any."

After breakfast next day I drove the pickup, loaded with split wood, up close to the woodpile stacked against the kitchen wall. I was going to Roaring River that morning to try and locate a new horse wrangler. I heard a noise as I was stacking the last of the wood, and it was the fat hunter starting to talk. He had reverted to his natural aplomb. "Thompson," he started out with, "if you'll come over to the cabin I'd like to have a talk with you."

Now, I'm not as cagey as some, but I had a hunch there was a Kroochef deal he'd figured out; but I followed Subsidy into the cabin anyhow. He goes over to the chair by the stacked up leather cases and sits down. He says, real gracious like, "Set down, Bill, set down." Long pursed up his thin lips at the ceiling, thinkin' like, then he reached over to a carved leather case on the polished table top and took out a bottle and a couple glasses. When he started to pour, I held up my hand. "Whoa, now, Mr. Long. All right f'r you or anybody else. But leave me out. I never touch the stuff. I don't hold against it, but me, I'm a teetotaler." Long nodded amiably and put the cork back in the bottle. He leaned back in his chair, holding the brimming glass up to the sunlit window. As he squinted through the amber liquid, he hummed contentedly.

Then he starts. "You know, this country is plenty rugged, and it takes a rugged man to hunt here." Long took a loud sip of whiskey and drummed his pudgy fingers on the table top. He pursed up his lips, and kind of gives me one of them loan shark smirks I've read about. You know, board of directors, the magazines say.

About then, I got to looking around at the boxes, cases, and bags stacked around the cabin. Looked like a sporting goods and gun crank's paradise: three big gun cases, hand carved, a couple pair of field glasses with leather scabbards, two long hunting knives, camp axes on belts, cartridge cases, and a long kind of spy glass with shiny tripod. There was a couple rolled-up sleeping bags and some leather-ended canvas sacks, besides several big leather bags about the size of a washtub. And when I saw the folding table and chairs and that collapsible toilet, I got sorta dizzylike. Somehow I got to thinking about Pete loading that stuff on his long-eared playmates, and about the tent this jerk would have to have out in camp. I reckon the buzzing I heard was Long talking, but I couldn't listen for wondering what kind of a six-legged horse to put him on, and if I could locate a two-headed guide to nurse him around the hills. All this time, Big Wheat musta been talking. Mebbe this *was* a dream, but when I finally got my dumb peepers focused on the mortgage factory sport with the silverplated "where-am-I" pinned to his shirt front, I come outa the haze. I damn well knew what was coming next.

As the man droned on about "what a nice set-up," I could feel a sorta cold sweat coming on; and when my mane hair started to tip my hat brim down onto my forehead, I could see through the glass. But the frame looked wrong. The money he'd paid down was only half in earnest, but winter was coming.

A few years ago, about the time hunting season started, I got a letter that still riles whatever principles I think I've got. The writer wrote that he, upon arriving at my ranch, would pay a stated sum for a couple of fresh elk and deer carcasses, dressed clean and hung up, at the writer's convenience. The letter also said that he, the under-signed, was a very close-mouthed individual, and that I had a very high recommendation from intimate friends, *and* he wished a very early reply, etc., etc.

Well, I know that us hillbillies haven't got a rep for being too bright, and mebbe I wasn't up front either. But if some star-polishing credit manager thought he could pin a poacher sign on this chicken, it would take more dinero than this floured-up numbskull could get hold of. But I got to feelin' about then that I hadn't been any too well lately,

I musta went Berkshire.

and that I'd been outa sorts besides. When I come outa that trance, I heard some snatches of what Mr. Long was saying. "And so, Thompson, if you will have one of your men, or you yourself bring in a nice bull elk and a good buck deer, I will pay . . ."

Well, you know, about then I was damned *sure* I hadn't been too well lately; and I knew I was *sure* outa sorts, when I jumped up and started to throw out them big gun cases and all the shiny hardware and carved leather gear outa that dad-burned contaminated cabin.

Well, sir, I musta went Berkshire, cause when I come to, I was sure there musta been some hella-ballo. I was standing outside leaning against the cabin wall, with Velma holding her hand on my briskit. I heard a car starting up close by, and there was that Kansas hunter driving past the bunkhouse. He had them big hunting glasses hung on an open car door handle, and leather cases jumbled up in plain sight on the dang seats. Velma had a rolling pin in her hand, and was laughing her fool head off. I looked around at somebody inside the cabin, and saw Sally sweeping up some broken glass on the dad-burned scratched-up floor. There wasn't much derbish around to show any subsidy had been left. Just as that big car started to speed up, I saw Pete gallop up on that big sorrel horse of his. He had a big grin on his lop-sided jaw. About then, them dang jacks down at the corral started the blamedest racket I ever heard. And then Moocher quit barking.

Everybody had different stories about what happened, but the main thing was, when the laughing got down to giggles, I was in the pickup headed for town to look for a horse wrangler and to get the mail.

Chapter Two

Good thing I had my ears lowered, because I met up with a man named Slim Wilson in the barber shop. Later he turned out to be a first class hand. About 45 years old. A fine wrangler and a good packer. By the time he had his bed, war bag and saddle loaded in the pickup, and had the mail and other stuff piled in, we were ready to go home.

"Slim, you mind drivin' this chariot?" I wanted to look over the mail. "Not atall, Bill, just tell me when ta turn off." Slim, I could see, was a good driver, so I got to reading what letters I'd got. Saw that I'd have to do down to the railroad at the county seat: Smithers, a hunter we'd had out last year was due in today. Well, I'll go tomorrow. Some more letters and lotsa bills. Mail for Hackett, the hunter out in our camp, and some more. Looks like those two friends Dr. Forrester and Mr. Parsin are going to show up in a day or so. From their letter they sound like fine people to hunt with. Well, I wasn't any help to Slim while I was going over the mail, but I did tell him some about our ranch and camp setup. He talked like he had plenty savvy about the life, but he was no phonograph.

Finally, when Wilson wheeled in to the ranch, I could see we had more company. A car was standing by the kitchen door, and I could see Velma talking with three men close by.

Naturally I hadn't told Slim Wilson about our big recent hunter, but Slim looked at me sorta sharp when I mumbled, "I hope these birds don't raise wheat!" When Slim stopped the outfit and we got out, I was relieved to recognize Tim Smithers, the big broker from New York. The other men turned out to be George Parsin and Dr. Forrester. I felt like a new man.

We shook hands all around, and everybody got acquainted. At our place we're not fancy. Everybody eats at the big table, old-fashioned ranch style, when we're operating. That Subsidy didn't know what he missed, but was he human?

Smithers wanted to know about "his old pal, Shorty: Mrs. Thompson, I'll bet Shorty learned how to cook from you, haw, haw!" Smithers had everybody laughting when he told about Shorty and the guides out in camp last year. "Best time in my life . . . best food

148

and best country . . . Been planning on it ever since last fall," etc. He asked about Tony Belknap, who wrangled and packed last year. "Leg broke? Well, well. Gotta watch them horses, haw, haw."

Forrester was a thin, gangly M.D. from Indiana. His friend George Parsin, formerly from Indiana, now with a museum, in New York, was a naturalist. Both were genial, friendly men, easy to get along with. "We drove out, taking out time. Lots of movies on the trip." Parsin said he was sure going to use a lot of film in hunting camp. "We met Tim this morning in the hotel, and when we found he was coming up here, he took a chance on two wild drivers." "Haw, haw!" (Smithers hadn't changed from last year). "That'll cost you a good picture of Shorty and me, George, haw, haw!"

The way these hunters were getting acquainted seemed to me a good sign. The first hunters we'd had out at the season's start had been an easy going bunch. They were fine hunters and good sports. Those men were back home by this time with their trophies and meat. Hackett, out in camp now, was kind of a stuffy sort, but it was Shorty and Buck who were stuck with him. Now it looked like we had three hunters again that were going to be as fine to get along with as those first. I thought of the slim hunting equipment these men had unloaded. "Just brought the needfuls," Dr. Forrester said, "too much is a damn bother." "Haw, haw!" Tim Smithers laughed about what "junk" he came with last year.

That evening, while I was visiting and talking over game conditions and camp with the hunters, Slim Wilson was visiting with Pete Elaby over by the big stove. Elaby was showing the wrangler a rawhide hackamore he was working on. Smithers and I were listening to Forrester and Parsin describe some happenings on their hunt in Alaska last year. I hadn't heard any car drive up, and didn't know there was a caller, until I saw Pete walk over to the door. As he opened it, a game warden we both knew came in. He said, "Hi, everybody," then he happened to look over at Slim Wilson. Wilson was standing sideways to the warden in the shadow under the gas lantern hanging from a roof log. He seemed to be making an intent examination of the headstall on the colorful hackamore. The game warden took off his hat and smiled around at the crowd, then he walked over to Wilson and stuck out his hand. "Why, hello, Slim." The new wrangler flitted a glance over in my direction. Then he quickly shook hands, said, "Hi, warden," with little enthusiasm, sorta nodded, and sat down to look at the hackamore. The game man gave Wison a queer sort of squint, and then I introduced Kompton to the hunters.

After we'd chewed the fat about this and that, he asked me in a low tone if we could have a few words in private, so I excused myself to the hunters. Velma and Sally were slicking up the kitchen for the night, and outside of friendly greetings, paid no attention to us as we sat down at a corner table.

"Bill, a hunter from Kansas showed up at my place this afternoon," Kompton had a cold left-handed grin as he said this. "Claims you're a crook." Warren Kompton had a reputation as a fine game warden and a square shooter, but the thoughts of Long began to get my dander up. He went on, "Says you threw him off the place, after you'd signed him up and taken his earnest money." I stewed that over, and told him, "O.K., Warren, I'll admit all but the crooked part. Now let's hear what else this bird has on me."

"All right, Bill, here she goes," Kompton said in a disgusted tone. "He said your food and service is horrible, your cabins not fit for a dog, and if your camp is run like your ranch, we oughta take away your outfitter's license."

No dishes rattled and no water sloshed for quite awhile. It was very quiet in the kitchen, when I saw the game warden staring up past me with an unbelieving look on his weatherbeaten face. When the smoldering cigarette fell out of his gaping mouth, I shoved back to get up out of my chair. To brace myself, I started to put one hand on the table. Looking up into the ferocious glare that little Shoshone gal of ours had riveted on Kompton, I put my hand on the - ah - sticky bleeding scalp of the wheat magnate.

When Sally cried out, "He pinched me," I come to. Looking down, I saw I had flattened out those slender brown fingers clutching a hot and soapy dishrag. Then that pretty little savage leaned over toward the dismayed game warden and burst out agin, "He pinched me, and that isn't all he did—that horrible man from Kansas!"

I didn't know whether to laugh or cuss. I happened to look over at the dining room door, and there was Pete Elaby's bony, freckled mug grinning past the tall horse wrangler. I don't know how *much* Slim had heard; anyhow, he was staring at me with accusing eyes. I started to look around for Velma. Just then, the jittered game warden gave a choky sort of grunt, and began to clutch frenziedly at his shirt pocket. His pain-contorted face—plucking fingers—could mean a bad heart, we all must have thought at the same time.

The small table overturned, as Wilson, Elaby and I made a grab for Kompton, to ease him down on the floor. He yelped, "Wait, wait, cigarette, cigarette." He was pinching at his pocket. The small wisp

The ferocious glare of the little Shoshone.

of smoke from his shirt pocket didn't have a chance. A big dipper of soapy water changed all that. Velma had pushed the little Shoshone warrior aside and put out the fire.

"That must have been a good one. Haw, haw, haw! Ol' Shorty shoulda been here. Haw, haw, haw!" Smithers stood in the doorway, with Dr. Forrester and Mr. Parsin, grinning at the jumbled-up show in the kitchen. I could see Velma with her arm around Sally, standing over by the big wood stove. Vel was smiling as she talked in a low voice to Sally. Sally, with one hand over her mouth, was staring, big-eyed, at the amused crowd. By the time we got a bunch of salve plastered on the game warden's burn, I began to think this was getting to be a ding-danged opry house instead of a ranch. Kompton looked down with a sad grin at his ruined red shirt. Suddenly Pete Elaby reached down to fumble around under the sink. He came up with Warren's scratched-up badge. "Do you reckon you'll need this, Warden?" Kompton sheepishly reached for it. "Thanks, Pete. Maybe I'd better have it. After all, I'm up here on business."

Nobody said a word. That whole procession just stood around and waited. A bunch of ravens looking for the carcass. The game warden pinned the badge back on his soggy pocket flap. He looked around at that bunch of scissorbills and then at me. "Looks like the gang's all here." He had a grin on his mug. "Think they might as well be in on this?" "O.K. by me, Warden," I told him. "Nothin' hurts like the truth."

Well, it's easier to suffer if you're comfortable. By the time we'd all got set at the big table in the dining room, Velma and the Shoshone gal had coffee poured for all hands. I didn't know hardly how to start the ball a-rollin'. Tim Smithers' buck teeth was a-shinin' over between the other two hunters so I could see that the stocks-and-bonds man was going to enjoy this here kangaroo court. More than I was, by a dern sight.

"Some of you fellers have heard what the game warden had to say, and some of you haven't. So, to put my head in the lion's mouth, I'll put you straight on whole deal. A hunter," (I had to gargle on that one) "beefed to our warden that I run him off the place, after takin' his earnest money. And that our food and service is horrible. Besides, his cabin wasn't fit for a dog. *And*, Warren says, this gent claimed that if my camp is run like my ranch is, my outfitter's license should be taken away. *Also*, that I'm a crook. So you birds can see just who you're 'sociatin' with."

"Haw, haw, haw!" Smithers couldn't hold it. "Doc, you and George here can see what us poor suckers are up against. Haw, haw, haw!" Being kind of jittery about this deal, I had my eye on Kompton. He seemed to look at Slim Wilson before he grinned around at Smithers. But the new horse wrangler was swirling his coffee around with a spoon and didn't seem to notice. Pete Elaby was seated in between Wilson and the game warden, and was smirking at me. He was having as much fun outa this meeting as the broker. Velma don't drink coffee, but she was standing in the doorway over by the kitchen watching. Sally wasn't in sight.

Well, I started out by telling how I started getting letters a long time before hunting season started from this gent in Kansas. "This Long inquired about rates I charged for huntin' big game. How far from ranch t' camp. Kind of tents." I had to think of the other sappy things he asked. "Oh, yeah, he wanted t' know did I have a good chef." I could hear Smithers snort at this. I could see the grins on Pete and Warren Kompton, who were well acquainted with old Shorty. I went on, "Did I have guides that knew their business *and* their places! Also did I have electric lights and heaters in camp. Was our water pure, and how about sanitation. He wanted to know if he shot some game he didn't want, could he exchange it?"

Nobody said a word for a while. Then Pete Elaby spoke up. "This jackass musta thought there ain't any more ethics in huntin' big game than there is in raisin' wheat an' storin' it for a subsidy." Oh, yes, I'd mentioned that he'd said several times he was the biggest wheat farmer in Kansas. Said he *also* had a big subsidy deal. Stored grain, too.

"Haw, haw, that smart damn sucker." Smithers was enjoying this.

"But when I wrote him that I required earnest money as a deposit, to book him as a *sure* hunter—that I could handle only a few, and that I could only run my business on reservations—well, he sent only *part* of the deposit."

The game warden had been listening intently to all this. Suddenly he said, "Bill, when you run him off, how about that deposit?" "You know, Warren," I found a paper I'd copied out of my account book, and handed it to him, "after th' ruckus I happened t' think of that. From our ranch rates for board an' cabin use, this geezer owes *me* around eight bucks."

I could see everybody smiling now, even the new horse wrangler. But the only one with a word to say was the broker. He says, "Haw, haw. That smart damn sucker. George, you and I, and Doc, here, we know how to get around ol' Bill now. Haw, haw!"

Kompton handed the paper back, but he still looked puzzled. "Warren, if you want ta look," I told him, "I still got all th' dern letters he sent." "Nope, Bill, the only thing left I'd like t'know," he was feeling better now, "why did you throw him and his hunting equipment off the place?

Little Sally was nowhere in sight, but Velma came out of the kitchen and got into it. "Bill, Sally finally told me all about it." Vel had a lopsided smile, but I could see she was still riled. "Day before yesterday, when she was serving Long the ham and eggs he asked for, Sally saw him pouring whisky into his coffee." She looked around the table with a grim smile. "When Sally put the tray down, that dumb ox threw his arm around her and pinched her. Then she slapped him as hard as she could. She said he shoved his chair back, stood up and roared, 'take that back and bring me something fit to eat! I don't like foreigners to handle my food anyhow!' " Velma started to swell up and get peeved then. "I heard what he said from the kitchen. Then the front door slammed and I saw him stomp past the kitchen windows towards his cabin."

Pete spoke up, "By hell, when Velma come down t' th' corral t' get Bill on th' job, I wouldn't got in that lady's way f'r seven hunderd dollars."

You'da thought this was a play the women's club down at Roaring River puts on in the winter time, the way this bunch was acting. Even forgot their coffee.

"Yeah," I told them, "when I got up ta where he was, I was about ta crown him where his little horns sprout, but Velma punched me in th' ribs. So I made him apologize ta Sally. Thought he'd pull out then, but he stuck around anyhow."

The game warden still wasn't satisfied. "You didn't throw him off, then?" By the time I told Warren about the visit in Long's cabin next morning, how th' wheat baron had built me up, and then the proposition to go bring in a bull elk and a buck deer for him, the game warden was mad. Velma said, "Just then, you know, Bill, there was a phone call for you that morning. I sent Sally over to Long's cabin to get you. You'd left the door open a bit. She got there just in time to hear Long's proposition. When you started throwing things, you just missed her with that first big gun case. I got there just as you hung that portable toilet around his neck."

Everybody was hee-hawing at Velma by this time. I thought Elaby's jacks must be there. Then she said, "I brought my rolling pin to help out, but when I got there I thought I'd have to use it on you to protect the man from Kansas."

154

"Haw, haw, haw, Bill, you poor damn sucker!" Smithers' teeth made me think of an alligator I seen in a circus one time.

It was about time to hit the sack, so I stood up and said, "I reckon that's about it, Warren. Th' show's over. If you wanta give my outfitter's license to th' man from Kansas, you're welcome."

That game warden had a big smile on his face when he rubbed at the bear's grease we'd put on his singed brisket. He stood up and put out his hand. "Bill, you're all there. I'm going down to Roaring River and see about some business.'" He wouldn't stay all night, said he had to go down to see about storing some wheat. He shook hands all around, wished us all luck, and left.

Chapter Three

Pete and I made sure the three hunters were comfortable for the night in the big cabin they were sharing. As we walked toward the ranch cabin, Pete stopped off at the bunkhouse. The tall wrangler had the gas lamp lit and was unrolling his bed. I was about to bid them goodnight when something itched me up above. "Pretty snug camp you guys got here," I looked at the pinups Tony Belknap, last year's wrangler, had stuck around on the log walls. They both laughed. "Plumb domestic," Elaby said, looking at Wilson. Slim had his boots off and was laying his socks across the tops. "Sure homey to have our girl friends' pictures around." I turned to go out the door, past Wilson's saddle with his blanket and chaps draped over it. "Oh, Slim, just happened to think. Did you know Warren Kompton? Had an idea you were old friends." As he gave me a quick glance, I saw Pete, hanging up his hat and jacket, watching Wilson. "You know, Bill, when I got a ride up to Roaring River with th' mail driver, I asked him if he knew anybody that could use a horse wrangler." He looked over at his saddle, then at Elaby and I. "He told me th' game warden would probably know. When I finally found him and we'd jawed awhile, Kompton said he didn't know, offhand. Said he'd keep an eye out." Slim looked at Pete and grinned. "If I hadn't needed a haircut, I'd a missed a payin' job, and a good show throwed in free."

The next morning after breakfast we were on the trail to camp. We left the ranch in good hands. I figured Velma and Sally could take care of most anything that came up. Pete Elaby would be at the ranch to take care of the wrangling and maintenance. He would pack supplies and gear out to the camp, and pack hunters, trophies, game meat and gear back to the ranch. " 'Pay Load Elaby,' that's what they call me, Bill." Pete had a homestead a few miles below Roaring River. With us four pack mules, saddle horse, and the bell mare, he made a good living in the life he loved. He'd packed for the Forest Service all spring and summer, and made a deal with me to do most of my packing, and was going to winter with us at the ranch. It wasn't far, only about eight miles, to camp. When we got there, Shorty Beel was cleaning up the cook tent and Buck Bruen was sawing wood. AND, dang my britches if MISTER Austen Hackett wasn't splitting and stacking it! In at the ranch, he was about the fussiest, most fidgity, "dang git on with the show," kind of geezer I ever saw. As Buck was going to guide him and Shorty was going to do the feeding, I was getting out of the maybe agony I figgered the guide and cook would have to go through.

For some reason, Hackett was a changed man. Now, he was the picture of a genial, hail-fellow-well-met, I-love-everybody kind of bird. This corporation lawyer said he'd had the time of his life; and that after ten days in camp with Shorty and Buck, he had an education, with a degree that he had, for *once*, really earned. And that now he was *blood brothers* with Bruen and Beel.

I noticed that he had a bad limp with his left leg, and was going to ask him how come, when my sweaty saddle horse started to roll. I forgot about it till afterwards.

When I asked him what kinda luck he'd had hunting, he sorta flushed up and said, "Well, you know, I passed up several shots at elk. Good ones. Missed several times." The lawyer gave me a grim smile. "You'll have to ask Buck about that. I'm going to take a big doe deer back home, though. Saw some bear, but passed "em up. Best trip of my life."

In the middle of the flurry of getting the three hunters settled in their tent, and helping the boys unpack the camp supplies and the hunters' gear, Al Neeman rode into camp. "Got to the ranch a couple hours after you'd all pulled out. Brought th' mail from Roaring River." Al got around to shaking hands with everybody. Just as Pete Elaby, with Mr. Hackett's deer and possessions loaded on his jacks, was starting back up the trail to the ranch, Al hollered, "Hold up, Pete. Here's a couple letters for Mr. Hackett."

Hackett on his horse, following Pete's big sorrel, pulled up and rode over to where I was standing by the corral. He leaned over, put his hand on my shoulder, and said, "Bill, those two blood brothers of mine over there took the *Mister* off my name, and now I'm 'Old Give-and-Take Hackett,' if any body should ask you." Hackett straightened in his saddle and took a long look back up the Buffalo Fork and around up to Terrace Mountain. "I'm coming back next year, Bill, if you'll put me in camp with my old professors, Buck and Shorty." *That*, coming from Hackett, made me sure he'd rolled in *somethin'* holy.

He shook hands again, hollered, "So long, everybody," and trotted his horse around the fringe of timber to catch up with Pete and his pack string.

After supper, when the three hunters had gone to their tent, I found

Hackett was a changed man.

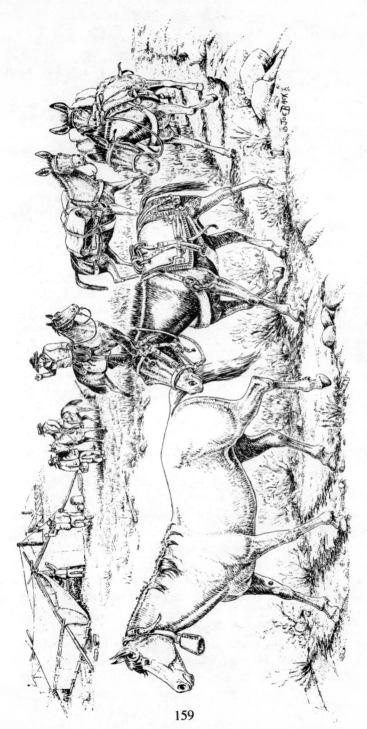

"They took the mister off my name."

out from Beel and Bruen about some of that "I dub thee knight" kind of gush that Hackett used, and about his gimpy leg.

I told the boys about poor Vincent and his arrest, and some about the wheat baron's hard luck. Looking around the cook tent I realized that now we had a full crew: cook, horse wrangler, and a guide for each hunter. Maybe this was going to be a good hunt without any more shenanigans.

Then I happened to remember about Hackett's stiff leg. So Buck and Shorty started to give us the deadwood.

"When Hackett shot, that sure ruined a good sneak we'd made on them elk. Good bull in th' bunch, too." Buck lit a match and got his smelly ol' pipe a-goin'. "That thick-headed sap was sure riled up when he heard th' branch-breakin' an' thumpin' when that band of elk bored a hole inta tha heavy timber. All we got outa th' deal was fresh manure an' plenty of tracks. All I could do was cuss," he sucked in some smoke and grinned, "when I looked past Hackett and all I could see was a mess of black feathers at the foot of a big fir tree." Buck frowned at the memory. "Seems like five or six big ravens had been havin' a hard time lately. You could see some of 'em on a high branch a-waitin'. They musta been arguin' about th' next move f'r a full belly. I figger they seen th' elk; then they seen us make our sneak. They wasn't born yesterday. They knew what we was up to. One of th' boss ravens got impatient about waitin', I figger. So he flew dow ta see what th' hell was holdin' up the' grub pile."

"Didja ever see them elk after that?" Wilson had listened intently to Buck's story.

"Hell, no, Slim," Buck shook his head at the memory of Hackett. "That lawyer had me half on th' fight 'bout then. Had spent three-four hours making *that* sneak. Hackett had missed a good bull an hour after we left camp that mornin'. An easy shot. 'So,' I told him, 'This fixes that bunch. Let's git back ta where we tied up our horses.' When we left, I could hear them ravens still a-flutterin' around an' waitin' for their pardner ta fly back with the news. Well, we angled around them parks below Nowlin Mountain and down Line Creek. Heard some bulls buglin' up high, about dark. It was plumb black when we rode inta camp, an' Hackett hadn't even opened his yap since he shot the raven."

"You remember that saphead from Kentucky?" Al Neeman really had a trigger happy hunter last year. "The one I give up on, Buck?"

"I sure do, Al. But you shoulda had this Hackett. Hell's bells. He damn near stampeded th' pack string after we left th' ranch, when he just *had* t' shoot a porkypine. I wasn't watchin' him that time. Bill, you remember that fat ol' rockchuck that's been thumbin' his nose an givin' us that monkeyface grin all these years on that rocky point about North Fork? Yep, Ol' Trigger-happy had t' blast him, too."

Shorty started filling our coffee cups and making a lot of racket filling the stove with wood. Al and Slim Wilson hadn't said a word for quite a while, but I could see Shorty was wrinkling up that seamy old mug to get in his half on Hackett. But Shorty didn't get his chance, because Buck Bruen was puffing that smoke like Casey Jones, and had just got warmed up.

"When me an' ol' Shorty was unpackin' the horses to set up camp, this gent blows a hole, big as a washtub, in a fat ol' snowshoe rabbit. Throwed blood 'n' guts all over his own fine eiderdown sleeping bag, a-layin' over by some panniers." Buck jerked his thumb at the grinning cook. "You oughta seen th' way Shorty watched him when he put th' grub on th' table. A few nights ago Hackett told us he's a-goin' t' make a *sportsman* outa his boy when he gits big enought t' handle a *gun*! Yessirree, he says, th' great outdoors and these here mountains is just th' place f'r a *he-man*."

"Yeah, he-man." Shorty had his sourdough keg on the table and was pouring a little potato water in it. "One mornin', while Buck was wranglin' horses, old Lead Spazzum was tryin' ta kill my chipmunks with that dang gold inlaid .22 that he'd had special made. What I told that gink wouldn't work out in Sunday School. I figgered mebbe he'd soon be outa shells. An' from what Buck an' I seen, his big gun was goin' ta go hungry. I keep mine hid, an' Buck's ought-six ain't his caliber." The cook stirred the sourdough with a long-handled spoon, and then started to wrap a blanket around the keg, but he wasn't through yet. "Say, you birds shoulda heard ol' Buck give 'im a talk about live and let live. Supprized me all ta hell. Didn't think Buck had it in him. Killin' them chipmunks got Buck's dander up, too."

Bruen, shaving a pitchy stick for morning fire lighter, was grinning at Shorty's cackling. "Yeah, when Buck give Hackett a lecture 'bout tit-f'r-tat an' survival of the fittest an' nachur's laws, you birds shoulda seen th' silly grin that lawyer give ol' Buck. I thought Buck was gonna blow th' plug when Hackett tells 'im, 'Who'd ever think you'd find a Holy Roller preacher out in these mountains?'"

When the cook took out his uppers and started to whittle on the plastic with a hunting knife, we leaned over to watch the operation. Suddenly Shorty waved the teeth in the air and dang near hit th' stovepipe. "Buck got red around th' gills at Hackett's crack, but he told th' hunter, 'sometimes th' cure is tougher'n th' disease, Mr. Hackett. Mebbe Mother Nature'll even up in th' long run.''

Slim Wilson had been watching the cook and the guide with more'n ordinary attention. Suddenly he punched Al Neeman in the ribs and slid his coffee cup over the rough board table. "Bill, you're nearest th' pot. An', while you're pourin', let me ask you an' Al here: did you ever see a cook an' a guide who could *ever* afford gold inlaid handles on their hunting knives? And look at them scabbards hangin' on their wore-out ol' belts! Hand carved an' fancy as hell!"

Beel and the guide leered at each other and Shorty snickered, "Let Buck tell yuh what happened that mornin'. Boy, I'd like ta seen that." I reached over on the Rema stove to get the big pot of coffee, and poured everybody a mug. The cook stuffed wood in the firebox, and tied the tent flaps down. The wrangle horse, Wilson had tied on a picket log out in the park back of camp, started to nicker. Wilson uncoiled his long length out from under the table, and untied the flaps.

Buck had just got started when Slim got back from his look-see in the dark. "Horse is O.K. Just lonesome."

Buck said he had wrangled late that morning, and as the horse wrangler sat down again, the old guide was saying: " 'Bout sunup that mornin', Hackett and I was on our horses an' leavin'. Snowin' a little when we left camp, an' th' white stuff changed th' look of th' landscape.

"I sure got a bang outa ol' Lead Slinger that mornin'." Buck was grinning kinda sly. "While we was ridin' up th' trail I could hear ol' Shorty, choppin' wood back at th' tents. So cold that it sounded as if he was slicin' steel with a sledge hammer." Bruen had that old mountain man smirk, when he said, "I looked back at Hackett, ridin' along behind me. He seemed kinda spooky at th' way th' weather had changed. Them rims an' ridges south of the Buffalo looked like dim, frosty, now-or-never ghosts from the Arctic. Th' timbered benches an' terraces on Terrace Mountain woulda sent a polar bear high-tailin' ta Florida, it was that frosty. Jest a sifty needle a frost a-fallin'. I'll bet Hackett," Buck gave an imitation of a he-man snicker, "wondered if them game magazines had told th' truth about huntin' in the' Rockies, haw, haw. . . . Well," he went on, opening up his shirt front, "Shorty, you sure banked this cook tent tight. That fire'll run us outa here."

Al shoved his shoulder against me and says, "Git over by th' tent flap, Bill. We ain't a-goin' ta let them hit the bed roll till these knife stealers tell th' truth. You gittin' sleepy, Slim?" Wilson shoved his coffee mug over again. "I'm just gettin' woke up," and he squinted at me. "We got to get t' th' bottom of this," I told Bruen. "That was sure some limp Hackett had, Buck."

The guide started fumbling for his tobacco sack. "Well, them ponies we was ridin' sure had rollers up their noses. They was shivery an' hated ta face inta them icicle snowflakes. After we had climbed above South Fork Falls, they got warmed up an' knew they was in for it. That trail is shore steep." He paused to light that smelly old thing. "A coupla miles below Pendergraf meadows, I heard some bull elk a-talkin' on them timbered slopes up north of the trail. Boy, on these frosty winter's-comin' mornin's them old bulls bugle their heads off. You'd think from the music they was puttin' out, that Nowlin Mountain was their last stand.

"Well, I turned Baldy up th' mountain. You fellers know that trail that finally zigzags up 'n' over, then down ta Crater Lake? One thing I gotta hand Hackett, he always kept up and didn't lag behind, like lotsa hunters do. I noticed he had his eye on me, and the way he handled that black horse mebbe meant he wasn't foolin'. We should be dressin' out a good bull pretty soon. Mebbe his trigger finger is numb, I hoped. The closer we got to them grassy benches and long narrow parks, the more bulls we could hear. We was a mile or two above the old Angle camp just up from th' White Canyon. The climb up that steep timber-covered mountain had our nags winded, so we stopped for a breather.

"You know, durin' all this time that hunter hadn't said a word. Mebbe too cold." Bruen tamped more weed into his pipe. "Well, the snow had let up a little. I wet my finger ta git th' wind, an' listened ta several bull elk. Most of 'em seemed ta be in these pot holes and benches below an' west of us. Them ol' stinkers was callin' each other bad names and darin' th' cowards. Sittin' on Ol' Baldy a-rubbin' his sweaty nose on a knee, I sneaked a look at th' Lead Slinger. He was kinda jitterin' in th' saddle an' nervous as all hell. But Blacky didn't give a damn. He looked like he was tired of us damn hunters anyhow . . . Say, you fellers gittin' tired of me an' Hackett?" We all told Buck to keep a-goin'. "Well, I made sign for him ta git off his pony. I got off mine, and took my '06 out of the scabbard. Then I tied both horses ta trees close ta th' trail, at the edge of a narrow park. Snow was three, four inches deep, and that high, snowy ridge between us and Sody Fork looked like friz crocodile teeth, up on end. All the heavy timber was ice frosted. Looked like Christmas with the Arctic D.T.s. Hack didn't look happy but he was game.

"Finally, seein' Hackett had his blunderbuss an' was set ta go, I whispered to him about how we was goin' ta pussyfoot west along this timber-fringed bench. There was a lusty bull soundin' off close by, just below in th' heavy pines. Hackett whispered, 'Buck, I'll do just what you say, this is for real.' Well, I figgered, we'll soon have this over with. So I took off, crunching along easy-like, stoppin' now an' then ta listen. Hack was watchin' close, followin' along O.K. Stoppin' - startin' - listen' - makin' sign ta Hackett - him noddin' - wind O.K. - bull below us - not movin' - gittin' louder - hear rivals blowin' off - gittin' close.

"Well, we went 200 yards, mebbe more, up - down - pockets - sink holes - alkali licks - blowdowns - deadfall jungle - then fine open timber - wind change a little - Hackett O.K. - followin' good. Well, I stopped, held up my hand. There, just below us - mebbe 60 yards - I could see a helluva good 6-point bull. We was behind trees. He was just below us - plain sight - buttin' an' slashin' small scrubby trees, an' gruntin'. Could see plain glimpses of fat cow elk slowly browsin' on th' snowy grass an' bushes. Those shadowy forms helped their blusterin' boss show up good. I looked around ta see if Hack was on th' job, cause there was his bull. Yessirree, I mighta knowed it. I looked around just in time ta see Old Killer throw up his highclass gun and *gut shoot* a big mule deer doe! She was jest about a throw rope's length away.

"While my yap was bouncin' around on my briskit, he snapped another shot, which missed, at her floppy eared fawn. It jest stood there, big wonder in its eyes, lookin' down at its dyin' maw, moanin' an' kickin' th' blood-soaked snow around.

"When that bull and his harem tore off down that jungled-up spruce mountain side, them thuds an' that limb-breakin' clatter woke up even that gut-shootin' jackass hunter.

"By hell, Bill, I done forgot my grandad was a hard-shell Baptist; or mebbe it come back ta me. I musta warmed up them frosty pines we was under, 'cause I got ta drippin' sweat. I told that Hackett bird just what a low, mother-murderin', two-bit, infantile, underhanded, gunpowder delinquent I thought he was. I sorta plain insinuated that he musta conceived himself, that no mortal man or woman coulda had any part of manufacturin' any such so-called two-legged human. That no animal I'd never seen would ever be caught associatin' with his lonely unethical carcass.

"I musta put over these playful remarks to this lawyer cause he didn't have no—what's the word?—no rebuttal! I admitted, though I

164

dang near didn't, that the game laws for this area allowed the hunting of deer of both sexes. It was legal, but even most human ghouls let the kids have their mothers awhile.

"Old Trigger Happy had set down on a log about then. He couldn't bear to look at that graceful fawn, she was a-hidin' close by in a stand of spruce, watchin' me clean the innards out of her maw. I couldn't hardly stand that, either. I cleaned my knife on the rotten tree he was a-settin' on. Real nasty, I was. A guide's got ta make a livin', an' most of us *are* meat eaters, but sometimes some people have a way of making a guide's life plumb shameful, I told him. Mebbe I was mean, but I was mad, damn mad!

"While Hackett was a-settin' there on that rotten deadfall lookin' at his imported gunbarrel he sorta looked homesick, and dammed if I didn't feel plumb ashamed of my damfool jabber. But thinkin' back, dammed if I didn't backslide again.

"I told him, 'Now, Hackett,' (no Mister, I'm a-tellin' you), I says, 'Hackett, I'm a-goin back t'git th' horses, so's we can take your deer back t' camp. If I find you gone when I git back in a half hour or so, you'll have t' *walk* back t' camp, and I don't mean *mebbe*!'

"Well, fellas, I grabbed my rifle and took off in th' direction of where we'd tied our horses. I figgered Hackett could build a fire (he had matches) to warm up his cold carcasss and dumb cranium. When I got to th' horses and was ridin' along leading his black, I figgered I'd put th' deer on Baldy an' I'd walk back t' camp. *That* hunter couldn'ta made it himself.

"Well, when I got back t' th' deer, that damfool Hackett wasn't there. Back when I was dressin' out th' deer it started t' snow. Now they was big flakes, big as a half dollar - fallin' fast - really comin' down. I tied up them nags, close by th' deer, made big circles around, huntin' sign. Snow'd even covered them runaway elk tracks. Finally I fired some signal shots - waited - snowin' like hell - fired some more - no answer - waited. Wind comin' up - snowin' hard - fired some more shots - waited - thought I faintly heard a shot - plumb faint - mebbe. Couldn't tell direction. Couldn't hardly see th' horses tied t' th' trees. Shot again. Well - I got ta lookin' in my coat pockets, then in my chaps pockets. Hell's bells - only got two shells left. Why, hell. I went over ta th' horses and felt around in Hackett's saddle-bag. He had two boxes - damnit - wouldn't fit mine - wrong caliber. Snowin' harder now. Dark that high up among the snow clouds - dark and cold.

"Well, I dunno what *you* birds woulda done. But here's what *I* done. I cut a lotta green branches with lots of needles. Balsam, I reckon. Put th' doe carcass, hair up, on some dead branches, then covered that warm meat with them green branches, I got that done. Oh, yeah I hollered quite a few times, figgerin' Hackett might be near or comin'. Didn't wanta shoot my last two shells. Heard nothin'. Hollered some more. Nope, nothin' but th' drivin' snow in that black timber. Naw, Bill, no echo, storm too low up in them timbered benches. Finally I could barely see, so I got them paper sack lunches Shorty give us. Put 'em in that old coat I keep tied behind my cantle. Wrote that dumb lawyer a note, and pegged it to a big tree trunk right next to Hack's doe. Hung the coat over it. then I got on Baldy an' led th' black. Got back down to Shorty an' th' cook tent 'bout midnight."

"Yeah, later'n that, Buck." Beel had followed every word. "Remember when you told me what happened? I ast why didn't you leave Blackie tied up so's Hackett could ride him t' camp if he come back t' th' deer. Buck told me that Hackett would probably git in more trouble than he was, if he'd left Blackie. Blackie'd come back t' camp if he had his head, but knowin' how Hackett is, he'd try t' guide th' horse, an' he'd end up on Buffalo Plateau or Blackie'd buck him off and come home alone. Anyhow, that's th' way it was."

" 'Anyhow, that's the way it was,' says you." I got kind of ringy then at Buck. Slim Wilson and Al Neeman stared at Buck and Shorty, then at me. "That's the way it was, *hell*! We're not goin' ta let two baby-snatchin' knife-stealers quit there, are we, boys?" Wilson and Al held their coffee cups over, and Shorty, grinning, filled them up. While Buck hammered out and refilled his briar, Shorty reached into some rawhide panniers and came out with a big pan full of raisin cookies. He set them down in the middle of the table, and then rushed around to the pile of wood behind the stove. He pushed Al out of the way to grab a stick, and rushed back to the panniers, mumbling, "Give 'em an inch an' they'll take a mile." Two big fat chipmunks appeared on the table top, running for their lives. When one fell in the pan of cookies, Buck got excited, dropped his pipe in his coffee mug, and started to shake the pan.

While everybody was laughin' and kiddin' the zoo-keepin' cook, Slim got the cook's dishrag, and was mopping up the coffee. By the time Bruen had his washed-out pipe a-goin', and all had started on the cookies, we got Buck goin' again on how Hackett got baptized into mountain religion.

"Neither Shorty or I slept much that night." Buck started to rub at his eyes and it must have been catching. All of us started to yawn,

166

but he was too close to the end to sleep now. Buck went on: "Well, we'll have t' tell it like Hackett told us. We wasn't there. Here's about how it went."

After Buck took off at a fast walk in the direction of the horses, he left the hunter to build a fire to warm up his chilling body and mixed frame of mind. He got it started after awhile, with bunches of dead needles, and squaw wood from the tree trunks. He turned round and round to warm up by it. He sat and squirmed kinda uncomfortable on his log. Hack finally admitted to himself that Buck's vociferous comments held a lot of honest truth. He churned over and over all the incidents of the hunt up to now. He saw what a figure he would cut, after all his brags, if he came back without a big bull elk. It started to snow harder, the hunter heard some trotting thumps halt in the open timber below him. Staring with unbelief, he saw a big antlered bull elk smelling and pawing with angry grunts at the tracks and sign of the recently departed band of elk. Slowly he raised his gun. As he was about to lower the boom on his trophy, the uneasy bull gave a whirling lunge, and swiftly faded into the jungle of dark timber below. The silent disappearance of his wildly revived hopes quickly erased the guide's instructions. Hackett jumped up and trotted off down the hill, right on the bull's plain tracks. The snow started falling again, right after a lull in the wind, but his new sign was plain to see and follow over the older tracks left by the other elk.

In about an hour, after a lot of false starts, stops, and hard tumbles over the now-slick down timber, and jumbles of brushy roots, the breathless hunter, heart thumping, saw close by a bull elk staring at him with an astounded air of "What in hell is this kind of animal?" The bull let the hunter get his trembling gun up. As he aimed, and started to pull the trigger, he slipped on a slanted wet branch and fell wildly, with the gun exploding, and a numbed feeling in his shaky left leg. When he slowly got up, he didn't look for the elk. He stared with frightened eyes at his bloody wool pants, and felt the burning shock of his wound. With shaking hands, Austen Hackett unbuckled his heavy pants. Exploring fearfully, he found the deep crease of a painful flesh wound, just above the kneecap.

He tore off strips of his underwear and wrapped them tightly around the shredded skin and the bloody groove. He painfully flexed his leg. It still worked. Thanking his Maker, he finally was able to stand up stiffly, and saw that he could still navigate. He brushed the wet soggy pine needles and clinging black dirt from his weak and shivering body, and looked around for his cherished rifle. The bolt and bore were chuck full of sandy dirt and snowy twigs and needles, as the gun had skidded under some fallen dead branches. It had stuck, butt up and barrel down, dug into the wet black earth of a pocket gopher's hill.

He cleaned off his gun, and blew and scraped the bore clean. Then he found he had just one live shell left to his terrified lonely name. His extra boxes of ammunition he'd left in the small saddle bag on his hunting horse. He groaned at the thicker falling big flakes, and hobbled in an aimless, painful circle. And now he remembered old Buck's final warning. He tried frantically to figure the direction up the steep, slippery mountain, back to the dead doe.

About that time, he heard three carefully spaced signal shots. As he slowly raised his gun to fire in answer, he heard another three shots. He pulled the trigger, and got only a dull click. As he pulled back the bolt to reason why, he heard a third salvo. Seeing nothing wrong with the firing pin, he shoved home the bolt, pulled the trigger, and felt only a dull ping. He had a dud, a dead shell. Listening, he heard three final shots.

The lost hunter tried to locate the direction of the signals, aware that the snow, now falling heavily, the rising wind, and the prison walls of thick timber were defeating his desperately straining ears. Listen as he would, he could hear no more shots. As he started up in the direction he hoped was right, he figured that the lunch he had tied on his saddle was worth a hundred bucks. He was lost and hurt, and his belly was empty. Finally, he thought of his own tracks—he could follow them back to the deer's carcass. Crestfallen, he found no sign, the falling snow had hidden them all. Anyway, it had to be up. Back and forth, painfully up and up, he hobbled. He found himself using his beloved rifle as a crutch. The cold, dismal darkness slipped up on the agony of his climbing and falling journey. He stopped weakly under a mass of dead trees, hung up slantwise in the crotch of an enormous green spruce's receiving arms. Just as the black snowy night fell, the crippled-up hunter finally got a fire going in the shelter nature had so conveniently provided.

Hackett's leg was bleeding slightly, and the makeshift bandage was clotted up. He managed to wash off the painful gouge with fresh snow, and ripped up the rest of his undershirt to fix up fresh bandaging. Now he felt some better; but the leg throbbed with pain, and had stiffened up.

That night was forever etched in Hackett's memory, he said. The sequence of fitful snatches of sleep, mixed with self-recrimination and anger at the fix he was in, putting branches on the sheltering fire, and shaking gobs of wet snow from his tired body, made a weary nightmare. Finally there was light seeping through his branchy roof. He was thankfully aware that he was still alive. His heavy wool pants and good hunting coat had protected him, his mountain retreat was fairly dry, and he had a sort of bed of piled-up dead branches, and pine boughs he'd hacked off with his hunting knife. Standing up and hobbling around was a harsh experience, but he felt no throbbing in his leg, and was much relieved.

About then, he heard a commotion of whirring wings and weird gobbling calls. In the clearing sky above him he saw a string of ravens, and he caught a glimpse of other birds, flying in a straight line, just about the height of the surrounding timber. He felt a wild jolt of revived hope. Shivering with excitement, he remembered some of Buck's remarks: something acid about city people with no more sense that to mistreat animals and birds that could really help them.

Old Trigger-Happy suddenly grabbed his three-hundred-dollar, walnut-butted crutch. Digging its blue barrel into the crusted snow, he took off on the black guides' raucous trail. He had to pause for agonized intervals of heartpounding, sweating gulps of air and rest, all the while wildly straining his ears. The noise was gradually receding over the tall timber tops. He climbed and staggered for nearly half a mile, seemed like a hundred. His leg-and-a-half gait was hampered by boggy swamps, willow clumps, blow-downs, and deadfalls. Now the miserable man came close to a jumbled-up noise of squalling, chattering, and calling.

He came out on a very small park, to view a couple of dozen or so of assorted sizes of ravens, camp-robbers, and Clark's crows, flying, dodging, in a frenzy of cleaning up the forest. Old Step-and-a-half had seen this spot before. The twitters, screams, and hoarse calls made the most welcome music he'd ever heard. Busy birds were flying about with scraps of bloody meat and entrails, perched on branches, chewing, pecking, scolding, and fighting for more food. Two or three enormous black members of the Sanitary Division had started to pull away the green pine branches off the deer's carcass. They had cleaned up the remains of the paunch, they were now going to uncover and work on the main course. This made up the most heartwarming picture old Trigger-Happy had ever seen.

His rescuers seemed to resent his blowsy presence. They were all busy at the serious business of making a living, so they gave him an angry cussing in their various squally voices. When he hobbled closer, to enjoy the location, they all flew up and perched in snowy treetops

He took off on the black guides' raucous trail.

and on various limbs and branches, there to stare with angry eyes at his bedraggled form. After the peculiar salutations and ceremonies of this welcoming committee of the cleanup squad had subsided into sudden squawks and muttered squally remarks, the limpy hunter took a better look around. There was an old shabby coat hanging from a snaggy limb on a near-by tree. When he hobbled over and took hold of it, he saw a piece of lunch-sack paper pegged on the rough spruce bark sheltered by it. Printed in heavy pencil was the message:

TRIGGER HAPPY—IF YOU GIT BACK HERE—*STAY PUT*— WE'LL COME BACK HERE—YOUR LUNCH IN COAT POCK- ET—P.S. *STAY PUT—YOU SAP*

As his shaking hands fumbled the lunch in its heavy paper sack out of the pocket, Mr. Hackett thought, "Why, that's the best love letter I ever read." And as he ravenously ate the tasty frozen sandwiches, grabbing up handfuls of snow to wash the food down, he thought, "Boy, can Shorty cook good grub!"

The storm had let up, now and then the sun came out, but the weather on that snow-covered mountain was still cold. When he had just about licked up all the crumbs and felt better, a great blob of wet snow fell off a straining branch, and he was the unwilling target. After he had brushed and shaken off this wet embrace, he got the shivers. He struggled with wet wood awhile, and finally got a fire going.

Suddenly the black clad members of the Sanitary Division flew up in excitement, and off over the timber tops on silent wings. Trigger-Happy looked around in fright, but he could see no reason for the alarm. The other birds paid no attention, continuing to chatter and whistle, flying down now and then as close as they dared, to snatch and grab at the visible scraps.

In a few minutes, even the hunter could hear the thumping, cloddy noise of approaching animals. Buck Bruen rode up, leading a pack horse. Close behind rode Shorty Beel, leading a saddle horse. Just about then, here came the giant crows, flying back to perch on tree tops and branches, muttering dark comments and watching with their cunning black peepers.

"Well, when ol' Shorty an' me rode up there that mornin'," Bruen shook his head, "yuh wouldn'ta believed it. I still don't."

Beel started to cackle in his squeaky voice. "Hackett was a-settin' on a big dead log kinda nursin' a smoky fire. It was blowin' right in his face. He was th' raggedest, dirtiest, ol' throwed-out lawyer I ever seen." Shorty watched as Buck started t' ream out his pipe with that gold-handled knife. "Yeah, danged if he didn't look glad t' see us.

171

He kinda staggered around when he stood up. He says somethin' t' Buck about gittin' a love letter Buck had left on a tree, somethin' about framin' the best love letter he ever got, t' keep on his desk." Buck swung at him. Beel leered, and finished, "I didn't know Buck could write love letters."

"Yeah, and that cook," Buck dug an affectionate thumb into Shorty's thin ribs. "When Hackett looked like he was goin' t' kiss Shorty, you shoulda seen him duck, an' lose his uppers in th' snow.

"When he started ta walk over ta us, I seen him stagger; he was talkin' kinda silly-like about my sandwiches. I see he's weaker'n a cat." Shorty looked at the new shoe-packs he was wearing. Kinda self-conscious, I thought.

Buck had his eyes squinted, thinking back. "While Shorty untied a sack of grub from behind his cantle, I tied our four horses t' trees close t' th' doe's carcass.

"We go ta lookin' over Hackett's leg, when he told us what happened," Shorty said. "He didn't wanta show us. But we built up a big fire, melted snow, an' made coffee in a big can I packed along. While he was gittin' stoked up, me an' Buck cut th' seam on his pants an' looked at his shot-up leg. Jest a shreddy kind of crease, clean, too. Didn't look bad. I took my bottle of iodine, I keep for wood ticks, and sloshed it good. Man, that lead slinger was lucky, Buck figgered we'd put salt poultices on it at camp."

Buck started to laugh. "Shorty, you remember when you sloshed that big bottle of iodine on him, an' he hollered?" The cook grunted, "Yeah, them big ravens, waitin' their turn, croakin' again. Damn things thought he was cheatin' 'em outa a good meal."

I knew Buck wanted to get this story over, he was yawning again.

"Shorty untied th' pack horse, and I started t' pull th' green branches, what them ravens hadn't, off th' doe. Th' cook was startin' t' tighten th' cinches an' I had just got th' sling rope fixed when Beel grabbed at my coat 'n' jerked his head. We looked over at the hunter. He'd just burned up the lunch wrappin's an' was tryin' t' hobble over to us. He'd start t'talk, then kinda gargle, 'n' git red in th' face. He sorta had us two birds worried, I'll tell yuh. Then, when we grabbed a-holt of the deer ta throw it across th' pack horse, Hack held up both hands, his wet mittens a-steamin' in th' cold. He said, kinda mixed-up an' choky, 'Wait a minute, fellas. Now this is hard t' say, but it's gonna be done.' That dirty mug, whickers, muddy kinda squint in his eye, looked sorta looney. He'd look up at them ravens, sittin' on their limbs, then further off at them others, waitin'. Then Hack would look

172

He said, "Wait a minute, fellers."

173

down at th' deer carcass, kinda limp an' hopeless it looked. I was gittin' spooked about then. I leaned up against Sleepy, that bay packhorse, and looked over at th' cook, ta se if he was seein' what I was.

"Ol' Shorty let go th' deer's leg, and scratchin' that empty gray noodle, was a-glarin' suspicious-like. He musta thought ol' Trigger-Happy was floatin' off, while we sorta stood around in a trance. An' then Hack said, 'Before you start that doe on her last journey, I've got t' say somethin',' an' he finally come out with somethin' Shorty an' I still don't believe. It was somethin' like "Boys, the teeter-totter of nature had me balanced on th' light end. Last night I saw that, to survive, I'd better get my big feet on *both* sides of th' middle. This morning proved that. I have lived in th' lonesome little world of *me and mine*.' By this time I figured I knew just who th' Holy Roller preacher was. This gent was really shook. Then he said, 'Now, if you'll let me into your friendly big world of *us and ours*, I'd appreciate th' favor.' Me an' Sleepy and Shorty was plumb petrified, but that's what th' man said! When we stepped over th' doe's carcass t' shake hands with Hackett, I looked up, and dang if one of them ravens didn't wink. When we shook hands, I says, 'Hack, you're 'nishiated inta our ancient an' honorable old club. We'll now call you Old-Give-and Take.' When us three members shook hands, them impatient members of th' Sanitary Division broke inta loud croakin' caws. Then they looked down at us with them smart beady eyes. I tell yuh old Hack was really shook!"

Well, now we got the lowdown on Hackett's limp, all hands settled down for a good night's sleep. We got an early start next morning, but by luck no one of our men connected. The hunters were all soft and not used to the altitude. By late afternoon, we were all back in camp. Shorty needed a spud hole dug in the back of the cook tent; he was afraid of a freeze-up; his spuds, onions, canned milk and tomatoes needed protection. So we cleared out some of this kitchen panniers and went to work. We soon had the hole dug, and the grub stored in it. Shorty got out some of his good doughnuts and coffee as a reward. While the cook carefully put some blankets over the stacked grub and boarded up the hole, Al Neeman and Doc Forrester told us about coming across the remains of two buck mule deer, which by the signs had locked horns and died on the battle ground. So the talk got around to the things that happen and could happen to the inhabitants of most any wilderness country.

"Reminds me o' findin' a horse skeleton up on a game trail one time. Was nothin' like what th' doctor and I saw today." Al took another sip of coffee and squinted back into his memory. "Huntin' elk by myself. Ridin' down this game trail on th' crest of a high ridge. Open timber on both sides. Head of Calf Creek, it was. Rode past a tree and then a hundred feet or so, recollected I saw somethin' outa th' corner of one eye, looked kinda strange. I turned my horse an' rode back. 'Bout five feet up th' trunk of this big lodgepole pine was an old rope, real old. Th' bark had grown over it, hid most of it but the end hangin' down. Was plumb rotten. I got off my pony for a better look. Th' rope crumbled up an' fell apart when I touched it. Got ta lookin' fer more story. Then I saw parts of a horse's skull, lower jaw in pieces, but the skull an' nose parts around. Grass grown all through it. Tied my horse to same tree, an' went down th' steep grassy timbered slope t' look. Kicked up an old rusty bit with small pieces of old leather hangin' on it. Some horse teeth. I kicked around some more. Found a buckle, and odd, chewed-up pieces of rein. Finally found some ribs hangin' on the' vertebray. Part of a shoulderblade an' leg bones. Down in a seepy willow clump finally I found an old saddle tree. Wooden parts an' iron horn. Stirrup bolts an' stirrup pieces. The cover an' skirts in curled-up pieces. Cinch rings an' old riggin' rings. Buttons an' part of an old wool coat.

"Finally figured from all th' sign that some bird had tied up his horse t' this tree a long time ago. Never come back to it."

Neeman looked around at the bunch at the table. The hunters and the rest of us were all tied up listening. Al was a real story teller. "Did you find anything more? George Parsin had started out the cook tent to hit the sack, but curiosity got the best of him. "Yeah, I did, George, but it ain't purty." Neeman was frowning down into his coffee cup. "It was clost ta noon when I found this. Got th' lunch off my horse, no use ta hunt elk fer two, three hours. Well, after I chewed on th' grub I got ta kickin' around in th' little dry park I found, where th' trees opened up. Finally found a bear trap. Sprung. With bones around. Course yuh know, mice, porkapines, coyotes, deep snow, and Nature had all worked over this whole deal. Found what I figured was parts of a grizzly. Bear claws, 'n' skull t'prove it. Human skull 'n' bones, too. Finally found rifle. Not too old a model. Lever action 1895 30-40."

"Al," I says, "is that th' old gun you've got hangin' up in your cabin?"

"Yeah, Bill, that's th' one. Plumb rusted tight. Well, I finally figured out what happened." He scratched his head and grinned. "From th' busted trap chain (had a wrench wired to it, too), and th' way th'

175

bones lay, what I could find. This man musta been a bear trapper. Caught a grizzly. Shot an' wounded him. But 'bout that time th' bear broke th' chain wired to a big tree. Killed th' man. Then died from his own wound. Horse starved t' death."

"Ever find out who th' guy was?" Shorty, next to his stove, was whittling some shavings for fire starter. Al looked around sad-like. "Nope, never did. Asked around fer years, too. Nobody I ever talked to could remember anyone missing. Musta been around 1900, I figured."

Chapter Four

It was starting to get dark by the time Al finished his story, so the two guides went down to the corral to help Slim turn the horses out. The three hunters went over to their tent. I was giving Beel a hand with his Dutch oven fire just outside the cook tent when it happened.

The wrangler, on his horse in the edge of the timber, was starting to drive the horses off while Buck and Al were shooing them out of the corral. Them 4-5 bonging clappers on the bell horses were pretty noisy; but I thought I heard a rifle shot from way off across the river above all the jangling clatter.

The biscuit-loaded Dutch oven had a broken lip on the rim. The shovel made a grating noise against it as I scraped a few more coals over on the edge. "Kinda late t' git a good shot this time o' night, ain't it?" Shorty stood in the cook tent door, holding the pot hook in his bent-up rheumatic fingers. He was peering over at the dark and shadowy cliffs, too.

"I couldn't tell whether the Ka-vroom across th' canyon was another rockslide peelin' off th' cliffs, or a shot from a high power rifle."

"Well, I thought it was a gun, too, but that jingle-jangle o' them horse bells throwed me off." Ol' Shorty turned around and bent over his cook stove. I thought, that boy's sure got a pair of ears yet, for an old throwed-out.

Back of us we could hear a couple of hunters talking in their tent—maybe they'd heard the shot, too. Sometimes in heavy timber the sound echoes from strange directions, but our camp was in a big grassy park. It was a good sound box, and the Buffalo River wasn't noisy right along here where it was flat . . . It must have come from over in the cliffs across the river.

"Well, whadda yuh know, Shorty, old boy, your nephew musta made you some teeth that fit." Tim Smithers swaggered into the lighted cook tent, and grinned down at Shorty, busy pulling brown biscuits out of the Dutch oven he'd just brought in. "Last fall, when I shot a horned owl out of that big spruce tree by the corral, your teeth fell out, and your cook fire dang near got 'em, haw, haw, haw!"

The short-coupled cook glared up. "I was a-tryin' ta ask yuh why did yuh have ta kill somethin' that wasn't a-harmin' yuh. Why, hell,

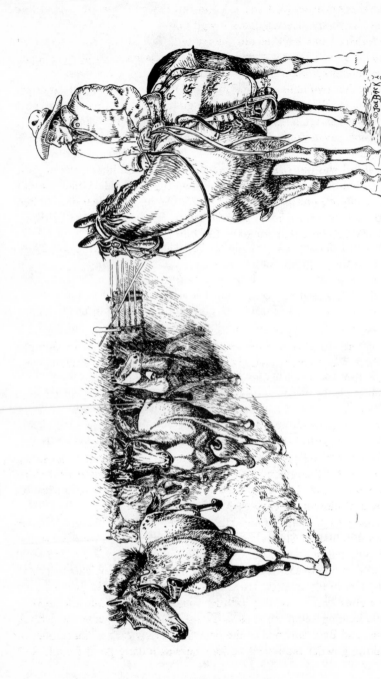

I thought I heard somebody shoot.

man, that big-eyed bird was a-killin' all the mice we git around this camp. Anybody else woulda knowed that."

Smithers came back at old Shorty with the sort of crack he loved to make. "Grinders that chawed on old bull elk meat for 40 years need better anchorage than you were givin' 'em!"

Our other two hunters came in out of the frosty night and sat down at the table. When we heard the two guides coming up, Shorty and I started to dish up the grub and get supper on the scrubbed old boards. The cook saved some back on the Rema cook stove, for the horse wrangler.

Last fall was our first acquaintance with Tim Smithers, the biggest stocks-and-bonds broker in his big town (he said). He killed a small bear, and got a pretty fair bull elk for his trophy room. All of a sudden he got a harebrained idea. He told everybody in reach that he'd pay anybody $20.00 a pair for good big bull elk teeth.

"I'm having the best tanner of the Shoshones make me a large beaded buckskin coat, and I'm going to decorate it with 1000 big elk tusks. Even Shorty is in on this deal, but I mean elk teeth, not cook's teeth, haw, haw, haw."

Johnny Beel hadn't liked that crack much. He was Shorty's nephew, in camp for a few days before he took off for dental school. He conived with Shorty to play a little joke on the broker. None of us thought Smithers was serious. And, we didn't think that dental student was, either. But you never can tell by the cover, what's in the book.

Tonight he brought up the subject again while we were eating—that Indian tanned coat with 100 elk teeth to decorate it. This got me kind of jittery. I knew by now he had lots of money and plenty of determination. "I suppose you know, Tim, that tusk-hunting is plenty illegal. Wasn't too many years ago that I knew of several gents who killed some elk for their teeth. These same smart gents ended up behind high stone walls. The spent a lot of lost time makin' horsehair bridles instead o' blowin' in easy cash from sellin' elk teeth."

What I said didn't bother that grinning hunter a danged bit. He speared another of Shorty's juicy steaks and put out his well-fed smile. "I'm just puttin' out bids. Several thousand bull elk are killed legal in these mountains every fall. Now, just where do their teeth go to? Well, I'm in the market. Good bull elk teeth only." He grinned over at the cook, who was busy rattling some split wood into the stove.

In a hunting camp the cook is the mainspring that keeps the gizzard going, and Beel was one of the best. He sure wasn't a can stabber or a baking powder bum, and besides he was a dang good friend. So I was beginning to resent Smithers' cracks at ol' Shorty. But I thought, better let it ride awhile.

Shorty wasn't even listening to that one. Buck was telling about a hunter he'd guided the year before, who wanted to keep a shell in the barrel at all times. Bruen refused to guide him unless he kept them all in the magazine until he was ready to pull down on the game. Ol' Shorty was about to shove a stick of wood into the stove.

"It's a funny thing t' me, anyhow, why a man has just *gotta* have a shell in his barrel when he's a-huntin'." The cook's piece of firewood was waving under the guide's apprehensive nose. Buck was relieved when Shorty shoved the wood in the stove, and went on, "Well, maybe not so funny, come t' remember what happened one time. Dad an' me, I was just a kid, we was camped over on Fish Creek huntin'. No game laws them days, anyways not like now. An' th' powder behind th' lead wasn't as hi-falutin as we got now; but it was just a-itchin' ta make itself felt, whether you pulled the trigger or that devil done it. Now, we was a-ridin' up this steep rocky draw. Dry, no snow. We knowed they was a bunch of elk in th' basin at th' head of th' draw. Gonna make a quick sneak on 'em, Dad said, Git th' job done. Three or four anyhow. About halfway up this rocky draw, Dad jist ahead o' me, both of us leanin' over our horses' necks, helpin' 'em climb kinda, well, it happened. We was all four of us busy, I can tell yuh. But all of a sudden when that gun went off we got a damn sight busier. My dad's horse, about t' go around past a big dead tree down crosswise of the game trail we was climbin'—he rared dang nigh straight up an' tried t' jump over the snaggy log. Well, Dad swapped his saddle f'r a mess a boulders without any boot. My nag, busy dodgin' rollin' rocks anyhow, whirled around before I knowed it, and headed down, me see-sawing my 16-year-old best on them reins. I got him stopped jist as he was about t' put a big puddin' foot on my new 30-30 I'd got for trappin' beaver that spring. Th' smoke was still comin' outa th' barrel, it happened so quick. But I seen an' felt more smoke, in a head-shrinkin' sort o' way, right sudden. That Dad o' mine wasn't tongue-tied, I can tell you.

"By th' time we'd ontangled th' bleedin' horse outa that tangled-up bunch a limbs an' rocks, an' was back down t' th' tent, doctorin' him up, I had a new education. An' th' mental part is still stickin'. My old Dad had told me a thousand times, he says, '*Never* keep a load in th' barrel. If you *ain't got time* t' throw one in th' chamber when yer onta game, you *ain't got time* ta git a shot anyways.'" Shorty was waving a spoon now. "Well, the strap on th' back end of my scabbard

All of a sudden, the gun went off.

broke an' my loaded rifle slid out. It musta lit on a rock, and bang! That horse got a crease on *his* rump, an' I got a lump on mine."

Ol' Shorty had the whole gang laughing at his long-ago story, but I was a-hopin' that story would stick in these hunters' minds. You never can tell a trigger-happy bird by the feathers he's wearing or the song he sings.

We were just cleaning up on the peach pie when we heard a horse trotting up the trail, and the little humming song Slim always had on tap. When we heard the pounding of the axe as the wrangler drove in a green stake on fresh grass for the night horse, Shorty started to put Slim's grub on the table. We could hear him over at the gear tent putting his saddle and outfit away. Soon he was swooshing and gasping as he washed up in the cold water at the wash block outside in the dark. He stooped to get his long frame into the cook tent door, and stood grinning down at the cook as he warmed his hands over the Rema stove. He laughed when the hunters kidded him about his icy habit of cold water. "Horse jinglin' in this altitude at night is a sleepy job. Too easy. You can't beat mountain water."

The crowd slid over and made way for Slim to get at the supper that Shorty had all dished for him. He just got started to eat, when suddenly he stopped. "Just happened to think, when I started to run our horse bunch away from the corral, I thought I heard somebody shoot. Did you fellers hear a shot?"

Shorty was starting to wash dishes. He stopped and looked around at me. "Yeah, me an' Bill thought we did, too. Couldja tell where it come from?"

"My horse bells was making such a racket I couldn't get the directions," Slim says. "Prob'ly just some elk hunter shootin' shadows in th' dark."

Dr. Forrester puts in, "George and Tim and I all thought we heard a shot, too, but we had our tent flap tied down. We couldn't tell where it came from, either."

Tim Smithers, like always the loud-talking man from the big city, claimed that if a sound came from the north, he knew, from all his experience in the mountains, that it was actually from the south.

Buck and Al were helping Shorty clean up the supper, and rattling the tin plates, pots, and pans at a great rate, while the talk went on about the way sounds carry and echo in the mountains. Slim wasn't saying a word, just forking food into his gullet and grinning down at his plate.

I knew now it must have been a shot fired somewhere that night.

Everybody was ready to hit the sack. As the three hunters started to leave for their own tent, Tim said, "Well, if that shot means somebody's lost, it's the survival of the fittest, here on these hills or on the sidewalks of New York. Maybe somebody sneaked up on a big bull elk that had good-lookin' teeth a-shinin' in the dark, haw, haw!

Buck Bruen lingered to tell us about George Parsin. He was kinda disgusted. "Naw, Shorty, we didn't get a thing, but wait'll I tell yuh: Parsin an' me was ridin' along on them benches above th' mouth o' Cub Creek. Heard a bull elk bugle down in them quaking aspen. We tied up our horses for a look-see, and George got his rifle, while I walked over a couple hundred feet t' look down in a little grassy park.

"A real good six-point was right in th' middle of this park, six or seven cows an' a couple calf elk feedin' in back of him, close t' them rimrocks above 'em. I made sign an' hid behind a big tree. George, he made a good sneak through th' open pine timber. Him an' that big bull elk saw each other at th' same time. Th' bull was puttin' out big wheezy grunts, an' slashin' at a little green spruce, but when he saw Parsin aimin' at him, he quit. He just starts walkin' kinda stiff-legged, gruntin' an' hostile, towards George, up above him an' in the trees. Them cows an' calves stopped feedin', an' the damn fools stood an' watched their bull. They musta not seen that hunter or me." Bruen snorted. "I was waitin' for George t' shoot. When he saw that sappy bull start towards him, he lowered his gun, don't even look at me. He walked back to his horse, put th' rifle back in the' scabbard. The' bull stopped an' put his head close t' th' ground and whistled. Them cows still standin' there. Me, I'm about t' come apart!

"While me an' them silly cow elk are still in a daze, that hunter comes over with his *movie camera* an' turns that whizzin' thing loose. What happens then, y' say, Shorty? Why, hell! Nuthin'! When that nut runs outa them film, that Barrymore bull an' his silly cows git spooked 'n' take t' th' timber. Me, I'm jist th' guide.

"When we untie th' horses, I ain't said a word yet. Couldn't. Parsin says, 'Say, Buck, you've got the politest elk I ever heard of.' 'Think nothin' of it,' I tells him, 'Wyoming elk don't ever see any damfools in th' fall. Hardly ever.' Say, Bill," Buck, was scratching his ear and looking out across the dark to the hunter's lighted tent, "I kinda like that there Parsin."

Well, we all got snuggled down for the night. The three hunters had a wall tent to themselves, Buck and Al had a big tepee close to the cook tent. Big Slim bunked in the gear tent, said he felt at home in with the pack saddles and the sacks of grain.

183

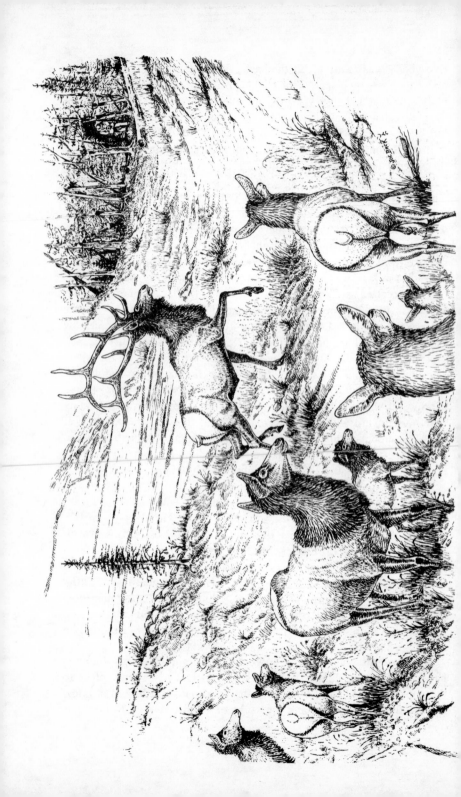

Shorty and I had our bedrolls back of the table in the cook tent. Just after Shorty wound his 4 a.m. alarm clock, and was squirming and grunting into his rolled-out bed, it came again. I had just faintly heard some wheezy bull elk bugling their brags to the frosty stars back up on Terrace Mountain, so I wasn't sure. The cook stopped rattling the bed tarp, and I heard some mumbling over in the guides' tepee. "That sure ain't no rock fallin' that time, that *was* a shot. Somebody must be strayed or lost," Shorty was sure about it.

"Hey, Bill," Slim stood outlined in the cold moonlight in his long underwear and boots, his wool shirt humped around his lanky carcass. "Somebody has got lost up around them cliffs. Didja hear that shot?"

"Yeah, me an' Shorty heard it, too. We'll have t'take a sashay over there in the mornin'. Break our necks tryin' ta negotiate in there tonight. Say, grab that 95 Winchester of mine on th' table top, an' shoot three times t' let him know we hear him." I reared up half outa my bed roll and snapped on a flashlight for Slim. He levered a shell in and fired a shot at the stars, then twice again.

We all listened for a long time, while Slim shivered in the frosty night, but heard no answering shot. The hunters and guides hollered out of their tents for the news, then after a while we all settled down for an uneasy snooze. Don't take long till morning in a hunting camp, no matter how early you roll in.

Chapter Five

Next morning we had our horses saddled before daylight. I'll say this for that tall horse wrangler, he always run the horses in plenty early, and no never mind at that. He always beat the cook up, and no noise either. Anyway, we rode across the river and up into that rocky cut-up scrub timber just under the cliffs, the whole seven of us, hunters, guides, and Slim. Ramblin' around spread out, we shot a few times and hollered a lot, then finally located a scratched-up and half-frozen hunter hunched up close by a cabin-sized boulder, over a smoky fire he'd got going. He was O.K., outside of a sprained ankle, an empty belly, and a powerful yen for some shut-eye. He had a rifle, but was out of ammunition.

Slim got him loaded on his saddle horse, and walked off, leading the pony carrying the dilapidated hunter. I knew the wrangler would get back to camp; he was humming that little tune and grinning as he picked their way down through the jungle of rocks.

Well, we split up after that. Buck and Al elected to take their hunters in different directions to prospect for elk. So Mr. Elk Tooth and yours truly headed over through some scrub jungle to the big parks above the Cub Creek rims. A good spot to maybe nail one of those big throwed-out bulls.

An elk bugled way up at the head of a steep grassy draw we were about to cross. We had just quit the heavy timber, and were riding down this steep game trail, when Smithers' horse gave a loud snort and ran slam-bang up against mine. Above Tim's furious cussing and the mixup of horses, I could hear "Yee-ough, Yee-ough," real loud and plenty close—a cow elk barking. That bond broker's horse whirled around and dang near knocked old Roany out from under me, then he started to gallop back up the trail, with old Elk Tooth cussing and see-sawing on the reins. The big field glasses strapped to Tim's neck hadn't kept up with the times; they were now hammering the hunter on both shoulder blades. The big rifle under Tim's leg started to come backwards out of the scabbard. When I saw about a foot of daylight between that big rump and the busy saddle, with the rifle telescope trying to pick up the pieces. But about then his fool horse stopped dead still, snorting and blowing at the crowd in front of him.

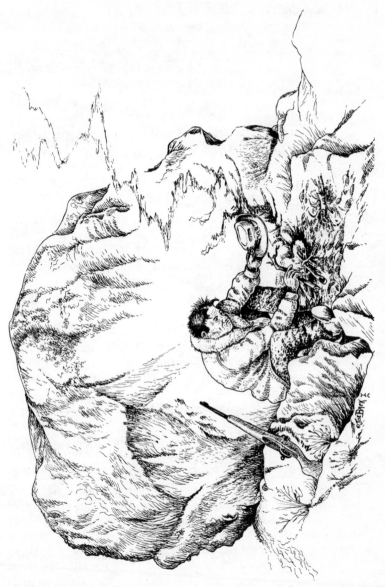

Scratched up and half frozen.

We were surrounded by a bunch of elk, it looked like. Up on both sides of the draw, in the edge of the timber, ten or twelve cow elk stood, bugging their eyes right back at ours. The few calves with them couldn't believe their eyes, either. But that silly old maid, somewhere in the timber close by, finally "Yee-oughed" loud enough to make 'em believe it. A few snorts and snuffy whistles, and we were along again. "That crazy dam sucker," was all Smithers had to say, by the time we got organized again.

In an hour or so, we located a big antlered old grunter and had the wind right, but that stocks and bonds magnate missed two easy shots. I found a couple of playful pine needles wedged in the front of the telescope sight. Then I had to stop the infuriated hunter from busting his four-hundred-dollar musket across a big rock. Can happen to anybody. Some days you can't make a dime, not even a ten-cent bond. He didn't love nobody by the time we walked back to our saddle horses.

We were circling through the timber, when a sudden squalling clamor of Clark's crows and whisky jacks drew us to a sight that made Moneybags grin. It brought back that uneasy feeling to me. There was reason enough for the gobbling racket of the shiny black ravens and the joyful screeching of the other birds. A couple coyotes trotted up the slope, looking back at us, then disappeared into the trees.

As we sat our horses in the long black shadows from the heavy timber behind us, the sun threw shutters of yellow light past us and on to the steep grassy hillside below. The carpet of gold light sloped on down toward Cub Creek, its beauty marred by the torn-up remains of five elk. Dozens of birds were in a frenzy of screaming delight at the clean-up job on four of the elk carcasses; while a huge old golden eagle, all by his lonesome, clumsily trundled around yanking shreds off the farthest one, a forlorn remnant of an elk calf close to the canyon's dropoff.

We worked our way down off the ledgy rimrock, got off our jittery horses, tied them up to trees, and walked over to look at this massacre. Two cow elk with their calves, and a young spike two-year-old, had been shot and left lay. But when I walked around the carnage, the birds jealously watching from nearby treetops, I found eight chopped-off big elk legs, scattered around in the heavy grass. Near as I could figure, the signs showed somebody had packed off two bull elk, and left the other five. Then I looked some more, and found that the tusks of the two big cows had been dug out. The tusks of the spike elk hadn't been touched. They're usually just a hollow shell. The vandals knew their grisly business.

A frenzy of screaming delight.

I looked over at my hunter. He sat on a big rock now, a sly grin on his big aggressive jaw. "Dog eat dog," he says, "and the devil take the hindmost." He waved a huge paw all around the scene. Well, that hunch, I've got a built-in one now, feels like what old Doc Rep says is an amateur ulcer just a-feelin' its oats in the fall.

We got back on our horses. While we were picking our way down through the jungly blowdowns towards the mouth of Cub Creek, I got to ruminating on this deal. Old bull elk stay by themselves at this rutting time of the year; at least that's the way I know it. Seems the lusty young bulls throw out some of these lecherous old boys. They may have passed their prime of virility, but their horns still seem to be as staunch and tremendous as their bodies used to be. They mumble along by themselves, sometimes tagged by an understudy or two of admiring spike elk. Sometimes grunting old grandpa picks up sympathetically with another wheezing big-horned old stinker, and they tromp from park to jungle, bugling their loud frustration from swamp to peak and back again. A lot of these bulls may have only their imagination left, but most of them have fine big tusks along with that huge rack of horns. Lots of times their remains are found on windswept ridges. Sometimes in mild winters they survive. It's risky for the ones who are overcome by optimism and elect to stay all winter up high. If the wind blows off enough snow so they can paw for enough feed, maybe they won't have to drift to lower altitudes. But the bark on quaking apsens and other trees sometimes gives out along with the browse. The deep snow foils their instinct to paw down. Their luck gives out right there. Goodbye, old wapiti.

Thinking of tusks of dead elk: usually hunters take them from their own legally killed animals. Human wanderers in the mountain country, summer and fall, sometimes come across the skeletons of winter-killed wapiti. They see the tusks in dried-out, coyote-drug skulls. They pry them out, to polish and treasure back home. Other times, elk meet with a natural accident; or are wounded, and cripple away to die unseen—it happens, even when the hunters are conscientious and try to find them. Most of the times it's hard to tell, when you find them, whether they've died of old age, natural causes, or found too late; though sometimes shattered bones tell of a bullet.

In these last few years, most of the carcasses I'd run across were elk; hardly ever deer, mountain sheep, or moose. Mostly elk. And in nearly every case the tusks were gone. Whether I found them in jungle pockets, on windswept ridges, or in grassy open valleys, these empty sockets told no tales. I'm no Sherlock Holmes in chaps, and most detectives don't have bow legs; but that hunch was with me just the same.

Well, it was nearly dark by the time we got to the park where camp was. The horse bunch had been turned out, for we could hear the belled ones jangle the direction they fed, over in the grassy park. I grained our two at the corral, for Slim to turn out late. I could hear Tim Smithers talking with the other hunters in their tent as I stumbled throught the grassy pine needles toward the lighted cook tent. I passed Slim's saddle horse tied to a tree by the corral. I noticed again that he had a halter and rope tied behind the saddle. May be a thrifty habit.

Buck and Al were helping Shorty clear up the camp table to put on supper for Smithers and me. Everybody else had got in early and were already finished. Slim left, and rode out to throw the last two saddle horses in with the grazing horse bunch.

"Your grub's too good, Shorty," Smithers loved to razz the cook. "This morning Bill had to help me get on my horse." "Yeah." Beel looked him over. "That bay window looks bad. I'll put rocks in yer biscuits from now on."

While Tim and I ate our supper, the boys told us the happenings. George Parsin downed a big bull elk a couple of hours after we'd all split up under the cliff, Buck said; and Al Neeman's hunter, Doc Forrester, missed a running shot at an enormous black bear; and late in the afternoon a couple of searchers came to camp looking for the lost hunter, and went back to their camp with him. They'd brought a led saddle horse, just in case.

Well, I finally told the boys what Tim Smithers and I saw on the hill above Cub Creek, after the hunters had gone back to their tent, and Shorty was slicking up his pots and pans for the night. He and the guides were all mountain men who had traveled these mountains for years same as I had. Al Neeman, sixtyish, and tough as a moose, says, "Sounds like some a th' new style hunters we got nowadays. Made what they call a drive. Killed too many, like a lot of them game hogs. Looks like th' game department oughta wake up. Them big tecknishuns won't have any animals left t' write them beautiful reports about."

Old Buck Bruen, helping Shorty, wipes the last tin plate and gets his say in: "Yeah, a lot of our game wardens are hard working and good men on th' job. But some a th' ones we drawed around these parts are home every night in th' fancy houses Game-and-Fish built for 'em. They stay where th' people are, not where th' game is. Badge polish don't shine up a saddle like use does. Bed rolls an' tents let in

191

more drafts than gas-heated houses with beds built for beauty-rest. I'm not delicate, so that job'll never be mine."

"Couldja figger how long them elk had been killed?" Shorty was stacking split wood behind the Rema stove.

"Musta been a week ago anyhow, near as I can guess by th' sign. Them chopped-off legs show that two big bull elk was killed right there, too; they'd been packed out. But th' ones that was left wasn't touched. Only th' cows, and they only took tusks offa them. A slaughter, an' they only used two outa the whole bunch."

We could hear the horse wrangler as he picketed his horse to a loose log. Now he stooped to come into the cook tent. He heard part of my last remarks, so I told him about the whole deal. He eased his lanky frame down on a saw block by the cook stove. "You say the teeth were taken out of those two cows? And the others left? If there's much of that goin' on, Wyoming'll be outa elk in a few years."

Old Buck chipped in, "Well, boys, everybody has got his own way t'hunt and his own ideas about how t' git onta game, any kind. We all know that. But when it gets so that people start t' ambush game like this deal was done, it's time fer some hell t' be raised. Legal or otherwise. If the game department don't start doin' somethin' about mass murder, the people will hafta."

Shorty was putting his sourdough keg to bed. He wrapped a towel around it, then an old coat. Now he got in his say: "I fed that lost hunter Slim brought in this morning, and put him t' bed in my rig. After he got a lot a shut-eye, he rolled out about noon, an' he and Slim an' me, we ate dinner, an' he give us th' lowdown on how he got mislaid last night. I don't reckon, from th' way he was teed off, that th' outfitter he was a-huntin' with'll be collectin' any dough f'r his hunt. If that's what yuh could call it.

"He said, yesterday four-five outa state hunters includin' him rode outa their camp with th' outfitter, th' wrangler, an' two guides. Well, this hunter says, th' whole outfit rode up a steep trail through a lotta timber, an' come out on them high timbered benches where they could see clear around th' country. He musta been up there above that slide rock country back of where we heard him shoot last night. The gent gits madder'n madder while he's tellin' us this yarn. Anyhow, th' boss 'n' his hands spot 8 or 10 head a elk down under this rim they're a-watchin' from. In a kinda pocket like. This gang o' big game guides stations him an' th' other city hunters on different spots about two or three hundred yards apart, all around a kind of natural pass. Tells 'em all t' stay hid, like. Tells 'em they, th' guides, are goin' ta ride down behind that buncha elk. Also th' outfitter says, 'Them there elk'll come through this pass here, when we an' th' boys git behind 'em t' spook 'em out.' He says, 'Give 'em hell, men. You c'n git th' whole bunch. Take yore pick,' he says, 'don't be bashful.' An' then they ride off down inta them breaks. Well, he waited an' waited, nuthin' happened. He stayed put for four or five hours, damn near froze, didn't hear a sound, not even a chipmunk, wore his eyes out a-watchin' th' pass, didn't hear a shot. Couldn't see where his feller sportsmen was stationed, prob'ly stayin' put, too, waitin' fer th' elk that was a-goin' ta come through the pass."

Slim was grinning at Shorty, telling the hunter's story. He nodded his head. "Yep, that's th' way he told it, all right. Before he got done he got hungry again, and Shorty had ta stoke him up, to hear about th' rest of his big elk hunt. Sure got weak when he got mad at th' way forty dollars a day was th' rate t' get lost."

Shorty puts in, "Anyhow, it gits dark on him, an' he shoots two-three times but gits no answer. He figgers he kin git back t' that stretch of timber where they'd tied up all th' sports saddle horses. If they've left him, mebbe his horse'll take him back t' camp. He stumbles around, darker'n hell, cloudy 'n' no moon t' see by, falls over rocks an' runs inta trees. Figgers mebbe he's close t' th' horses when he hears some snorts—prob'ly was that band of elk they didn't get. Finally takes a hard fall in a rocky willa bog. Can't see, no moon yet, but his ankle is sprained. Loses his rifle, then fumbles around an' steps on it, gits scared, fires th' shots we hear down here last night. Finally hears ol' Slim shootin'. Then he figgers he better stay put, when he finds he's lost his extry shells. Stays all night up there an' then you find him. Sure lucky, he says, but ta hell with huntin' elk if that's th' way it's done."

Me and this crew of mine talked awhile about this ruckus, thinking of all the hunters lost in the mountains, ones we knew about and others we'd heard of. Our hunter, Hackett, had lost himself, while this stranger we'd collected had his hard luck through the dumb tactics of a crooked outfitter. When ol' Shorty said, "Looks like th' Man up above was a-watchin' both a them gents; them fellers coulda got inta worse jams than they did." We all agreed with those sentiments, and then decided to hit the sack, too.

I couldn't sleep for quite long time. No, I didn't start counting sheep; I was counting elk, but the way things were stacking up, I figured I was going to run out of elk, and maybe would have to stay awake all night. Old Shorty's rattling snores flopped the tent flap, but

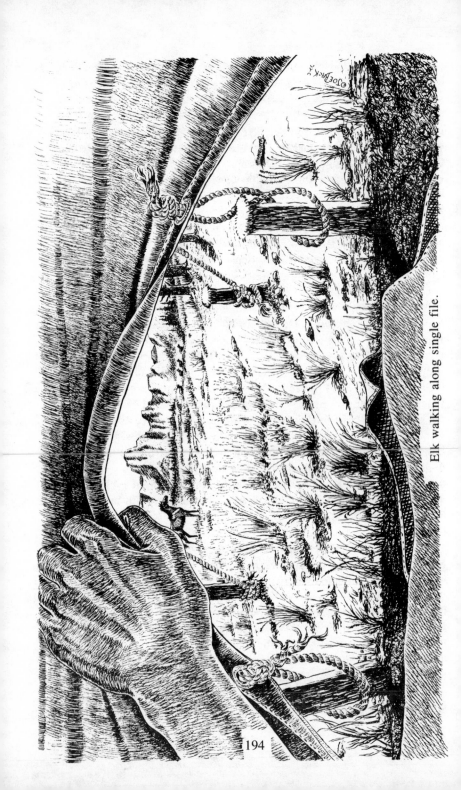

Elk walking along single file.

didn't bother me. What did jitter me was his scattered mumbling about big elk teeth, so I had to try to think of something else.

I shoved the blankets and tarp to one side and lifted up the bottom edge of the tent wall. No clouds. It was bright moonlight now. Looking past the frost on the tent rope and pegs, I could see Slim's night horse, tied with a long rope to a loose log. Once in a while he'd quit grazing, throw up his head, and listen, lonesome-like, to the far-off horse bells on some of our horse bunch over across the Buffalo on the grassy benches. Then, big as a elephant, a mouse humped along past the forest of tent ropes, pegs, frosty grass blades, and distant tree trunks. After he left, I was getting frosty myself around the withers. I was about to lower the curtain on this show when, way off, past the glittering grass tops, I caught sight of two or three cow elk walking along single file toward the river. A big bull was in the rear.

All I could see was their bodies from the belly up. The moon cast silvery glints of light on the big boy's antlers, and on the body outlines of the darker cows. I could even hear the faint clattery splashes of young ice broken, as they disappeared over the river to the dark spruce jungle beyond.

Well, we got a few elk left, anyhow, I figured. At some more elk teeth mumbles from over in the dreaming cook's bed roll, I dropped the canvas edge on the ground, and drug the stiff tarp over my head; elk teeth or stomach ulcers, here I come! But even then, I was a-doin' it again; so I got a new line of thought; and there it was, all elk. The fact is, I thought, when the moon is full like now, the elk feed at night, and mostly leave the grassy parks by early morning. Then they go back into the timbered jungles to chew their cuds, rest, and ruminate on the perfidy of all mankind, until in early evening when they get hungry again; all this depending on their appetite and the kind of feed they're on.

Oh, sure, some big-headed old bull, throwed out of the harem by some smart and tough young upstart, gets foolish ideas and crosses open spots going from one stretch of timber to another. He's looking for a grass-widow elk; but not finding any unattached, he grazes along timbered fringes of meadow, bugling and grunting in angry perplexity. Also, sons or stepsons, spike elk, tag along or try to. And some old maid elk looking for sympathetic company may stray absent-mindly across openings. So hunting elk in the fall (if you get trophy heads) seems to me either plain happenstance luck, or knowledge and strategy and skill at outwitting. This gang killing is foreign to most people's instincts, I thought; and with that I musta dropped off.

Chapter Six

We started out after daylight the next morning. Smithers had spend half the night cleaning his two-eyed fancy blunderbuss. He went out with old Buck Bruen, whose hunter had got a big-headed elk yesterday. They'd packed it in, and the meat was now cooling off on the meat pole back of the tents. Buck told me privately that Slim didn't need anybody's help on packing. "That guy slung them elk quarters an' horns on them two horses slicker'n a whistle, an' throwed as good a diamond as any hand I ever worked with. He didn't need me at all." Now Buck's hunter, George Parsin, wanted to try for a bear; so he and I rode off together, after we talked over with the other guides our plans of where we were going.

As we rode through a stretch of lodgepole timber, I got to thinking about how Slim Wilson was handling our horse bunch. His quiet self-assurance and his friendly ways were easy to get along with. He was darned good with horses, and it was turning out that he could pack and shoe with the best of them. He never talked much about himself and claimed to be a stranger around these parts. He made comments about packing and hunting in Idaho, but that was about all. He'd been running the horse bunch in before daylight. After we had the horses we were going to use that day, he'd keep the rest of them in the corral for four or five hours, then run them out on good feed until evening. Then he'd bring 'em in to grain up. When we had all come in, he'd put our saddle horses with the bunch, and then locate the whole bunch on new grass for the night. When I kidded him about the halter behind his cantle, he said there seemed to be a bunch-quitter or two in our string. Slim said he missed one or two lone feeders when he rounded them up in the dark early morning. After we'd got our hunting horses out, and left after breakfast, he'd ride out and locate the lost one, catch him, and lead him in to the corral to put with the bunch. That was reasonable, all right, but I noticed the three or four wrangle horses he'd changed off on seemed to be rode down more than they should be. He took good care of 'em, though, and grained 'em plenty. As we were riding off this morning, Shorty was cleaning up around the cook tent and Slim was busy at the wood pile, so I reckoned the horse bunch was all there.

I'd noticed bear sign up by those elk carcasses above Cub Creek the day before. Parsin and I got up there pretty late, but we did see a big black bear and her two cubs having the time of their lives trying to put the run on the birds yelling around. No soap on a mamma with kids. But the big buck deer in a stand of quaking aspens didn't have a chance. George Parsin nailed him first shot. I dressed him out and throwed him on my big roan. George rode ahead and I walked, leading old Roany and his fresh load. Maybe in the morning we'd find a new bear on the buck's entrails back there. Good bear country up there by the Buffalo Falls.

We tied our horses and ate lunch in the shadow of a clump of lodgepole pine. Sitting in the dry grass, leaning up against a big limby deadfall, George says, in between bites of Shorty's juicy sandwiches, "Smithers is sure enough set on having those elk teeth, isn't he? Must have a lot of dough to go with such onery ideas. If the wrong kind of money-hungry birds try to supply him, they all ought to land in jail."

"Th' game laws say that no edible portion of game meat can be sold or bartered," I says, "but that lets out tusks. I don't reckon Tim can find any jackass dumb enough to kill elk for their teeth. Like you say, they could both git years in the hoosegow for that, if caught. Don't see how he can contact enough hunters or owners of legal teeth, either."

"Those elk carcasses we saw the bear family chasing the birds off of, what do you make of that?"

"Could be that somebody got too excited when they run onta that bunch of elk. Trigger-happy gents, maybe. Killed 'em all before they realized what got into 'em, then they got scared. They come back, though, an' packed out th' two bulls; I'd a taken the' cows myself. Better meat. But they did rob th' cows o' their tusks, an' that's what bothers me."

While we were talking, I was glassing the country with Parsin's powerful binoculars. Might pick out some bear snoopin' around out in the open. I caught just a blurry movement of something through some tree clumps across the South Fork, over close to where the elk carcasses lay. Boy, those glasses were powerful. Sure like to have that pair. We were around two miles from the grassy slope above Cub Creek. . . . But there he was. It was the wrangler, a long ways from camp, riding the big snorty buckskin. He was staying in the shadows of the timber, but now and then a sunny spot would show him riding slowly around, in and out of the trees above the dead elk, and he wasn't leading any lost horse.

Our two horses tied just behind us started snorting and faunching around. When I lowered the glasses to look, a big brown bear was just disappearing up through a heavy growth of spruce. Parsin was right on the ball; he had his rifle up, aiming, but he was a little too late. That brown was sure fanning his ears. He was in a hell of a hurry.

Goerge had a big grin on his angular face when he slowly lowered his rifle and looked around at me. "That bear wants my buck deer, not his entrails back there. But he doesn't seem to chase us kind of birds away from the meat . . . Bill, just before the bear broke up our lunch hour, I was about to ask you if game wardens ever come up into this part of the mountains."

"You know, that's what bothers me. Years ago, when I started huntin' 'n' guidin' in this here same country, they would show up pretty often. Mostly they were ex-guides an' packers. I knew a lot of 'em and sure liked to have 'em around. They knew th' game an' the mountains an' all their ways. I ain't had any game wardens check any o' my hunters or camps for a long time now."

"When we stopped down in Roaring River, the day we came to the ranch, seemed like there were quite a few game wardens in town, and I talked with several of them. They seemed like fine, upstanding young fellows."

"Yeah, the ones I know are. Lots of 'em are able game wardens; but in th' old days you'd meet em out in th' hills more 'n y' would in town."

It was dark by the time we got into camp, what with George lallygagging around with short stops taking pictures. Then it was too late to get the best picture, Parsin said, of the whole trip. For in front of the cook tent was Tim Smithers seated on a block of firewood, and in the light of the big campfire was Buck Bruen, grinning and pouring iodine on the big hunter's bowed head. As we came closer to look, Buck let the bottle slip, accidental like, and some of the stuff trickled down in the back of Smithers' shirt, and must have went pretty far down, for he jumped up with a big yelp and grabbed himself.

Shorty was standing in the door of the cook tent holding the gas lantern for Buck to see better. He cackled an old man's giggle, "I'll betcha that big horned owl that tried to scalp ya t'night was cousin ta the one you shot outa that spruce tree last fall."

Smithers grimaced over in Shorty's direction and surprised us all with, "Let the punishment fit the crime."

We found that Buck and the stocks-and-bonds man had got to camp just a little before we did. Out in the big park, Tim had rode under a low tree limb and had his hat brushed off. A big swoopy flash of wings, and whango! a horned owl out hunting for supper mistook that white head bobbing along beneath him for a snowshoe rabbit. All he got was a shreddy clawful of outraged white hair. Buck, riding ahead in the dark, said he didn't know a leading millionaire could scream such horrible lowbrow bad words.

Smithers was sure defensive at supper. If he even thought anyone was looking at his dyed head, he'd switch the conversation around to his so-called achievements. Doc Forrester wondered at the fact that there were no wolves left in this part of the country, nothing in the dog line but coyotes and some red foxes. Smithers had the answer for this one. "They all went to the big cities," he cracks. "It's dog eat dog, there, if they're tryin' to make big money. It takes a wolf to catch a wolf, no panty-waist coyotes there. And me, I've got the best and biggest business of its kind in my town."

After he went to his tent, George Parsin and Doc Forrester lingered over more coffee with the bunch. Looked like they got a band out of the comments on Smithers' declaration. Al poured himself some more java. "Shore, shore, when this rich yak-yak kicks that golden bucket, he'll have a newer and bigger tombstone put on his grave each year. Prob'ly leave that pervision in his will." Slim, he never says a dad-blamed word about all the deal. Just swigs coffee and grins. Finally, before we all turned in, Buck has his say: "In old Full-pockets' game of put and take, I'll betcha he's gotta cinch up his light *put* side o' th' pack a damn sight tighter 'n th' *take*."

The next day we all saw game but no trophy heads; except Doc Forrester and Al Neeman. The good doctor had no trouble getting in one good shot which done the business, according to Al. Neeman's little brown eyes twinkled when he told us, "You'd oughta heard him namin' all the innards while I cleaned out his elk. The hell of it was, they was all in Latin or somethin', longest tongue-twistin' I ever heard. I told Doc, I could clean out a critter without them big words; but if a M.D. had t'know words like them t' put th' innards back in so's they'd work, why, I was sure gonna stay jist a guide."

That evening Dr. Forrester and Smithers caught a few trout in the big bend of the Buffalo, just below camp. Tim spied a large cow moose in the edge of some heavy timber; he laid his fishing rod down and unlimbered his camera. Sneaking in closer for a better shot, he ended up climbing a tree when the moose charged him. Doc had to rescue him by thowing rocks at the jealous mother. Forrester said, "I never did see the calf, but I knew there was one back in the trees."

"You birds sure had a streak of luck, when that cow moose went back to her calf," Slim Wilson told them. "If it had been spring, and that calf was plumb new, I'll bet you'd a had a jangle. Over in Idaho, one time, a moose cow, with a new addition in th' family, didn't like publicity. She musta figured her baby was either too snooty or too homely to have its picture taken. Anyhow, I was drivin' down th' highway a few miles below th' ranch I was workin' for, headed for town. Come to a big bend along th' river, timber 'n' willow bottoms on both sides. I saw a new-lookin' car parked a few feet off this oiled road, and there was a screamin' woman alone in it. I stopped my pickup an' looked around. Couldn't see another soul, until I happened t' look down th' steep grade to the river's edge. There was a big cow moose standin' on her hind legs in th' water, strikin' a man with her front feet. She had 'im pawed down to his knees on th' bank. Her squealin' an' them huffy grunts had that hollerin' woman in th' car beat all to thunder. This bird wasn't sayin' a word, but he didn't seem t' be enjoyin' this kind of affection. So I jumpted outa th' pickup an' ran down there, grabbin' up a short tree limb a-layin' in th' rocks. I whunked this mad female on her snoot a time or two. She whirled around an' splashed back across th' river, to a calf I saw, barely hidden in the willows over there. I helped this gashed-up gent to his feet, and finally got his wobbly carcass back up th' grade to his car.

"Naw, his wife'd quit screamin', but she never did get outa th' car. Too scared t'move, I reckon. You know, this gent finally sorta come to when he got close t' his car. He suddenly jumped in th' driver's seat, started up th' motor, an' took off down th' road. Nope, neither him or his old lady said a word all this time. Them nature lovers didn't say howdy, kiss me, go t' hell or even goodbye, just took off in a hell of a hurry down th' road.

"About that time, wonderin' if I was goin' deef, dumb, or blind, I sorta come out of it, an' curious about why th' man an' th' moose got into this jamboree in th' first place. So I walked back down to th' battlefield. I looked over cross th' river, but that bogtrotter wasn't in sight. Then I saw something glisten in th' roily water. I fished around with a stick until I hooked out th' sad remains of a stomped-up camera. When I got back t' my pickup an' started her up, I got ta thinkin', sometimes it pays t' ask first."

Smithers took all this in with a big grin. "Well, if any long nose sucker like that one ever chases me up a tree again, I'll start collecting moose teeth, too."

She had him pawed down to his knees.

Chapter Seven

Next day started out about as usual, with nothing happening out of the ordinary. But when we got back to camp after dark, I found that something had happened there that changed the whole hunting camp to something else. Pete Elaby had packed in some supplies we'd been looking for, and brought the accumulated mail—and little Sally!

Al Neeman told me about it. "By golly, Bill," Neeman was squinting at me, "Doc went out with Slim 'n me t' git movies while we packed his elk in. He run outa film f'r his camery. We wasn't far f'm camp, so I come in with him t' git some more."

Forrester and Parsin had gone over to their tent, and Buck was helping the wrangler stack some sacks of grain in the gear tent. We could hear Shorty out in the dark throwing some cans into the garbage pit. "I hope Johnnie ain't in some jam, back east, Bill." Al had a hoarse whisper. "I figure on him doin' my grinder work some day." From the lighted tent we could hear Shorty's shovel scrape on the rocks at the pit back in the timber, and Slim's and Buck's voices over in the gear tent.

"I saw Sally holdin' Shorty by th' wrist and talkin' like a Dutch uncle. She was shakin' her finger under th' ol' boy's nose, an' boy, was she mad!" Al kept looking furtively out into the black night. "I saw all this while I was helpin' Pete pack Parsin's meat an' heads on them jacks of his. Ol' Shorty wasn't sayin' much an' he sure was listenin' close t' that mad little Indian." Neeman stopped to listen again, then he said, "All I could git outa th' deal was 'city slickers!' She hissed it real loud a coupla times. Sally was shakin' her head at somethin' Shorty was sayin', she was holdin' Shorty by th' wrist by one hand an' th' other was held straight back of her. Looked like at letter she was holdin'." Al was getting excited. He kept listening to make sure Shorty was still covering up the garbage." "Bill, all of a sudden, th' cook made a grab and got that letter outa Sally's hand, and that little Injun slapped him one alongside th' jaw, an' kinda wailed, 'Oh! Uncle Shorty!' Then ol' Shorty kinda trotted up towards th' cook tent. Nope, he didn't say a word, jist kinda mumbles somethin', didn't even look back at that poor kid.

"What did she do? Why, she jist turned around an' run up t' her

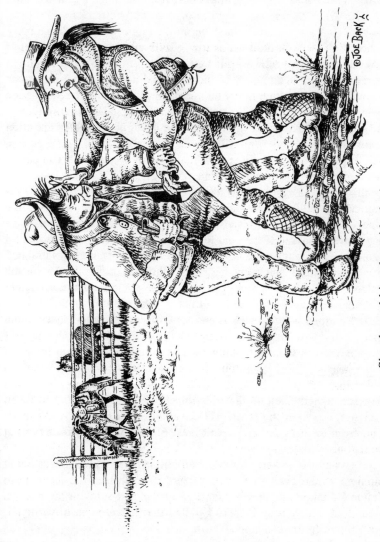

She slapped him alongside the jaw.

horse, grazin' over close t' th' corral. She was up on that surprised critter like a flash an' was poppin' him on th' belly, lopin' down th' trail an' outa sight before y' could say Geronimo!"

About that time the cook come back into the tent, and that's all I got outa Al. He sure ain't no stool pigeon, and he thinks a lot of old Shorty, so I figured this must be another one of them dang belly wobblers. The cook didn't mention Sally's visit, and I didn't ask.

While we were eating breakfast next morning, Shorty was sure grumpy. "What's the matter, old boy, did a mouse fall into your sourdough keg last night?" "Sure did, Tim," Shorty gives Smithers a grunt, "Cantcha notice th' taste?" Didn't bother old Elk-Tooth a bit. He just grins, and snares another golden cake, and dribbles syrup on it, for answer.

Slim put in, "You shoulda seen th' show in th' gear tent last night. Somethin' woke me up and I snapped on my flashlight. A big snowshoe rabbit was at th' foot of my bedroll, eatin' oats out of a hole in a grain sack, and perched right up above him was two white-footed mice a-watchin'. They musta give up an' come over to the cook tent." Doc Forrester asked if the gear tent put on any other shows. Slim had a good one: "Night before last a loud thumping woke me up. I grabbed for my flashlight, but something had a-holt of it. Finally I won the struggle, and there under a pack saddle was a big pack rat. He made a last desperate grab for the flashlight, but he seen I was the biggest, so he thumped a time or two, and took off, mad as hell. Mebbe his eyes are haywire. It sure gets dark in these mountains." The hunters and the rest of us had to laugh at Slim's description of all the activity in the gear tent, but Beel didn't seem to get any bang out of it.

We didn't go hunting till afternoon that day. The hunters all decided they had to write letters that morning. Pete Elaby was due in again with supplies from the ranch. He'd take our mail back in with him to send from Roaring River, and the rest of the meat and trophy heads we had accumulated.

When I saw ol' Shorty fumbling around in his private set of rawhide panniers at the back of the cook tent, I recollected the letter from Velma I'd taken off the cook table last night and stuck in my pocket. I was too tired to read it then. I pulled it out, and went to sit on the wash block in the sun:

Dear Bill,
   Things are going all right here at the ranch. I hope the list of supplies and the things the hunters wanted sent out to camp are all

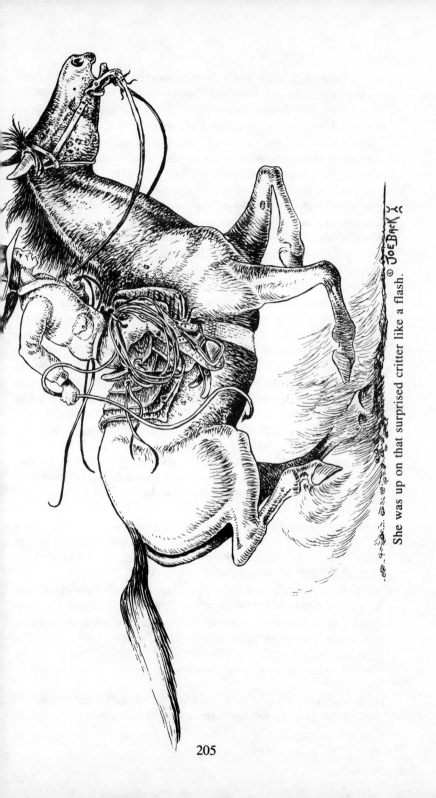

She was up on that surprised critter like a flash.

in Pete's packs. Sally and I double checked with Pete and think we got everything you and Shorty had on the list. You'll be surprised to see Sally (of course, you'll probably be out hunting away from camp and won't). Anyhow, that girl *sure* got in a dither when Elaby brought the mail from Roaring River late last night. She got a letter (I think from her Johnnie), and after she went in by the dining room stove to read it, she came running out to the kitchen table where I was peeling apples for some pies and was just about to cry which I've never seen that kid do yet. She was trembling all over and she got her coat and that old hat of Johnnie's she wears all the time. She said she was going to to the bunkhouse (this was after supper, Bill) and get Pete to saddle up a horse for her. "Have to go to camp to see Uncle Shorty," she said, and "This can't wait." She took off, left the door open, and ran out in the dark towards the bunkhouse. I thought that child had gone out of her mind, so I grabbed that long flashlight of yours and took out after her.

Bill, you would have laughed, I did, and later nearly cried too. Pete's bell mare, Maw, got into too many oats and was sick yesterday (you know, those blamed mules, hee-hawing all morning, looked scared if a mule can). Pete worked on her half the day and she got O.K. Then he drove into Roaring River for more horse medicine, supplies, and the mail. So poor Pete had a hard day.

Well, when I caught up with Sally she was in the dark bunkhouse pounding on Pete's bed tarp to wake the poor guy up. When I came in with the flashlight, Pete must have thought the man from Kansas had shown up again and Sally figured it was him. He was hollering and the little Shoshone was yelling at him, "Please get up and saddle a horse for me."

When Pete got his wits about him, he told Sally. "There's only th' wrangle horse in th' corral besides that sick bell mare, and that pony is a bronky outfit. Yuh couldn't ride him. It's all I can do to stay on th' side-winder. Jest a-breakin' him." Pete hunched up in his tarp bed and rubbed his eyes. "The horses and mules are all turned out down on 4-mile Meadows. Yuh'll have to wait. I've got to take the pack string to camp in the morning anyhow, and you can ride out to see ol' Shorty then."

Sally is on the peck this morning. She's done her hair in a pony tail, so I know she's mad at somebody.

There was a little more in Vel's letter but it didn't help clear up the rest of the puzzle I felt a-comin' round the mountain.

Shorty's woodpile looked kinda gant, so Buck Bruen, Al Neeman and me, we got the long cross-cut saw and axes together, and walked over back of camp to cut down some standing dead pine. When I came back to the tent to rummage around for a file, the cook was at the back end of the board table writing furiously and mumbling to himself.

We had four or five good trees down, and were chopping limbs off and sawing the logs into shorter lengths. The wrangler, on the big roan horse, was a-snakin' them over to the woodpile close to the cook tent. One log saw its chance and got an end wedged into a waiting loopy root. Slim was a-whippin' his rope back and forth to drag the log free sidewise, when a big black notebook fell out of his jacket pocket. I was trimming knotty limbs off one down tree close by, so I stepped over, picked it out of a mess of tangled branches and pine chips and handed it up to Slim on his sweaty horse. He reach down, put it into his coat pocket, and buttoned down at me, "If you're curious about the book, it's a diary I put down ideas in." I noticed Al and Buck and listening as Slim went on. "Some day, when I'm old and more harmless, I figure on quittin' this horse jinglin', and I'm goin' to try writing up some stories. The whoppers these locoed guides, the cook, and them hunters tell around these camps is a-goin t' waste. Other damn fools write stories and peddle 'em, maybe there's room for one more."

Buck was sitting on the butt end of a big tree he had just dropped. "I think Slim's got a good idea at that. Here's one for him. A couple days ago Smithers an' me got inta camp kinda early, so Tim went over ta his tent sayin' he was goin' ta take a little snooze. Well, I was over in Slim's bunk and gear tent a-gittin' me a strap ta fix up my knife scabbard." The big guide looked around at the hunters' wall tent over in the edge of the timber, then went on, "Whilst I was a-rummagin' around in there, I heard, right close, a couple uh big *Ka-whoom, Ka-whooms.* I looked out past th' tent flap, and there was that nap-takin' tooth hunter just a-goin' back inta his tent with his cannon still smokin'."

Buck felt of a crack in his axe handle and looked up at the wrangler with a big grin. "I heard some kind of screetchy mumble about that time, an' lookin' over t' th' cook tent, there was ol' Shorty standin' out in front. He was shakin' his fists up and down, an' that flour-sack apron he wears was a-flutterin' in time. Well, I ambled over t' git th' deadwood on this shootin' deal.

"Shorty kinda glares at me, then he says, 'I was a-peelin' these

The wrangler was a-snakin' 'em over to the woodpile.

here spuds an' I happened ta look over inta tha big grassy park that other side of the corral. There was a big mamma coyote a-teachin' her pups how ta catch mice. Them big fluffy pups was pouncin' an' hoppin' in that tall yella grass. An' then all of a sudden that big game hunter starts bombardin' at 'em!' Now you fellas ain't seen nothin' yet, if you never seen Shorty mad."

Bruen carefully looked around at the cook tent. "Then ol' Shorty really gits ta goin'. He says, 'I ain't got enny patience with fellers who's *always* a-tryin' ta kill everything that lives. 'Specially when they don't need 'em t' eat an' they ain't harmin' nobody. Survival of the fittest, Smithers was a-sayin' last night. Why, hell, Buck, many more uh these kind uh leaders uh men, and they'll trail th' whole population right inta purgatory.' "

"Yeah," Al Neeman's a-sittin' on a log over there, filin' on the teeth of the log saw. "Last night I heard Smithers say he came up the hard way, damn hard, he said, an' made a fortune by follerin' his own beliefs. He said he figgered on stickin' with 'em. He says, do onto the other man as he would do onto you, but do it first."

"Well, mebbe he does go by his book," Buck put in to say, "but only a few days ago he saw Pete Elaby showin' me th' gash on his arm where that kickin' mule got him. Tim went 'an got his first-aid kit, a real fancy job, made Pete take his shirt off, an' done as handy a job of dressin' a bad cut as Doc Forrester could of. When he gits done, he says t' Pete, 'O.K., Sucker, you better watch them long-eared politicians. Don't foller 'em, Sucker, lead 'em!' "

Al put in, "Yeah, mebbe he packs a first-aid kit and can use it, but he sure is blind in other ways. He don't seem to *mean* to be vicious to a horse, even if he does put kidney sores on the few he's rode. I showed him one, after I jerked the saddle off his nag last night. He says, 'What th' hell. A horse is only a horse, the poor damn sucker.' "

About that time, a bunch of hee-hawing and wheezy braying down the trail brought Pete Elaby and his packs in sight. We all helped the packer take off his panniers and mantied-up cargo. After dinner, we packed up the quartered meat of Doc Forrester's elk, and his trophy head, on Pete's long-eared partners, and he took off for the ranch, to put the meat in the cooler there.

We spread out for an afternoon hunt in three directions. Parsin got lucky about three miles from camp. I didn't even see him shoot. I was riding up ahead of him, going into a stretch of quaking aspens on an old game trail, the dead fallen branches and leaves making snappy crackles and pops. I thought he was right behind me, when I

A big mamma coyote a-teachin' her pups to catch mice.

heard just one KA-BOOM back in the dark swampy spruce jungle I'd just come out of. I trotted Roany back down the trail; and there, stitting on a very dead glossy big black bear was old Dead-eye George. He said, "I happened to look back down the trail, and there was ol' Fatty following along, dumba as hell." Well, that's hunting, you never know.

After I got back from rounding up that damfool Blackie that George was riding, I tied the two snorting, bear-hating horses close by George's prize. It was pretty dark in there, but George said he was going to take pictures anyhow. I skinned out the bear. When I got through, we decided Slim could pack the meat and hide in the next day. George wanted to take a few movie shots from up on the timbered bench above us, so we rode up there and tied up again.

While he was angling around getting pictures, I was using them high-powered glasses of his looking over the country. Saw a little band of elk, a bull and five cows, grazing high up on Terrace Mountain, partly in the shade of some timber. Suddenly they all spooked at something below them, and took off into the shadows.

Finally I spotted the cause. Those glasses showed two men sitting on the ground close to their tied-up horses, down in a grassy pocket. They'd talk awhile and point around, then get up and walk in and out of sight in the open timber. I finally got the hair focus on these two birds. One of them was a stranger, as far as I could tell. He had a red cloth on his hat and looked like a hunter. The other one, a tall lanky guy, was our horse wrangler. He was only a couple of miles from camp, but it was away off from where we grazed the horse bunch. Just about then, Parsin got his film all used up, so we stepped on our horses and hit for camp. I got to wondering why was Slim pirootin' all over the country. Yesterday Buck told me that while he and Smithers ate lunch a day or so ago on a slope of Terrace Mountain, he was glassing the country with that highfalutin spotting scope of Tim's, he swore he spotted the horse wrangler riding across Nowlin Meadows way down below. Buck was busy trying a new mantle on the gas lantern in the cook tent while he talked. The rest of the gang were out at the meat poles helping Doc Forrester measure his elk head.

"You know, Bill, this Wilson is a good mountain man. Six, eight years ago I was workin' for an outfit on th' other side o' the' mountain. The biggest man in th' crew was an ex-football player. He wouldn't git off th' blazed trail. Nossir, I wouldn't a believed it either, until his hunter beefed about it. If he couldn't find a nich-an'-a-slash ranger blaze on a tree, he wouldn't go. 'A game trail is a snare an' a delusion,'

The other guy was our horse wrangler.

he said. 'Damn elk especially, tryin' t' foul yuh up, every time.' Yuh kin sure git some queer ones. Th' boss of this outfit said he hired a cowboy once, fer guide. Good man with horses, go anywhere, up, down, through th' worst jungle y' ever seen; or try it. The hell of it was, this bird would never git off his horse. No sir, he wouldn't. Eat, sleep, help good around camp, split wood 'n' help wrangle. But he wouldn't walk a hunderd yards. Once he had them legs clamped around a horse, he was set till he got back t' camp. So th' boss tried it different next year, he said. He put an ad in th' paper, which read: 'Wanted—Experienced Guide and Packer. Cowboy will do, if willing to learn.' Out of five he tried out that year, four were cowboys, but three of 'em made th' grade. Their legs an' dome hadn't been warped too bad, an' they never took th' movies an' Will James too serious. No shadow riders. Slim, he's no shadow rider, either. Mebbe he's a mystery, but he shore is a good hand."

This traveling wrangler sure done all the horse work O.K., helped with the wood, and packed in all the game the hunters killed, so I had no kick. But he had an uncanny way of getting around in a bunch of mountains strange to him. He sure was a mountain man, anyhow. Shorty mentioned a time or two that Slim often didn't show up for dinner, and all Slim packed for a gun was a battered old .38 six-shooter.

George and I got back to camp early, and all we found there was a crummy old porcupine trying to rustle his way into the gear tent. He hadn't made the grade, so we run him off. George got his fishing gear and went over to the river to try for trout. I got some chores done around camp. It began to get dark, and no cook yet, so I started up the fires— Shorty's stove in the cook tent, the Dutch oven fire outside, and the stove in the hunters' tent. Just as I shut that one down, I thought I heard two quick rifle shots somewhere in the heavy timber above camp.

Wilson and Shorty Beel always had got along fine. They seemed to be friends from the time we brought Slim out with us. But I'd noticed lately a peculiar coolness in their attitude towards each other. Was it just since Smithers started up his talk about collecting elk teeth?

This here Terrace Mountain had some copper veins. An outfit had put in two, three years exploring, digging shafts, looking for the mother lode. Had a big camp once, just below where our camp sets. An old fell-down cabin or two around here yet. Mebbe one of these two birds had hit it rich, and figured the other was a claim jumper. The cook had guided and packed over this country for years, before arthritis had bent up his carcass. He knew the whole country like the back of his hand. The horse jingler had been around these parts maybe a couple weeks. Sometimes a newcomer finds things an old-timer has seen for years and didn't see for what it was. Or had he?

I tied up the tent flaps and stood outside listening for any more shots, when the horse bells started up their music, and soon Slim was driving the bunch into the corral. I called when he was putting the poles in the gate, "Didja hear a coupla shots up on th' mountain, just now, Slim?"

"Sure, Bill, but them horses had me busy an' I couldn't tell where from. Al and Buck and their hunters went down th' Buffalo to hunt, so it couldn't a been them." The wrangler gave a quick look up Terrace Mountain. "After all you fellows left this afternoon, Shorty told me he was a-goin' to walk up that steep draw back of camp. He said, he thinks Terrace Mountain might have some uranium, and he could use a few shekels." Slim grinned. "I was tackin' a shoe on the buckskin when he left, so I don't know whether he packed a gun or not. Mebbe elk teeth are surer'n uranium, haw, haw."

"That remind me, Slim," I said, trying to catch him, "I spotted you on Terrace three or four hours ago with Parsin's glasses. Looked like somebody was with you."

Slim never batted an eye. "I sure was up there." He had a big grin. "I thought I'd look at the formation, too. Horses O.K. down here. I met a hunter from a camp on Sody Fork across the ridge. He hadn't shot an elk, he said, but I learned a lot about the country from him."

The wrangler went on up to the gear tent and came back with a sack of oats, so I helped him grain the horses. About then George Parsin came through the timber with a string of big trout. "I got enough for supper, with that liver Smithers is sure to bring in. Maybe those two shots awhile ago mean Tim got a bull with two more teeth."

The Dutch ovens were on the hot coals, and I had started to cook, when Shorty showed up in the dark, outside the tent. He looked sour and grumpy, but says, "Thanks, Bill. I'll take over now." He didn't even ask who got the trout that I'd rolled in cornmeal and had ready for the Dutch oven. About then Buck Bruen and Smithers rode in. "Tim got a big bull three hours or so ago, down below Bear Cub Pass," Buck said. "Good big rack and two big teeth. All he needs now is nine hundred and ninety-six more, haw, haw."

Al Neeman and Doc Forrester rode in right after that, and Doc untied a big deer liver from the back of his saddle. "Hey, Shorty," he hollered, "More meat for the pan." Shorty didn't even look up from the Dutch oven, just waved his pot hook and grunted in Doc

Forrester's direction. He pried up the Dutch oven lid to take a peek at how the trout were doing, and Smithers got a whiff of the real thing. "If I could cook like you can, Shorty, I'd have the best restaurants in New York." "Yeah," Shorty grunted at him, and looked out at the still night, "Sure windy tonight, ain't it?"

We all just got set down to eat, when we *could* hear a big wind come up all of a sudden. Doc Forrester was telling about killing his buck deer down in the vee west of Terrace Mountain, and was waving his fork with a piece of fried liver on its business end, in his description of the running deer. We could hear the timber tops moan and whistle, up back of camp. The wind interrupted Doc, whipping up the loose cook tent flaps with a tearing pop, then something plenty heavy smacked down on the tent pole. The chimney wires whangled, and down comes a pipe section. Smoke, sparks, and powdery soot came pouring out of the stove, choking and blinding the whole crew. We all got up and ran outside in the dark, in a tangled mess of arms and legs.

Tim Smithers was last, being clear in the back of the cook tent. He was on his way, when the gas lamp shimmied off the wire wrapped to the shaking tent pole. The lamp fell smack dab into a platter full of French-fried spuds, and sizzled out. The big-footed hunter got tangled in the bail of a Dutch oven. He fell flat, his high-priced nose buried in a pile of piping hot liver and onions. Old Shorty, first out, was hollering real frantic, "Look out fer my sourdough keg, yuh damn fools!" By that time he got his flashlight going. When we got the liver-cured millionaire and the hot stove pacified, we found it *wasn't* a crazy grizzly, it was a big dead flowzy branch that had busted out of a all tree quite a ways off. It musta come pinwheeling down in the wind dead center for our tent.

We finally got the sections of stovepipe wired back, and the liver and onions off of Tim's face and ears. Buck started the gas lamp up. Al and I were a-cleaning the soot off the table boards. The genial doctor from Indiana and George Parsin were washing some tin dishes and kidding Shorty, who was a little happier, having found his keg as safe as ever. We were ready to eat again.

We just got set down to have at it, when Smithers, in a clean shirt, showed up in the tent door. He looked all around with a greasy smirk, pulled a hand out from behind him, and held up a big piece of fried liver. "To the victor belong the spoils, suckers."

215

Chapter Eight

The next morning George Parsin had a bad attack of rheumatism, so Doctor Forrester wanted to stay in camp and doctor up George with a few rub-downs he was sure would help. Buck and Al Neeman helped Slim tighten up and re-shoe a few of the saddle horses during the doctoring. Smithers said he'd like to hunt up around Nowlin Mountain again, so he and I took off. Besides, we decided to look at the bear bait, an old worn-out pack horse we'd planted a week or so before, in a timber surrounded park close to Line Creek.

After he missed the bear, Smithers had dirty looks for anybody who mentioned how handy a flashlight was. Early in the evening we tied our horses in the timber a hundred yeards or so from the dead horse, and made a sneak through the trees to where we could see the bait. Sure enough, it was ripe enough to have a visitor. On the opposite side of the carcass, we could see the big black. Standing upright, he'd stoop over from the hips, to gnaw and tear at the paunch of the old sorrel pony. Then he'd straigthen up bloody nose snuffling and paws dangling, to look over at the timber diagonal to us. His chompy growls in that direction looked like he figured company was coming. About half of that timber surrounded park was in the sunlight. The long shadows, cast by the spruce timber we hid in, reached out just to touch the carcass.

A small breeze sprang up, rippling the tall yellow grass, and bringing the perfume straight from the dining room. It didn't seem to bother the broker. At a nod from me, he started to raise his rifle. I held my nose to keep down a cough, while I watched his finger take up the slack on the trigger. Just as Smithers shot, the bear jumped over the horse and tore off, coughing and snarling at something over to our left. "Why, that lucky dam sucker!" Smithers jammed the butt of his rifle on the ground, and started to cuss.

While we walked back to the horses, I tried to console that mad hunter. "Hell, Tim, that bear didn't even know you shot. He was chasin' some other bear off. We can come here early in th' mornin' and you can git another shot at th' same bear, I'll betcha."

By the time we walked around a small swamp to within sight of

216

our horses, I forgot about bear and done a little cussin' of my own. There was only one horse in sight and he looked mighty lonesome. "Any horse-thieves in these parts, Bill?" was Smithers' comment as we walked up to my horse. "Nope, I don't reckon so; but a big Boy Scout from New York" (I see Smithers starin' bug-eyed at where he'd tied his horse) "is plumb afoot, bear or no bear." Tim always insisted he was able to handle his own horse, so he felt flabbergasted to see nothing but the wrong end of the neckrope tied to the tree. Also, a long-handled flashlight was lying on the ground where it had fallen from the saddlebag of his departed horse. "My bowline musta slipped," he says, fingering the rope, "but we can see, if it gets dark. Good thing the horse left the flashlight." From the sign and tracks I found, I figgered our bear, or maybe two, had come this way and scared the horses. I cast around, making circles, trying to find which way the stray horse went before it got dark.

Finally I told Smithers to ride my horse back to camp, about two miles. I'd walk up to a high grassy park, just above us a hundred yards or so, get the lost horse, and ride him into camp. "I know old Prunes drifted up there," I told Smithers. "That's an old campsite of ours. His tracks head that way anyhow." I saw Smithers ride off packing his flashlight under one arm, down toward the ranger trail that led to camp. He'd put his rifle in my scabbard, and I carried mine as I climbed up the hill.

Well, I found Prunes right in the old pole corral. He was licking at a small lump of salt and looked plumb at home. It was plenty dark when I rode up to the corral at camp. I expected to hear Smithers haw-hawing up at Shorty's cook tent. I could hear all the others talking, and see the shadows they made around the table, but no Tim. I tied Prunes up to a corral pole, with the horses inside nosing at him for the news. As I walked over towards the cook tent a horse nickered in the trail. Turned out to be my horse, that Smithers had rode off. I was looking Roany over in the dark, when Wilson opened the tent flap and came over to where I was.

"Hi, Bill, where's Tim?"

When I told Slim about the bear and about when I last saw Smithers and his flashlight, he started to laugh. By that time, Buck, Al, Shorty, and the two hunters came out of the cook tent to hear the palaver. We found Smithers' rifle in the scabbard under the left stirrup leather of my saddle. Outside of the absence of the broker and his flashlight everything was O.K.; Roany himself acted plumb spooky. You know, that dang Wilson is a sharpie. When he started to *laugh*, it kinda got my dander up. But Slim musta seen several flashlights and horses in his time.

The boys saddled up horses, and I got up on Roany, leading Prunes. We trotted back up the trail, wondering if we'd find shreds of stocks and bonds clear to the upper canyon. That roan sure acted real spooky. I wondered what he'd done to Tim. We rode a mile or so up the trail, dark as the inside of a tar barrel, when there come a big circle of light and a loud holler, and there was Wilson in the light, imitating Booger Red coming outa chute number three. Wilson was riding the freshest horse and was in the lead; if he hadn't been plumb forked he'd a lit in the rocks. By the time Slim got his horse under control, we found Smithers in the trail mumbling, "Why, that tough dam sucker, why, that tough dam sucker!" And that danged money bags was still waving that blamed flashlight around.

All the broker would say, when we asked him how come, was, "Got tired of riding that dam sucker." By the time we got back to camp and had shoveled in some of the cook's good food, Smithers was in a better mood. He got around to noticing the puzzled grins, and finally come out with it. "If you birds want to get a good education, just show one of these western horses the Great White Way." He started to rub his knees. "I thought Roany had lost the trail, so I snapped on my flashlight to show him the way to go home. He put me right where the beam lit."

We got a real early start next morning. Buck, with Tim, and Al, with Doc, went off toward Pendergraf Meadows; but George Parsin had a moose permit, and I thought I knew where a big bull hung out; so we were touring across the river in the spruce jungle, cut up with willow bogs and swamps, looking for a big-nosed gent with panned horns. When we got up on a knobby ridge, down there feeding in a floating bog was old record-buster himself, him and two floppy-snouted lady friends. George whispers real quiet-like, "I'm a-going to lower the boom on that gent." We were in the shadows of some big spruce trees and were off our horses. The pleased hunter got his gun laid across a down log, and was getting set to aim at the unsuspecting bull, when a dead quaking aspen tree decided to liven up the proceedings. Just a busted-up second before George could shoot, this tree gave up its shallow-rooted ghost, and fell, KA-WHOUNCHY-BANG, right in between poor old George and the three swamp lovers. Them three moose had plumb evaporated when George got through swearing.

As the moose hadn't seen us, and was used to the tricks trees play in the mountains, we went after them. We were riding real cagey-like, with stops and starts, through that messy pothole country, and hadn't got sight of our quarry yet, when we came up on a spiny open ridge. We stopped to take our bearings. I got off my horse, and was using George's fine binoculars again. I happened to swing them past old Tinsley's mine shaft hole up on the side of an open draw a quarter of a mile away. Dang my wrinkled-up old hide, if I didn't spot the cook, old Shorty; he had a sack on his back, and was just about to enter that black hole on the steep sidehill. I held the glasses on Shorty till he disappeared. I moved them a little, and then spotted a movement on a timbered point two or three hundred yards above the long-abandoned copper dream of old man Tinsley.

Hell, no, it wasn't that big bull moose that George Parsin had his soul set on. It was Big Slim the horse wrangler. Why, dang my miserable wrinkled-up hide all over again.

Parsin was sitting impatiently on his horse. He whispered a real anxious Jim Bridger whisper, "Do you see any sign of our friends yet, Bill?" I gave a fool grunty "Not yet," because up there was the horse jingler sitting behind a log, with a long telescope trained right down on old Shorty's hidey-hole. And right now he wasn't my friend.

I figger I'd better get my mind on normal moose instead of crazy men, so I told George we'd probably better make a big circle up around the blown-down timber we'd got into, and hit them beaver pond pockets just below the ridge. Well, we did, finally, and after about two hours of hard traveling, I'll be dad-burned if we didn't see old Pappy Big-nose himself, with his two snooty girl friends, and he didn't have any jittery trees to help him this time. He seen us, too, and blustered up into a mud-slinging trot right out of a beaver pond. He had a water-lily root in his dripping schnozzle, but that didn't camouflage him a bit. He was in a big splashy hurry, but my hunter was faster. The old willow-cruncher fell just on the slippery bank of the boggy pond, but his discreet lady friends didn't wait for the ceremony.

While I cleaned out the moose, the happy hunter took a lot of pictures. When I got through, George helped me turn the huge carcass over on some limbs to cool out. After that, we cut and piled green branches on the roan hide of the old monarch of the timbered jungle. It looked like snow was coming, and we probably wouldn't pack the old boy in to camp till next day.

All this time I'd forgotten about that scene played by Shorty and the horse wrangler. But now, old Doc's idea of a mountain ulcer

I held the glasses on Shorty.

started gnawing at my innards again. I thought Shorty was the wrong kind of mouse if Slim was paying cat. Mebbe Slim *was* going to write stories someday. If so, he sure was getting plots, but this one had me stumped.

It was a big surprise when we got into camp, early in the afternoon, to find the whole gang there, except the horse wrangler; and I soon saw him on the bench across the river, rounding up the horses to bring to the corral. The cook was bustling around, banging pots and pans. He was even grinning at Tim Smithers' big haw-haw cracks about Shorty's "square-rumped gait." Al Neeman told me "The Big Haw-haw" bagged a buck deer on the way back to camp—that was why he felt so jovial. "Too bad bucks don't have tusks, ain't it, Tim?" came from Shorty this time. Smithers puts out another of his so-called quips: "A tooth for a tooth," he says, "I'll trade anybody all my buck teeth for just one elk tusk." When the whole gang started haw-hawing, he saw his crack had backfired: that big freckled mug of his had a whole mouthful of buck teeth. He musta got mad then; anyhow, he flushed up and grunted, "To hell with you suckers," and stalked over to his tent.

Just before supper, George Parsin borrowed a needle and thread from Shorty, to patch his jacket, and mentioned how he'd got snagged by some tree limbs he'd rode under. "You sure don't dare to go to sleep riding through the timber. I thought I was low enough to clear that limb." That started talk about how much wear and tear clothes take to survive. The cook laughed, "when I was younger, I used to buy guaranteed britches; 'ten cents a button, a dollar a rip,' that's what th' label read." Buck said, "You ain't as old as I thought you was, Shorty. I used t'wear that brand, too. Can't buy that kind any more. They don't make 'em."

Shorty put the grub on the table, and we all started to eat. Buck went on talking: "Damfool things happen, to clothes and people, too. By hell, you'd a thought, as much as I've rammed around in th' hills, it would never a happened to me. We was huntin' moose, an' was headed for them willow bottoms on Soda Fork. My hunter an' me had just rode outa some heavy timber onta a grassy hog back. Then we started ridin' down a steep game trail slanted down a gravelly hillside. My hunter was comin' along about thirty feet behind me. When he whistled, I looked back an' up ta where he pointed, an' saw a big ol' osprey a-glarin' down from a snaggy limb on th' top of a tall dead pine. I waved, 'Come on,' an' turned back, jist in time t' have a small dead tree fall over on my saddle, between me an' th' horn. It knocked th' reins outa my hand, then that damfool horse spooked an' ran between two trees an' hung up. My knees were too wide f'r th' door-way, an' that ever-lovin' tree had me by th' chin. Yessir, I was dang near chokin' t' death, spread out on the horse's back, when th' hunter rode around an' grabbed my horse's head." Buck grinned and rubbed his belly. "Any you birds wanta see th' scars them branches made? My hunter called me 'Fish Hawk' th' rest a that trip. And, y' know, them pants still held together."

After this early supper, here come another puzzle. I hadn't heard it for days, but Wilson was humming a little tune, as he put the horse bunch out. . . . And a while later, the two guides and I were over in the trees, looking at the game carcasses hung on the meat poles back of the tents. We could hear Doctor Forrester and George comparing notes on the day's hunts. Hearing some large haw-haws in another direction, I looked over; and back of the cook tent, there was Shorty listening to Smithers, and derned if he wasn't nodding his head and grinning as that big beefy millionaire waved his hands around. Tim's loud voice sure carried, but the only words I heard plain were: "Can I depend on this, Shorty? It'll be cash every time, and I don't mean maybe." The cook grinned and nodded his head, and it looked like they shook hands. Why, damn it all, them belly wobblers of mine started up again.

The hunt was about over, but that was the one I'll never forget if I live to be 100. As Smithers started to walk over to his tent, I happened to think of his yen for a bear hide, so I sang out, "Oh, Tim, how about us takin' a look at th' bear bait? We'll still have shootin' light. This is your last chance if you're goin' in, in the mornin'." "Thanks, Bill," Smithers still had a big grin on is mug, "I think I'll pass it up. No bear's going to make a sucker outa me twice!"

For some fool reason, the cook and the horse wrangler, who'd been good friends the first part of this hunt, had in the last few days been as distant and suspicious of each other as two turpentined strange bobcats. But as we started to gab around the table this evening, Shorty pouring coffee all around, I noticed he and Slim were burying the hatchet. Wilson was cracking jokes at Shorty; and the cook, looking puzzled, was meeting the friendly cracks with some salty comments of his own. Al and Buck were staring at them, too, with odd grins at their horsey humor; here were these two porkypines about to be lovebirds. I thought about mine shaft holes, lost horses, shots in the night, the wandering horse wrangler, and the deal behind the cook tent. Was there a Smithers in the woodpile?

Well, Pete Elaby got into camp next morning with his jacks, and he brought some mail. We were going to eat dinner, and then pack all the hunters' meat and trophies and their camp gear on Pete's mules and some of our pack horses. Their hunt was over, and they were going on in to the ranch and then home. I spotted a letter for me from Velma, so I went over to the woodpile and sat down in the sun to read it. I noticed the rest of the crowd had mail except Slim Wilson. He was helping Shorty set the table, and joking about something.

Velma's letter was good; it read, among other things; "Bill, you'll be interested in a note from Warren Kompton. Sally and I were, to say the least." I found the note, and it *was* interesting.

"Dear Bill, Hope your hunting camp is operating O.K. Regards to the crew and hunters. When I got back to Roaring River, I couldn't find hide nor hair of your friend from Kansas. But a couple days ago a warden stopped in. He told me that the law down at the county seat had a hunter from Kansas in jail there. Seems like this gent got more than fresh with a lady he somehow mistook for a wayward waitress. Evidently he had a snootful at the time. The lady turned out to be the mayor's wife. Anyhow, there he is. Story is, he refused to use any *dumb, local lawyer* for defense. He said the governor of Kansas will raise hell with the *hillbilly mayor* for this outrage. Yours, the Game Warden."

After that, I felt pretty good, and hungry. We ate Shorty's fine dinner, and soon the hunters were all set to go with the pack string to the ranch; they'd all settled up their bills with me, and they and the rest of us were visiting around for the last time.

Then I noticed the cook, off to one side, halfway hidden by the cook tent, talking alone with Smithers. They seemed kind of furtive, and it looked like Smithers was buttoning a package into a large pocket of his heavy hunting coat. I saw him handing Shorty a handful of bills, which the cook carefully counted. Old Money-bags watched Shorty, then he started hee-hawing. "I'll sure be looking for the rest of 'em," he said. Pete Elaby and Slim were throwing a diamond hitch on the last jack loaded with the hunters' gear, and Slim was watching the cook and Smithers over the mule's back. Damned if *he* didn't have a sly grin on *his* face under that big hat. I wondered if *all* the wolves had gone to the big cities.

The wrangler was going to help Pete take the pack string in to the ranch, and was going to come back with the pack horses. Just before the hunters got on their horses, we shook hands all around. Doc Forrester and George Parsin planned on a hunt with us next fall, and said they'd write. The big hunter, Tim Smithers, said, "I don't think

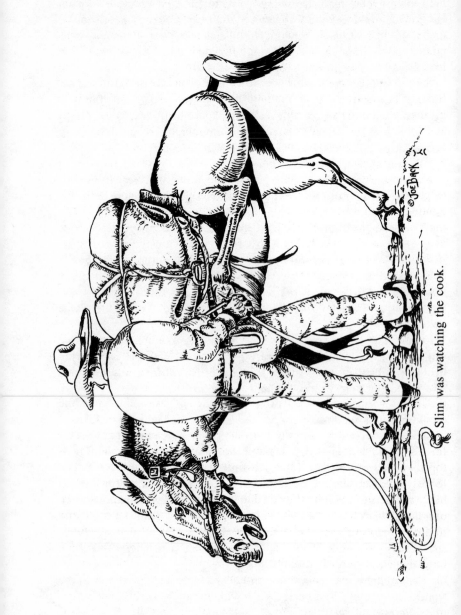

Slim was watching the cook.

I'll be out. I'll have what I want out of these mountains by Christmas." He grins a big toothy grin. "If any of you birds need any good stocks or bonds, just write old Timothy Smithers and Co." As they disappeared down the trail, that big voice boomed out of the timber, "So long, suckers, haw, haw, haw!"

Shorty was hanging some wet towels he'd just washed on a tent rope, as I came over. He was mumbling to himself, so I says, "I didn't git that, what didja say, Shorty?" He hung another towel on the rope, and looked at me kinda grouchy-like. "I said, that trail Smithers is a-follerin' ain't a straight one. Many a long, smooth trail has a lotta big slide rock at the other end."

Now that we had the hunters off our hands, us four fellers decided to get our own elk for our winter meat. We had only a few days till hunting season was over. I told the other boys they could hunt where they pleased, but I was going to hunt across the Buffalo Fork till evening. I saddled up the big roan and took off.

When I got across the river, I rode up on a timbered point where I could see camp. Al Neeman and Buck were a-ridin' off up the trail towards the falls, and the cook was busy taking down the hunters' tent, so I knew I could do what snooping I had on my mind without getting caught at it.

Finally Roany got the hill climbed and I got off and tied him up in the shadow of the heavy timber, just above Tinsley's shaft hole on the steep sidehill. I knew where Slim was, and I was dern sure Shorty wouldn't have time to git up here, as I slid and stumbled down into the pile of rocks and rotted timbers at the entrance of the long-faded dream of a copper empire.

Looked safe enough, so I went in. There was a hole for about twenty feet. Beyond was just a pile of shattered greenish rock all fallen together. A huge pile of sticks, old rotten pieces of moldy canvas, leaves, pine needles, fuzzy remnants of hair and grass, along with a bitter acrid stink—all this showed that here was the high-class mansion of some industrious pack rats. That's all I could see at first. Sun was in the wrong direction. I lit some matches. All I found was some odd sprinklings of a slick white odorless powder, a lot of candle ends burned clear to smears, a couple poles laid side by side, with four-five old gunny sacks on top of the poles, and a couple empty bottles. They smelled something like hack-sor-been liniment. I dug around in the mess of pack rat nests, ran out of matches, and gave up. A hell of a Sherlock on horseback, I was.

Roany was fidgeting around, snorting at nothing, I thought. He had wound around the tree he was tied to, so his neck rope was tight. I was winded from that climb up from the mine hole. After I'd got him unwound and got on him, I found the cause. A band of elk were bedded in the heavy timber right behind him and he tried to tell me; but by the time I got my rifle unlimbered they'd got away. It was getting dark by then, so I turned him downhill and headed for camp.

When I got close to camp, I saw old Shorty's shadow moving inside the lighted-up cook tent. It was getting colder'n hell, and he had the tent flaps down, but I could hear that old Bill Rema stove a-panting. The boys hadn't got in yet, so I unsaddled and got some oats from the gear tent. I was graining the horse bunch Slim had left in the corral, when Buck and Al rode in and got off their ponies to help.

Well, we put the bells on the bell horses and they throwed the bunch over on the big bench and anchored their picket horses to a couple logs. By that time it was plumb dark and Shorty was hollering, "Grub's on, come an' git it," so we rambled over to the cook tent.

Old Shorty was humping around the table, filling our tin plates full of that good grub of his; then he sat down himself, to start in. Al and Buck had got lucky. They had both got a cow apiece, after running into some, skirmishing around in the quaking aspens long Line Creek, above the falls. They were going to pack'em into camp in the morning. I finally got the talk see-sawed around to the old copper mine that was just below camp—the whys and wherefores of the mother lode, sudden fortune, frustrated hopes, and hard work for nothing. Had it going strong, and was about to get the talk wrangled around to Tinsley's dream of a copper fortune, when the cook blew my Sherlock Holmes idea all to hell.

"You birds know that old shaft up th' draw across th' river? Well, that old hole, that Tinsley spent a year or so diggin', is youranium 'stead of copper. I ain't got no reglar Gigglin' counter, but my arthuritis has got that beat. No matter what you wise birds say, every time I'm a-travelin', afoot or a-horseback, I know when I'm over rich youranium country. If my joints gits ta feelin' O.K. all of a sudden, then I know I'm over rich stuff. All I gotta do then is ta move so far thisaway or thataway, and when she gits to givin' me hell again, then I know I'm past th' lode.

"Now, you smart gents think yore a-goin' ta git rich a-guidin' people like ol' Elk Tooth Smithers all over these hills. Now, me, I ain' a-goin' ta have ta rob no poor widders an' orphans t' git mine. I've tromped 'n' rode over these same mountains a-doin' th' same thing you're a-doin' a long time before you gents was weaned. I've got areas

226

mapped out, with my built-in Gigglin' counter, in places you fellers wouldn't dream of. I know you boys won't try ta jump my claim up in that hole. But I'll give yuh each a share as witnesses."

The cook has got all steamed up now. William J. Bryant woulda had his jaw fractured on his own briskit-top to have heard Shorty's oration.

"You fellers probly wondered where'n hell I was a-wanderin' off ta when you was a-huntin'." Shorty had done forgot to eat his own vittles now, he's goin' so strong. "Well, youranium's a hell of a good cure for arthuritis, as I was a-sayin'. Pervided yuh c'n stand th' strain of th' pain a-leavin' yuh sudden-like. I go up ta Tinsley's lost hope hole, rub my liniment an' medicine powder around on my joints, an' lay down on some poles I got up there. Bin a-doin' it ever chance I git, between cookin' fer dude hunters an' damfool guides. Feel a damn sight better'n I have fer years. Mebbe I c'n git 'nough grub up there, an' stay all winter. I gotta notion ta try it."

That wrinkled-up squinty blue-eyed cook had us breath-bound with his story. But when we got our wind back we couldn't hold it. Shorty acted sore as hell at our haw-haws. If he ain't a hillbilly Barrymore he sure as hell means what he says. I got dizzy about then. That package I'd seen Smithers button up in a coat pocket. That roll of bills that'd choke a moose. That haw-haw hand-wavin'. That "Can I depend on that?" and, "It'll be cash every time, Shorty." Hell, yes, I got it now. Must be!

Old Full-pockets is grub-stakin' Shorty. He's taking rich uranium samples back with him. Old Stocks-and-bonds is going to get more samples of uranium, and big Smithers Uranium Corporation is a-going to beat some more widders and orphans. Is Shorty turning crooked or is he being took? That elk tooth business is just my own hell-lucy-na-tion. Boy, my belly-wobbling settled down now. And, man, did I eat Shorty's good cooking?

What with one thing and another happening, Shorty and me, we got our elk, too. The wrangler and Pete Elaby came in from the ranch with their pack string in a day or so. By that time, we had everything ready to go. By noon we had the whole camp, meat and all, packed in to the ranch. The snow started to fall just as we pulled in.

Vel had the corral gate open for us. Her eyes were sparkling, and she was just a-bustin' with something she wanted to tell.

"You throw off the packs and hurry up to the house, she says, real sassy. "Dinner's all ready, and you want to hear the latest about the man from Kansas!"

Chapter Nine

Turned out to be quite a tale Vel told while we ate.

"Yesterday, I went to town, mostly to see if my sister Minnie was over her sick spell. She was entertaining the 'Top of the Mountain Club' and looked as healthy as any of Pete's mules." Velma had a bad case of giggles.

During the luncheon with this group of Roaring River's housewives and ranch-women, she heard the man from Kansas' name mentioned, she said.

It seemed that Bessie Brumley, the veteran nurse at Roaring River's doctor's office, observed that very peculiar wounds seemed to pop up among hunters during hunting season. According to Velma, Bessie went on to say, "This bird showed up in the waiting room, banging the door and mumbling to himself. The place was plumb full of people, most of 'em with appointments, some of these really needing the doctor's help. Well, when I told this man to write his name and address down on the pad and sit down to wait his turn, he got real uppity. I didn't cotton to this gent atall, looked like a heavy drinker and a big eater. See 'em alla time. All alike, too. Big bay window and back porch to match, plus that boiled beak, all gave him away.

"Well, girls, you see'em all th' time! Figured he had a hangover and needed an aspirin.

"I thought I'd humor him, so, real sweet, I told this character, 'Well, Mister, if it is urgent and you are a-hurtin' real bad, tell me what's it about, and I'll get word to the doctor. He's setting a kid's broken leg right now.' Well, girls, you'da laughed, too, if you'd a seen this guy then. He swelled up like a pouter pigeon, glared around at the other patients waiting in the chairs around the room, glared at me, and then leaned up close to the counter I was behind; and then he started to unwind a long and fancy muffler he had twisted around his neck. I could see some scratchy cuts on top of his ears and underneath 'em. He also had some fuzzy cuts on his chin, and a little cotton pad was stuck up on a singed place on his bushy hair.

"When I saw that, and those little pig eyes a-glarin' at me, I remembered the badger that got caught in old Harley Dedrick's chicken house on the ranch. The hen's private door was a little too small and the badger too big. I couldn't help but think this bird must have something in common with the badger, so I just had to laugh, even if he didn't have any feathers in his mouth.

"That tore it. This gent whipped the muffler around his neck and stomped out, snarling something about hill-billy pill peddlers and their no-good help."

The crew had a big laugh over this news about Kansas, and Pete says, "That's our boy, but how in thunder did he git them cuts?"

Vel had another giggle for this. "I'm saving that story for you, too." She went on, "While Bessie was telling about Kansas and his cuts, Pauline Bucknem started to laugh, and she told the interested ladies that she had the answer to that one."

Seemed like the day before Bessie had the encounter with the hunter in Doctor Mack's office, the six-year-old son of Pauline's had a cold, so she let him stay home from school. She hadn't told Willy, her husband, about it, as he started out to his welding shop in front of their house. "Willie's Welding" was known for miles around the mountains as the best in the business, and he was always busy.

The boy with the cold looked out the window when he heard the loud blaring of a car horn. From his bed on the couch he could just see the front end of a big car peeking past the shop building's front door.

His curiosity hurt him more than his throat did, when he saw a bare-headed man with a wide white collar going into his dad's shop. Just as soon as he made sure that his mother, in the kitchen, was washing dishes with her hands and reading a who-dun-it with her eyes, he felt safe enough to ease out the front door. Sometimes his favorite knot hole was obscured by some piece of machinery leaned up inside the busy place, but this time he could see nearly the whole shop's inside. Billy could see the barrel-shaped man waving his hands and taking to Willie. The breathless boy saw his dad nodding his head and taking a bill from the man. Then he heard Willie say, "Sure, Mister, I won't tell a soul. The price is right, but it'll be a ticklish job."

Billy looked over towards the house and sw that he was still safe. He stuck his runny nose up against the rough board, and glued his eye back to the hole; this was worth any strapping his dad could give him. He noticed the long hunting knife strapped to the straining belt, and decided this hunter was different, this one must have a bad cold and his collar was hurting. After he saw his grinning father break several hack saw blades on the collar, Billy suddenly realized that the collar was a *white-enameled toilet seat*. His dad finally had to resort to the cutting torch before the collar gave up. Billy decided he'd seen enough. He barely made it to the couch, before his mother came in from the kitchen to see about her ailing scholar.

Pauline told the ladies that Willy, during meals or at odd times while in the house, would break into fits of sudden laughter, then clam up. She took to watching him, as welding is a chancy life; but Billy, sensing the undertow, told his mother all about it. Pauline finally got Willy to squeal.

"Well," Velma ended, "of course, I had to tell them the rest. The poor guy—that's all the use he ever got out of that toilet seat."

Slim commented, poker faced, "He got more mileage out of his than most men expect to."

"So much for Kansas," says I, getting up, "She's snowing pretty hard, and we got lots to do."

Pete, Buck, and Al were going to help me put up some cabins. But Slim said he was going down to the lower country for the winter. So I settled up with him, and told him that if he ever wanted a job with my kind of outfit, just to holler, for I could use an A-1 hand any time. He said, "Bill, it's been a pleasure to work for you. I've learned a lot about the country, and some new things about people. If there is a finer bunch of fellers to work with, I ain't seen 'em. I'll drop you a line soon to ask how you boys are stackin' up." He shook hands all around, and threw his saddle, bed roll, and war bag in the pickup. Pete Elaby had to go to town and was taking him in. As they went down the road and through the trees, I was thinking of the warm way Slim Wilson had shook hands with old Shorty. The cook was grinning, and sorry to see Slim leave. The riddle was Slim's last remark to the cook, "So long, old-timer, take care o' yourself, and don't let them elk teeth get mixed up with that uranium." Then I saw Shorty, his face all squinted up in a puzzled frown, leaning against the kitchen door. He watched the old green pickup disappearing through the falling snow, till it faded out of sight in the timber.

Well, here it goes again; why didn't I tell Pete to bring back some more Rocky Mountain ulcer pills?

Shorty Beel, the cook, had a few acres close to town. A lot of the little town was built on land Shorty had sold from his homestead to late settlers. He rebuilt guns, saddles, and pack outfit gear, and was a clever tinker with a lot of things. He was an industrious and thrifty old mountain man. When my wife and I would go to town, sometimes we'd stay over with this old friend for a few days. Come holidays, the old boy would stay with us.

The only person closer to Shorty was his nephew, who was now pretty close to being a full-fledged dentist. He was in school in the same big town Smithers called his. Old Shorty planned to stay at the ranch a few days to rest up; but right after Slim pulled out, the cook get restless and said he had to go home. There was some things he wanted to fix up and send to Johnny in New York. He says, kinda worried-like, "I shoulda went in with Pete an' Slim. I plumb fergot about that stuff fer Johnny."

This sudden yen to get to town had me up a stump. It didn't help the stump any, even when here comes the pickup back, with Pete and Slim a-grinning in the cab. Pete had forgot the chains, and that snow was getting deep and slippery. While Pete went over to the shop for the tire chains, Slim and I helped Shorty get all his gear and them big private panniers into the back of the truck. After seeing him get in between Pete and Slim, I said so long again to Slim and told Shorty I'd drop in for a visit soon. Away they went the second time. Pete was sure making good time. The clackety-clack chain end hitting the fender was real noisy. I figured, by the jumped-up Judas, I oughta feel better now, getting rid of two ulcers at the same time.

Chapter Ten

During all the flurry of unpacking the mules and horses; stacking panniers, tents, stoves, and the rest of the camp gear; taking care of our meat; eating dinner; and now all this goodbyeing, I'd forgotten to ask what happened to Sally. We expected to find her at the ranch with Velma, but she was gone.

"You know, Bill, that girl was sure changed when she came back with Pete from camp, after she saw Shorty." Vel was unpacking some kitchen panniers, and putting left-over camp food supplies into the store room off the kitchen. "I had to slow her up. She jumped into the ranch work with such vim, I thought she'd have a nervous breakdown. I really got worried about her. She lost that sunny disposition, and several times I saw her stop and stare at nothing, like she was in a trance. She wouldn't tell me anything. All I could get out of that kid was mumbles about 'sneaky city slickers.' Then, the day before the hunters came in to the ranch from camp, Sally had a phone call from Tom Hoster, her brother-in-law down on the reservation. He was calling from his ranch to tell Sally that her sister was very sick and it was serious. . . . Yes, Pete took her home in the pickup. He said she hardly said a word during the trip. That packer sure is a driver, he got back here just at dark. Bill, I hope Johnnie isn't in trouble. I tried to pump Sally, but all she did was set her jaw and work a little harder."

Before my imagination caught fire, and I swallowed some, I got busy and started to catch up on the ranch accounts. While I was trying to find out who won, me or the tax man, Al Neeman and Buck Bruen got all our tents, pack saddles, panniers, rope, and the rest of the hunting gear, slung up and stored away for the winter. We'd throwed all the horse and mule bunch in that good saved-up pasture below the creek. Getting ready to cut logs for some new cabins was next.

We just started to eat, and was all talking about beginning the log deal, when Pete Elaby came in through the kitchen, and Velma set another place for him. He said Wilson was sure lucky. Pete pulled in to the gas station for some fuel, and Slim caught a ride with a hunter going below in a truck to the town on the railroad. Pete took Shorty over to his cabin, helped the cook unload his gear, drove over to the store and post office to get the stuff for the ranch, had a bite and a cup of coffee at the greasy spoon, and came on home. "Dang road's sure glassy," he said, "and that snow comin' down sure looks like business. Winter's about ta ketch up with us. Woulda been back earlier, but that loggin' truck for th' sawmill in town was crosswise th' road fer awhile; sure slick travelin'. "

I kept quiet about Sally. That dog Moocher had a good house and was friendly, but I knew he'd have to move over if I said anything about the Sally-Johnnie rattles in my head. Velma's got a mother complex about both those kids, but I had that buzzing up above.

That night I was visiting with the boys over in the bunkhouse. We got to talking about the mystery of Johnnie and Sally, when Al Neeman spoke up. "I hope it ain't so, but I'll betcha Johnnie has fell fer some floozie in th' big town." "Happens alla time," says Buck, cutting the top off an old boot to make a staple bag. "Yeah, Johnnie workin' hard, an' lonely, probly met some swivel-hipped, eye-rollin' little tart on th' make. Yeah, hear it on th' radio' an' see it in th' papers any day o' th' week." Pete had it a little different but it ended up the same. "Well, I'm like you fellers, too, I think th' world o' them kids, but that's life, yuh gotta live yer own and God help you. Yessir, I can't help thinkin' about stoppin' by last summer, Bill. Stayed all night. I can't help rememberin' Johnnie playin' on his guitar an' Sally singin' with him. Th' tune they played was, 'The Sidewalks of New York.' "

What with building log cabins, ranch work, and odds and ends of things going on, we got back into a restful way of life in these hills. Buck, Pete, and Al got to see Shorty every time they went to town, and said he was really doing fine. They would razz him about his arthuritis and his youranium, but he claimed he'd planted some rich stuff under his cabin floor, and was gitting younger every day.

"Well, I seen Shorty in the Post Office when I got th' mail this afternoon," Buck said one evening. "He was lookin' sassier'n ever. He was mailin' a bundle of stuff, ta Johnnie in New York, I thought mebbe. But when he told Whiskers behind the bars that it was C.O.D., I peeked, and danged if it didn't say 'Smithers' on th' package!"

Damn! Did you say belly-wobblers? I'd visited with the cook a time or two, and thought all my suspicions was a hell of a reflection on an old friendship. Now, that squirmin' started all over again.

It kinda let up, but in a week or two, on a hell of a cold day, it started up again. I was in the old storehouse where we keep our gear; I was a-tryin' to ketch a pesky pack rat. I pulled down the cook tent, all folded up on a rafter log. Damned if a couple of wadded up pieces of paper didn't fall out. Woulda thought they was lunch paper or somethin,' except they was covered all over with scribblin.' Looked like several tries at writing a letter. Couldn't tell whose it was. It was plenty cold in that building. The logs in the walls looked like big freckled horizontal icicles. Thirty-five below, the thermometer said that morning. But when I finally got the wrinkled papers outa them folds of canvas, and flattened out, and figgered out what they said, who from and who to, I got the tropical tantrums.

When I galloped outa that frigid log building, I was a-sweating like an amature bridegroom. Pete was a-warmin' up the pickup for a town trip, an' it was right in front of the bunkhouse, with a pan full o' hot coals under the oil pan. The steam and vapor round it looked like Niagery Falls to an old maid. I took me a runnin' jump inta that mumblin' gas wagon an' got her started. That hell-bent wheelspinnin' throwed me and that fool pickup around in a circle. I could see my wife lookin' out th' kitchen door, then Al, Buck an' Pete run outa th' bunkhouse t' watch th' crazy man. But I didn't have time for any damfool palaverin.' I was goin' t' town t' have it out with that connivin,' bandy-legged, grub-spoilin,' crooked old cook. Friend, hell.

As I was a-grittin' my teeth down that frozen, rutty old road, I looked in th' glass. Back there was the boys a-throwin' snow on the coals throwed into th' bunkhouse. One was holdin' th' run-over biscuit pan, and Velma was a-wavin' her hands up 'n' down alongside the snowdrift by th' house, an' I could see she was hollerin,' too—I dang near got stuck a time or two in them big drifts, crosswise th' road. —Why, damn that frosted windshield. —Shorty musta lost them tries at letter-writin'—probly thought he burned 'em up—somehow got caught in th' folds when we took down that cook tent. —Man, is this road skiddy—that letter t' Johnnie—that crooked stock deal, yeah—damn that moose an' her calf—always gotta git in th' road—so Smithers took th' kid fer his school stake—wouldn't yuh know it—I better watch her—comin' back now—Hay, yuh damn flop nosed fool!—jest dented the fender—If I git t' town without wreckin' this outfit, I'll be lucky—Damn kid tryin' t' increase his school money—dang near graduate dentist now—I guess that moose ain't hurt none—there, she an' her calf are goin' through th' timber—windshield foggin' up again—hope Pete put oil in this engine—yeah, Shorty tells Johnnie t' stay in school—damn that big-shot Smithers—so Shorty tells th' kid he'd make a deal—git th' money from that damn Full-pockets, come hell or high water, Shorty writes—Why, that damn crooked

234

cook!—hope these ol' tires hold up—windshield foggin' up again, damn it—old friend, hell—hell—I'll fix that old so-and-so—Betcha Slim's in on this—them shots we heard—somethin' haywire about that mine hole deal—good thing I found them tries at letters—boy, it's a wonder I c'n stay on th' road—this zigzaggin' snow—damn him—his false teeth an' th' same kind o' friendship—that crooked ol' sharpie *couldn't* be killin' elk now—fer th' tusks—season's closed—or could he?—mebbe that dang galoot's arthuritis is a plum fake—an' that youranium!—damn—I hope I c'n make it t' town—that gas gauge sure is gittin' low—why'n hell do elk have t' have tusks anyhow?—I always tried t' run a square outfit—this's gotta happen—I have a good rep—I think—outfitter's license—bonded guide, too—for years—I'll give that crooked ol' youranium elk killer what he's got comin'—Damn that kinda friend—

The closer I got to Shorty's the madder I got. Take *me* for a sucker. I skidded past the gas station, but I figgered I better stop at Uncle Sam's an git th' mail right now. Because after I see that grub-spoilin' ol' mountain canary and give him what he's got comin', I'll be too wore out t' stop then or any other damn time.

I fumbled that two-bit ketch on the frustrated cab door open and stomped through the deep snow to the Post Office. I was reaching for the door knob, I was in a high lope by then, when some fool yazoo opened the door to come out. I missed that ding-danged knob, slipped on the icy board walk and fell flat. My drippy cold nose rested on one of the wet shoepacks of that toothtimin',' grub-spoilin,' mountain Methuselah, Shorty John Beel, his crooked old self! He reached down, got me by one outraged arm, pulled me up, and says, "Old Bill Thompson's a-hittin' th' mountan dew, shore as hell. Got a snootful, Bill?"

I shook that bent-up knobby old claw off my holy old mackinaw, and yowled, "Listen, you unnameable excuse of a fatherless old sidehill wampus, what I got ta say ta you won't work in this cheap emporium of Uncle Sam's. You just git on th' outside till I git my ding-danged miserable mail, and I'll fix your arthuritis without any antidose of that counterfeit youranium." I waltzed over to my box, yanked out my key, opened her up, and out fell two lonely hi-falutin-looking long envelopes. I looked out the steamed-up window, and that onery wrinkled-up old Shorty was tryin' t' peer in at the locoed packer, Bill Thompson, his former good friend.

Well, the first letter on that splintery old fir floor was marked *from*:

James (Slim) Wilson
Field Inspector
U. S. Game and Fish Comm.
Washington, D.C.

It was marked IMPORTANT.

The other one I turned over right quick, and caught that whiskery, small-time politician of an old postmaster a-peerin' out of his mangy cell, with his mouth open clear to his purple-green gizzard. I throwed him the right kinda glare and looked at th' top corner of this letter. It says plain: *from*

Mr. George Parsin
Chief Technician
Natural History Building
New York 92, N.Y.

It was also marked IMPORTANT.

I ripped the first one open, give her a quick goin' over, an' I dang near fainted right on them squeaky floor boards. Then I peeked out th' frosted-up window, and there was poor old Shorty, still standin' outside, slappin' his cold thin arms agin his sheepskin coat, an' stampin' his cold feet up an' down on the old board walk.

Then I jest had t' rip Parsin's letter open. What I saw quick there made me want to go suck onto that puffin' exhaust pipe of the chewed-up ol' pickup, still achuggin' out there on high priced gas. Then I jest had t' go over t' that window, that my good friend, that fine postmaster Whiskers O'Leary, was a-starin' out of, shake his suspicious and gentle old hand, and say, "I wasn't mayself, Whiskers, old friend. Next time I come t' town th' drinks are on me. Merry Christmas, old boy!"

I run out of that lovely old building of Uncle Sam's and grabbed my fine and cherished friend Shorty by his freezin' lonely old arms, and I be damned if I didn't hug that angelic old mountain purveyor of fine food and intellectual integrity.

But when I kissed him, damned if he didn't bust me between my miserable, close-together, dumb peepers. "Look out!" he yelped, "Yuh crazy counterfitten four flusher. Are yuh nuts? Mountain sickness agin. Why, DAMN YUH!"

"I got over bein' nuts, right in Whiskers' stamp shop just now," I said, and meant it. "Shorty, you wily ol' wolf, you are as of now elected chairman of the festive board, and you won't be the cook." He put up an argument, but I wore him down, and persuaded him to come up to the ranch for the holidays.

After he wrapped up his sourdough keg in a couple of blankets and started to take it down cellar, I throwed down them two letters on his bed, and told him to read them while I went over to town. Just as I started out the door, I said, "Shorty, it's sure tough that Johnnie and Sally busted up." "Whaddayuh mean, busted up?" Shorty came out of the cellar, keg and all, so fast some sourdough slopped out and hit him in the eye. He wiped it out with his fist without even noticing. "They're gonna git married right after Christmas! Sally's on her way t' New York right now. Johnnie's done with school in a month er two. Th' army's got him then an' Sally'll be with him." He set the keg down on the floor and reached over to the window sill. "Here, you dumb sap, take this along with you. Read it. It's a letter I stoled offa Sally last fall. I'll be ready when you come back."

While I'm still in a daze with the letter he hands me, I drove over to town and read it right quick. That envelope was post-marked New York City, too. It was from Johnnie by way of Sally, and was old, a couple months maybe. Was waterstained and kinda fuzzy.

Dearest Sally,

This is going to be hard to say, but we might as well call it quits—You never in the world should marry as big a fool as I've turned out to be. —Here it is, I may as well get it over with. When we made our plans to get married after I got my degree in dentistry, we figured that by another year we would be on our feet and be a going concern. Well, I thought I could speed it up by taking the advice of the big stocks-and-bonds hunter that Bill had out in camp when I was there last fall. Smithers is his name. Well, to make it short, he had a private talk with me, before he took off for the east after his hunt. He showed me a list of what he called confidential reports of several industrial ventures, just putting shares on the market. —Gilt-edge, he said—can't lose—get in on the ground floor—secret Government contracts about a new uranium process— hush-hush weapons manufactory—State Department friends in on the deal. He said that Uncle Shorty, Bill, and Velma, and the mountain people, were out of touch with the *real world outside*. Especially the business world. Why, he said, they don't even have television! "In the mountain country," he said, "living like your people do, they naturally wouldn't know how many ways there are to double your income and more, by taking advantage of the progress and rapid change in the outside world." He said he knew if he showed Uncle Shorty or Bill or Velma this group of confidential investment stock plans, they would just laugh at him. —Well, I thought it was hooey, too, until I got back here in school. I talked with some of my classmates, and showed them the list of big name investors. Several of them were very much impressed.

Well, a fool and his money are soon ———— that's me! I put the whole six thousand I had left in his confidential secret shares deal. Floated on air for awhile, and now WHAM!

So, to go on, I'm going to have to leave school. My tuition and living expenses are going to be due before long, and I'm broke.

Please, if you love me, don't tell Uncle Shorty or Bill or Velma what a stupid fool I've been. I have a chance to take a job in about 30 days as a purser, a sort of bookkeeper, aboard an oil ranker on the South American run. The wages are good, and maybe in another couple of years I can save up enough money to finally earn that degree as a dentist.

Please don't tell the folks what a jackass you let yourself get engaged to.

Sally, dearest, forget me and look for someone worthy of you.

Until now,
Your Johnnie.

(Part of letter from Slim Wilson) . . . And among other things, Bill, I did tell some white lies. That halter I kept tied to my saddle was to lead a relay horse, as I had to cover a lot of country in my investigations. The enclosed check is to pay for his use. I was in touch with state and government game men some of the time. I am happy to report to you that several unprincipled outfitters and some wanton game killers are in custody, awaiting trial.

In our books, you and your whole crew have the best A-1 Rating as outfitter and guides in your whole area. And, Bill, you paid me for the best vacation I ever had. I am now putting into effect some of the ideas and suggestions you and the boys unconsciously gave me, as to a game warden's real duties; and some on game management that are practical. The men will have to live more with the game and less with the people. I'll never forget one of old Buck's remarks: "Some of our game wardens are people wardens. They know a damn sight more about people than they do about game."

And, Bill, please give my affectionate regards to Buck, Al, and Pete, and especially to that good old pal of mine, Shorty. He is a fine cook, an expert mountain man, and is sure handy with his fingers. Did that old boy have me fooled! Those extra rifle shots!

Please ask him to forgive me for being a snoop. I looked over those false-elk-teeth molds he had cached away. Best counterfeits I ever saw. That dental office he had in Tinsley's old prospect sure fits the country. Some day I am going to come out and have a hunt with the best outfit I know of, if you'll let me.

Please give my best regards to Mrs. Thompson, and have some yourself, Bill. And when you see her, my best to litle Sally. Merry Christmas to a fine outfit.

> From your friend, the "sneaky" horse wrangler,
> James (Slim) Wilson

(Part of Parsin's letter) . . . What you'll be most interested in, Bill, is a party at Tim Smithers' sportsman's club. He invited me, and I'm glad I went. A bunch of his hunter friends were gathered around him admiring his coat—the one he bragged about getting made, with 1000 elk teeth to adorn it. Well, Bill, there it was. A beautiful white buckskin, Indian-made coat. It was really decorated! We all admired it, handed it round, tried it on, and so forth. While a big young man about Smithers' size was admiring it, he remarked to Tim, "Man, I'd sure love to have this." Smithers said it wasn't quite complete, "I need one elk tooth to make up the thousand. It should be here tonight." Well, would you believe it, about that time a messenger came in with a special delivery package for Smithers. He signed and paid for it. Then he opened it with a big flourish. But when he read the note enclosed, he seemed to shrink, then I thought our big friend was going to have a heart attack. He dropped *two* elk teeth out of the box on to the table, threw the note on the floor, and stood up. He was flushed up like one of your beautiful Wyoming sunsets. But he wasn't pretty: he was mad, and trembling like a quaking aspen leaf. He said in a raspy little voice to the young man who'd "love to have this:" "Take the coat, my friend. It's all yours, as of now!" Then he stomped out the closest door. I heard him mumbling as he went out: "Oh, that smart damn sucker! Oh, that smart damn sucker!" And, Bill, did he slam that big oak door! The crowd stood watching Smithers' exit, so I picked up the note, and here is what was on it: "inclosed is a extry unfinished false tooth to show how they was all made. Thanks for th cash. Let the punishment fit the crime. So long, sucker. From the Country Wolf."

I am enclosing five sets of colored pictures I took around camp. Please give one set each to Buck, Al, Shorty, and Slim. One set is for you, Bill. I also enclose a good one of Pete and his pack string, which I hope he likes. Doctor Forrester and I plan on a trip with you and the boys next fall, about which you'll be hearing from us soon. My best regards to you and all the boys, and the pretty Shoshone girl, Sally. Please give my best to your fine wife, Mrs. Thompson.

Merry Christmas to you all,
Your friend, George Parsin.

Well! By th' Jaysus! For *one* time I'm gonna fall off the wagon. So I drove that faithful pickup over to the right place, and got a jug of the best. Then I got a couple of the fattest turkeys they had at the store, and all the fixins, and a tankful of gas for the chariot. When I got back to the cabin, Shorty was sitting on the bed with a big grin on his wrinkled old mug. He had his best clothes on, all ready to go. He handed me the incriminating letters and pushed me out of the door.

He says, "Let's go home, sucker."